DEADLY DYNASTY

D. L. ASTLE

This book is dedicated to my wife whose steadfast support and enthusiastic feedback were the motivating force that propelled this manuscript to completion.

CHAPTER 1

2012

It was two oh eight a.m. on a warm Thursday morning in Huntsville, Alabama. Another of many calls came into the overworked and understaffed 911 emergency call center for the greater Huntsville metropolitan area.

Dispatcher- "911, what's your emergency?"

Caller- "There's been a wreck out on Magnolia Drive at the old Rock Island railroad overpass. Looks really bad. Don't see any movement in the vehicle."

Dispatcher- "We'll have a unit on the way."

Officer Bobby Greene, a rookie cop, responded to the dispatch. Shortly after Greene pulled up, Robin Taylor, a seasoned officer with ten years of experience, heard the call and arrived to assist. The patrol units' strobing red and blue emergency lights pierced the night's inky darkness, reflecting off the twenty-foot concrete abutment of the railroad overpass like a neon light show.

"What've you got?" Taylor asked.

Officer Greene shook his head with a look of shock at the sheer carnage sprawled in front of him. "Looks like a fatality wreck. I was able to reach the driver's left arm to check for a pulse. Didn't find one. I checked for breathing. It's bad. My God, it's bad. His face was crushed into the back of his cranium. His head looked like a smashed cantaloupe covered in blood and hair."

Greene pointed his flashlight into the crumbled mass. He motioned for Officer Taylor to move closer.

"Take a look at this. I've never seen anything quite like it."

The two officers stood silently as the beam of Greene's flashlight danced across the interior of the wreck. Officer Taylor leaned through the broken passenger side window, peering into the interior.

The scene was ghastly by any measure. The violent impact of the driver's body against the steering wheel and the instrument panel festooned the crumpled SUV with human tissue splayed throughout the interior of the vehicle. What little remained of the pulverized windshield and mangled dash was soaked in blood, creating an eerie crimson rainbow, arcing across the twisted vestiges of the passenger compartment.

With her years of experience, it was obvious to Officer Taylor. The conspicuous pattern of blood spatter was consistent with the violent disintegration of the driver's head at the millisecond of impact.

The truck body and metal undercarriage were a contorted mass of mangled steel and shattered glass. The remnants at the scene were so severely mutilated, they were barely recognizable as a vehicle.

Based on the misshapen hulk and excessive speed, Taylor concluded that the rear of the truck had momentarily continued forward after the front half collapsed on impact against the massive abutment.

The extreme force deformed the SUV's frame into an eerie U-shape, reminiscent of a boomerang upended onto its point. Despite Officer Taylor's years of service on the force, she was deeply moved and unnerved by the gruesome sight of the crash.

While Taylor checked the wreckage, Greene initiated a search of the area surrounding the vehicle, looking for any additional victims. No other bodies were found.

Officer Taylor noted that the vehicle was a 2009 Mahetsi Liberty SUV. Based on the condition of the truck, it was obvious the SUV hit the abutment head-on at high speed. The force of the crash drove the engine compartment into the front portion of the passenger area.

Taylor walked slowly toward Greene's patrol unit, nervously touching her forehead.

She remarked, "This is the worst crash I've ever seen."

"You've got that right. This is as bad as it gets. The death of the driver must have been instantaneous. What a waste of a life. I'll call EMTs. They'll confirm the fatality and transport the body to the morgue."

In the accident report, Greene noted the incident involved excessive speed. The report mentioned the fatality may have been intentional due to the absence of skid marks and the position of the truck smashing head-on into the concrete structure of the railroad overpass.

Within minutes after the call, the EMTs arrived. Following a quick check for vitals, the medical personnel loaded the body onto a gurney, into the ambulance, and left the scene.

Greene pointed toward the mutilated carcass of the SUV impaled on the railroad trestle. "I won't soon forget this."

"Amen. If you've got all the photos you need, call for a wrecker and get this heap of metal off the overpass."

"Will do. Have a good rest of your night."

As Officer Taylor drove away in her patrol unit, Greene paused to assess the scene and to contemplate what had happened only a few hours earlier. He knew the horrific experience on this desolate road made him a little less of a rookie than he was the day before.

In the following days, the Madison County medical examiner's office conducted an autopsy of the body. Due to the unusual nature of the incident, the medical examiner was unable to determine whether the death was an accident or suicide.

The bizarre circumstances of the wreck triggered a referral for review by the detective division of the Huntsville Police Department. Lieutenant Roy E. Mercer, a slender, athletic-looking man and an eighteen-year veteran of the department, was assigned to the case.

After obtaining a warrant to search the contents of the mangled SUV, Lieutenant Mercer drove to the police property yard on the east side of town to inspect the remnants of the vehicle.

On arrival, the yard manager, Bryan Younger, a stocky man with salt and pepper hair and a ruddy complexion, directed him to the location of the crumpled hulk at the back of the lot.

"It's one of the worst wrecks I've seen in a long time," Bryan said. "There's not much left to inspect, but good luck anyway."

Lieutenant Mercer walked to the back of the lot. As he approached the vehicle, he was shocked by the sight of what remained. The collapsed metal hulk was half the size of an undamaged SUV. Checking under the seats and the center console of the vehicle's passenger compartment, Lieutenant Mercer, with some effort, was able to pry open the glove box. The contents were mostly miscellaneous clutter- -straws and napkins from too many trips through the drive-through, a couple of packets of condoms, a roach clip, and wrapping papers. Nothing particularly helpful in his investigation.

Lieutenant Mercer had previously reviewed the initial accident report filed by the patrol officers. The report noted the airbags on the vehicle had not deployed. But, for some reason, the report failed to state whether or not the driver's seatbelt was in use. With his many years of experience investigating car wrecks involving a fatality, Mercer knew what to look for to help resolve the question.

He instinctively pulled up the carpet on the driver's side. He looked behind the mutilated seatback to check the anchor hardware. The sheet metal of the floor pan was not bent or distorted at the point of connection of the seat belt anchors.

That's odd. If the seatbelt was fastened at the time of the crash, the floor pan metal of the passenger compartment would typically be distorted.

Mercer's report noted that the metal around the seatbelt anchors was intact and undamaged.

The obvious question was, why did the vehicle veer off the road and strike the abutment? Roy checked under the truck to see if anything was amiss. At first glance, nothing seemed to be significantly askew. As he directed his flashlight toward the steering linkage for the front wheels, something didn't look quite right. The linkage appeared to have been damaged, but Roy didn't know for sure.

Lieutenant Mercer had a real dilemma. There were no witnesses to the "accident". Magnolia Drive was often used for drag racing. The kids liked the challenge. The road had several sharp curves in the vicinity of the railroad overpass. It was quite possible the driver had simply been out for a thrill ride, driving at high speed through that winding stretch of road.

As he left the property yard, Lieutenant Mercer stopped by the yard office.

"Bryan, you were right. There's not much to inspect in the vehicle. Something odd, though. It looks like the driver wasn't wearing his seatbelt. I know some people don't wear seatbelts. It's kind of a Bubba thing here in Alabama. But I'll have to tell you, it's a damn sure way to die in that type of crash. Makes you wonder if it was an accident or not." Lieutenant Mercer shook his head. "Well, anyway, thanks for your help."

Before returning to the office, Mercer stopped by the city garage to talk to George Alderson, the senior mechanic. George had a reputation as the go-to guy for anything mechanical. Alderson started his career at the garage twenty-five years ago. He'd worked his way through the ranks to become a master mechanic.

"Hey, George. How you been? I need a little help. I'm investigating a car crash. Looking for the cause. It was a head-on crash into a massive concrete railroad abutment. The wreck was just off Magnolia Drive at the Rock Island railroad overpass."

Lieutenant Mercer paused. "I'm no mechanic but when I checked the undercarriage of the vehicle, I noticed the steering tie rod for the right front wheel was damaged. It looked to me like the rod was completely severed. Would that cause a vehicle to lose control?"

Alderson furrowed his brow. He glanced over his shoulder. "Oh, hell yes. It would be bad news. It would be like a total break of the bone in your arm above the elbow. You'd lose the use of your arm."

"Did the accident cause the damage?"

Alderson slowly stroked his cheek. "Could be. Don't know for sure. It may be something that began to fail sometime back and finally broke driving down the road."

"You know, the driver was going at a high rate of speed when he hit the abutment. I suppose that may have caused the linkage to fail."

Alderson instinctively ran his fingers through his thick gray hair. "Yeah. I agree, but who knows for sure?"

"I see what you mean. By the way, the accident report said the airbags didn't deploy. What could have caused that? The force of the crash should have triggered the airbags, don't you think?"

"Should have, but the system controlling the airbags is complicated. If something went haywire with the seatbelts, the airbags won't inflate."

"Well, it looks to me like the driver's seatbelt may not have been in use at the time of the crash."

"That could be the culprit. In some vehicles, the airbags won't go off if the seatbelt isn't fastened. The seatbelt slows the person's forward movement so the airbag won't cause serious injury."

Mercer turned to leave. "Okay, thanks. I'm headed back to the office. You've been a big help, as usual."

As Lieutenant Mercer walked down the hall at police headquarters toward his small, cluttered office on the north end of the building, Corporal Mark Davis stepped out of his office with a look of excitement.

"Hey Roy, did you hear who the crash victim was in the fatal wreck the other night out on Magnolia Drive?"

Before Mercer could respond, Davis continued, "It was Jarod

Harrington, the son of Clevis Harrington of Harrington Industries. Clevis was that guy who was murdered not too long ago."

"Yeah. I know. I just found out the crash victim was Jarod. I hated to hear he's gone. Man, I'm telling you, it was a real tragedy. I learned a lot about Jarod in my investigation of the deaths of his father and mother. Right now, I'm trying to determine if his wreck was an accident or suicide."

Davis, ignoring Mercer's response, elaborated, "Mr. Harrington made a fortune over the years in the aerospace industry as a subcontractor and supplier to the space program. That family was a dynasty. Practically owned this town." Corporal Davis, a bit of a local history buff, continued, "Did you ever hear the story about Mr. Harrington? I read a feature article about his rags-to-riches life. The story said the family is worth about 1.5 billion dollars. He was truly a self-made man. The article said Harrington grew up in the Huntsville area, the son of a rural mail carrier. You might say his life growing up was modest, dirt poor, actually."

Walking briskly to keep pace with Lieutenant Mercer, Davis asserted, "Harrington went to grade school in Brecksville and high school right here in Huntsville. The story goes that he was a star quarterback on the Huntsville High School football team. Back in the day, the team won the state championship three years in a row. Kind of surprising to me. Harrington was over six feet tall. Such a good quarterback. What a runner with those long legs and athletic build. From what I've read, Mr. Harrington went on to college but dropped out his junior year to seek his fortune in the world. I guess it worked out pretty good for him."

Mercer glanced at Corporal Davis. "Yeah, as I said, I knew Clevis Harrington. But not under the best of circumstances. You may already know I've been working the homicide case in which he was brutally beaten to death."

"Yes. I heard the story just the other day. That's why I said he'd been murdered." Davis pointed down the hall. "I saw on the assignment board that you're the lead investigator."

Lieutenant Mercer continued, "I also knew Jarod Harrington.

Jarod's name came up in my investigation of Clevis's death. I interviewed Jarod a couple of times. You know, there's a whole lot more to the story. I've seen the other side of the Harringtons. From my investigation of the homicide of Mr. Harrington, I learned that Jarod was a complex person leading a challenging life. Based on what I've determined, Clevis made Jarod's life a living hell."

Davis furrowed his brow. "What do you mean?"

Mercer explained, "Mr. Harrington was hard driving. He never cut Jarod any slack. As I understand it, the tension between Harrington and his son was through the roof. The article you read probably didn't mention that. The whole thing about the Harringtons is a tragic story, to say the least. Not at all like the public image the family sought to portray. There's been multiple deaths in the family. Mr. Harrington's wife, Veronica, died mysteriously in a drowning incident. We now know that, at the time of her death, Harrington stood to get a multi-million-dollar payout from life insurance on Veronica, along with an undisclosed amount of money from a personal injury settlement. That money would have come in very handy for Harrington since his aerospace company had fallen on tough times."

Lieutenant Mercer unlocked the door to his office as Corporal Davis followed him in. "You know, Mark, this has been a very complicated series of events. We don't yet know if Jarod's fatal crash was an accident caused by mechanical failure or a suicide or what."

"Which do you think it is?"

"Too early to tell. I was recently asked by the brass to look into Jarod's wreck to see if there's any connection to the killing of his father. You've probably read some of the recent news stories about the deaths of Veronica and Clevis. The news media was all over it."

Mercer dropped his file on the desk and turned to Corporal Davis. "We've made a lot of progress in those two cases. There's definitely more to the story than what I've told you. Remind me to give you the inside scoop on this whole thing sometime."

CHAPTER 2

1995

"Dad, can I go to the office with you today?"

"Don't you have school?"

"No. It's teacher's professional day or something like that."

Clevis hesitated for what seemed like an excruciatingly long time.

"Okay, I guess. I won't have a lot of time to spend with you. I have a management staff meeting this morning. I have a troubleshooting session with the engineering department this afternoon. We have to resolve some issues with our primary production unit. One of our biggest customers, Aztec Engineering Components, is threatening to pull their contract if we don't get the vertical stabilizer trim tab servos up to spec and delivered to their west coast facility by the end of the month."

Jarod was used to that type of response. All business. Way too much information. No dad stuff at all.

Clevis's sleek black Mercedes S Class coupe swung around the gentle curve in the road just outside the main entrance gate at the North Bay plant of Harrington Industries. The bright morning sunlight glinted off the ostentatious chrome grille as Clevis pulled up to the main entrance.

The guard at the security gate waved him through onto the massive parking lot overlooking the cluster of industrial buildings. Clevis flew across the parking lot in his usual high-speed manner as he approached the main office building at the edge of the complex.

A large door to the executive parking garage opened on cue.

"Well, we're here, son. Hope you can find something to keep yourself entertained today. I'll meet you back here later this afternoon."

Jarod wandered into the industrial complex, unsure why he wanted to come to the plant with his dad.

Assembly Building 1A was bustling with activity. From overhead, it resembled the interior of a beehive in early spring. The noise was something hard to imagine. Despite the large number of employees, almost everyone knew who Jarod was.

"There goes the big man's kid." Bob Miller, an eight-year journeyman mill operator, remarked to co-worker Fred McCormick.

Fred responded, "Yeah, he's got it made, but I wouldn't give a plugged nickel to be in his shoes. From what I hear, his old man is on his ass 24/7."

"Heard the same thing. Not an easy life." Bob replied.

Fred continued, "Mr. Harrington casts a big shadow. I'd guess it's very intimidating to such a young kid. Not a pretty picture, in my opinion. Definitely, not an easy way to grow up."

"If Mr. Harrington runs his personal family life like he does this company, I'd say he's probably a pain to be around. That hard-driving overachiever syndrome and asshole personality can get old fast."

Cleve was running late for his afternoon meeting with the engineering department. The meeting with the Aztec executives did not go well at all. The pressure to ramp up production for Aztec and yet maintain quality was wearing him down.

Clevis had heard some competitors had been fudging the quality control lab results to get the products "in spec" in time for shipment. He knew that was not the way to go in the long run. He was already running two shifts each day at the production facility but still couldn't seem to keep up with the contractual deadlines for Aztec.

By the time Clevis finished the meeting with engineering, it was six-fifteen in the evening. Not all that unusual for a day at the office.

Jarod sat in the main lobby of the front office building, waiting for his dad. He had walked all over the industrial campus, ate lunch at the company canteen, and later spent a sizeable part of the afternoon watching TV in his dad's private conference room.

"Hey, son, you ready to hit the road?" Cleve asked.

"Yes sir, I was ready a couple of hours ago. Kind of boring around here."

Arriving home, Cleve pulled into the motor court area of his sprawling estate. He had an obvious penchant for accumulating high-end cars. His collection included a 1963 split-window Corvette, a 1989 BMW Z1, a Maserati Biturbo Spyder, and his Mercedes S Class coupe.

Soon after entering the residence, Cleve poured a scotch and water at the bar in the family den. The room resembled an English pub with old-growth imported library-style wood paneling crowned by heavy quarter-sawn overhead timber frame beams creating a medieval cathedral ambiance.

The last remnants of daylight pierced the skylight window near the crest of the twenty-foot ceiling, casting a warm auburn glow onto the bijar blue oriental carpet as the final vestiges of the day steadily sank onto the western horizon.

Cleve sat down in his favorite chair just as Veronica walked into the room. As if thinking out loud, he said, "Next year, when Jarod turns sixteen, I plan to put him to work during the summer in one of the plant buildings at the North Bay facility. That way, he'll be there where I can keep an eye on him."

Veronica nervously stroked her temple and exhaled with an audible sigh. "I don't know if he's ready to work at the plant. He's so young. I don't want him to get hurt working around all that machinery."

Cleve fired back, "Oh, hell, he'll be fine. It'll be his baptism by fire. I want him to be self-reliant and resourceful. You know, the way I was at his age. I don't want to raise a shrinking violet or a pansy kind of guy. It will be good for him. He'll have to hold his own against the other workers. If they give him any crap, he'll just have to grow a set and deal with it."

Veronica pursed her lips as she glanced at Clevis, shaking her head disapprovingly.

Over time, Veronica became even more uneasy about Cleve's decision to let Jarod work at the plant. She implored him to reconsider.

"I don't like the idea of Jarod going to work. He's too young. He just turned sixteen. I would prefer he stay around home. Maybe take some tennis lessons or do some volunteer work. Something like that. You and I both know Jarod is a very sensitive boy."

Cleve responded emphatically, "I know you have concerns, but my mind's made up. I don't want him living in a protected bubble through his adolescence. It'll be good for him in the long run. If things get rough, he'll just have to learn to deal with it. To act like a man. Trust me. I know what I'm doing."

The next year passed quickly as Cleve tackled the myriad of problems and challenges he faced at the plant. Harrington Industries had experienced a phenomenal rate of growth and was facing many tactical and managerial hurdles.

In a recent meeting with his top tier of management, Cleve informed the managers, "The company is approaching a critical point to achieve a balance between sustaining adequate access to financing and maintaining a cost of production in line with the cost of capital. If either the aeronautical or aerospace markets decline significantly in the foreseeable future, we will likely experience a cash flow dilemma that could jeopardize the viability of our future growth and sustainability. I'm counting on each of you as department managers to maintain our production level while avoiding any unnecessary costs related to our overall operation."

At a personal level, the business environment of the aeronautical industry was all-consuming for Cleve. The demands of the company had taken a toll on the family life of the Harringtons.

Clevis and Veronica had always been partners in their lives. However, as time progressed, Cleve became more rigid in his approach to everything, including his relationship with Veronica and Jarod.

By May 1996, Jarod had completed his sophomore year at Huntsville High. True to his promise, during summer break from school, Cleve assigned Jarod to work at the North Bay facility of the company. Jarod's first responsibility was to work in the supply room of the fixed-wing production unit.

Jarod tried to hide his anxiety about working for his dad. He didn't want to screw up. He knew why his father insisted he work there. It was a test. To see what he was made of. To see if he had the Harrington DNA. The ability to persevere. The ability to achieve a successful result in everything he undertook. It was the "Harrington way."

"How was your first day at work, honey?" Veronica asked.

"It was okay, I guess. At least they didn't fire me. They told me to read one of the parts manuals from cover to cover. God, that was so boring. It would help if I knew what a hydraulic bleeder valve and a reciprocating actuator were."

"Oh, you'll catch on fast, I'm sure. Just keep trying. I know you'll do really well. If you have any questions, I'm sure you can ask your father. He can help you."

Jarod sighed as he responded sarcastically, "Yeah, like he wants to be my life coach. You know him, Mom. He throws you in the pit. It's up to you to figure it out. He'd just tell me how he did everything on his own when he was my age. It's bad enough I've disappointed him miserably by not turning out to be some big high school football jock like he was."

"I think your father loves you just the way you are."

"That's not true, Mom. What he wanted was for me to have

turned out to be an exact duplicate of him. The last thing I want at this point is to seem needy and ignorant in his world. Sometimes, I just wish I'd been born the son of a factory worker. Not the son of the founder of this juggernaut company with our last name blazoned all over the buildings and on the huge sign at the plant entrance. I have to admit, Mom, sometimes life just sucks."

Veronica tenderly hugged Jarod. "I know it can be tough. Your father is very proud of the fact he's a self-made man. I guess I just have a genuine understanding of what makes your father tick. I was around him back in our college days. I know he had that fire in the belly drive to succeed, even back then. I just wish you could understand. He's driven. I know it comes off kind of hard and cold at times. You know he loves you and always has."

Jarod nervously bit his lower lip. "He's easy on you. He drives me like I'm never quite up to his standards. I dream of the day I'm out on my own. Maybe then I can feel good about who I am and what I want to do in life."

Veronica reached out and gently touched Jarod's cheek. "I'll always be here for you. It will all work out."

By July 1996, Jarod had been working every day in the supply unit of the company, assisting in the distribution of parts throughout the production units. He had learned the names of many of the parts needed to assemble the various components for the aircraft sections in production at the company.

At that point, Jarod was anxious to extend his capabilities and learn new skills. He had become good friends with several of the personnel working on the assembly lines near the supply department.

He had gotten to know Jimmy Boswell, a senior crane operator in Assembly Area 5. Jimmy, an affable thirty-four-year-old father of two, was the type of guy who never met a stranger. He had taken a liking to Jarod.

"Jimmy, can you show me how to run the crane? Looks like it would be cool to lift some stuff."

Jimmy responded tentatively, "I don't know. Probably

shouldn't let you do that. You know you must be eighteen to run a crane around here."

Jarod pressed, "I just want to give it a try. I'll be careful, I promise."

Jimmy hesitated. He felt conflicted. He wanted to please the owner's son but knew the OSHA rules about crane operation. Despite his misgivings, Jimmy finally relented.

"Oh, what the hell? I'll be right here to keep you out of trouble."

Jarod couldn't disguise his excitement. The crane system in the various buildings looked like a giant erector set. Huge overhead steel I-beams were mounted near the roof of the building, with motorized wheel dollies running the length of the facility. The lift portion of the crane was powered by a fifty-horsepower electric motor attached to a chain driven by a cogwheel sprocket bolted to the motor driveshaft. The crane was operated by a control box attached to a long electric cable. It was a massive and powerful system. Designed to lift and move large pieces of production components and equipment to any point on the factory floor.

Jimmy was still feeling uneasy about letting Jarod operate the crane.

"You have to do what I tell you. It's important you follow all of the safety rules. Listen carefully. This is the control box. It runs the crane. It has four buttons. Up, down, forward, and reverse. The forward and reverse buttons move the crane along the overhead track. The up and down buttons do just what they say- they either lift or lower the chain. You got that? It's very simple."

Jarod responded with obvious excitement, "Got it."

Jimmy continued, "You need to remember that once the load is secured to the chain, you have to watch the position of the load at all times. You have to make sure the crane doesn't get in the path of someone or another piece of equipment. Don't forget, the load stops moving quickly once you release the forward or reverse buttons. Sometimes, when you stop, the load will swing like a giant pendulum. If that happens, someone can get seriously hurt."

Impatient with all the training tips, Jarod said, "Okay, okay, let's get going. I want to try this."

It seemed like only a few short minutes had passed since Jimmy gave Jarod the crane operation safety instructions. But it had been almost two hours. The scene had become disorganized and chaotic beyond description. The deafening sound of the company accident alarm pierced the morning air like the scream of an eagle circling aloft.

"I don't understand. I did everything you told me!" Jarod shouted, his voice tinged with panic.

The workers in the immediate area quickly gathered around the injured employee. Everyone could hear the approaching ambulance siren wailing in the distance.

The comments and questions of the co-workers came fast and furiously. "Who is he? What happened? Oh my God, I can see his leg bone sticking out of his thigh."

The femoral artery had been severely cut. Blood pulsed out of the victim's leg like an artesian well.

The EMT team arrived and immediately administered emergency first aid. A tourniquet was applied to stop the bleeding, and an IV was started to provide plasma to counteract the effects of the loss of blood. As the ambulance pulled away, speeding toward the hospital, John Bowers, an EMT supervisor, began to gather information about the accident.

"Does anyone know the name of the injured?"

A journeyman machinist, Travis Weaver, responded, "His name is Scott Westby. He's fairly new here at the plant."

Bowers asked, "Can you tell me, in your own words, what happened?"

Weaver explained, "Well, I didn't actually see the accident up close. From where I was standing, it looked to me like Scott was in the wrong place at the wrong time. The big receiver drum being lifted by the crane apparently came loose from the tension clamp holding the drum. I guess it fell on Scott's leg. Looks like the drum must have fallen about twenty feet before it hit Scott. He's lucky to be alive."

Clevis was summoned from a meeting in his conference room shortly after the accident. His executive assistant, Rita Goodman, told him, "Mr. Harrington, there has been an accident in Assembly Building 1A. You should come quickly."

Cleve arrived on the scene to find Jarod in a state of shock. The other employees had returned to their respective job assignments. Cleve sat down next to Jarod. "What in the hell happened here?"

His hands trembling, Jarod replied, "It's my fault, I guess. I just wanted to learn something new. I asked Jimmy Boswell if he would let me run the overhead crane. I was being careful, but something slipped all of a sudden, and ----"

Cleve clenched his jaw. In his booming voice, he interrupted Jarod midsentence. "What in the hell were you thinking? How can you be so damn stupid as to think this ten-ton crane is your personal plaything? This has to be the dumbest goddamn thing you have ever done in your life! I'm very disappointed in you."

Cleve abruptly stood up without saying another word. He immediately left to stop by the hospital to check on Scott.

The news was not encouraging. Due to the extent of the injury, the medical-surgical team had extremely bad news. The leg was not reparable. They had no choice but to amputate the left leg at mid-thigh. The doctors mentioned if they had not done the amputation, gangrene would have set in, jeopardizing Scott's life.

Cleve waited for an hour to meet with Scott's parents. Cleve tried his best to console the Westbys.

"I'm so sorry. Please let me know if there's anything I can do for you."

Mr. Westby pursed his lips. He nodded as he tried to speak. But no words emerged.

CHAPTER 3

As Clevis drove home, his mind raced through the day's events. He tried to get his head around the situation to analyze the risk to the company for personal injury liability.

His psyche consumed him. His thoughts ran wild.

Just when we were hitting a smooth stretch with a decent balance of production and financing, this happens! I don't know what the hell Jarod thought he was doing. The company will be sued for a lot of money. It's inevitable in this litigious age. I could kick Jarod's ass into next week, but I know that won't make matters any better. I just hope we can survive.

After the accident at the plant, Jarod felt it would be almost impossible to show his face again at the company. He told his father he didn't want to return to work. Jarod pleaded with him, "Dad, I don't think I can fit in after what happened. I know everyone will be talking about me. I'm sure no one will have anything to do with me anymore. Being around everyone, especially Scott Westby's friends, would be too painful."

Clevis clenched his jaw. He aggressively pushed his index finger against Jarod's chest and emphatically asserted, "I don't give a damn what you think about this, son. You're going to go back down there and do your job! I can't have people think you are some sort of privileged character who gets by with anything without consequences for what you do. If you didn't show up, the family would lose the respect we've worked so hard to earn. Everyone has to know that the Harringtons don't quit. Plan on showing up for work on Monday morning, as usual."

Jarod complied with the wishes of his father. On Monday morning, he reported for work. The treatment by his co-workers was mixed, at best. To Jarod's surprise, some people showed compassion for what had occurred. Others, more closely tied to Scott Westby, avoided contact with Jarod or stared at him as he passed.

Jarod was unnerved by that type of treatment. At some level, he fully understood why they reacted as they did. The comradery and interaction between Jarod and the other workers had totally disappeared. From then on, Jarod dreaded going down to the plant each morning. He couldn't wait for fall so he could return to school full-time.

Several weeks passed. Rita Goodman, Cleve's personal assistant, called Cleve on the intercom. "Mr. Harrington, there's a gentleman here to see you."

"I'm really busy right now. What does he want?"

"He said it's personal business. Said he only needs a minute of your time."

The visitor entered Cleve's office through the large double doors.

"Mr. Harrington, I have something for you."

"What is it?".

The visitor gave no response. He simply handed an envelope to Harrington.

Clevis opened the envelope. As he stared intently at the papers, he quickly realized what this was. A summons for a lawsuit by Scott Westby for the crane accident in Assembly Building 1A.

The lawsuit sought twelve million dollars in actual damages and forty-two million in punitive relief. Cleve shook his head as he muttered, "Damn it! This would bankrupt me. I don't carry that kind of liability insurance. This is ridiculous."

After an extensive investigation, the Occupational, Safety and Health Administration assessed fines against Harrington Industries totaling over one million dollars. The violations included disregard for age limitations for the operation of inherently dangerous machinery and unsafe operation of mechanical equipment.

In the long run, the Westby lawsuit proved to be the most problematic, time-consuming, and potentially expensive circumstance for Clevis and Harrington Industries. The liability insurance provided coverage up to policy limits and legal representation for defense against the suit. However, Clevis knew any judgment over the total coverage amount was his responsibility.

Cleve realized he had to settle the matter. It was essential he avoid the possibility of a gigantic judgment in a jury trial. Cleve's thoughts quickly focused on the worst-case scenario: *If I ended up with a multimillion-dollar judgment, the company's credit rating would plummet. That could force me into insolvency.*

After many grueling months of depositions and negotiations, the attorneys representing Cleve finally reached a settlement. The amount was never disclosed. Only Clevis and his attorneys knew that the total liability for the accident far exceeded the dollar amount of insurance held by the company.

Clevis mused, *I don't have a clue how I'm going to keep this together. I can't afford to lose my line of credit. I have to think creatively. I've got to find additional financing. The last thing I want is to have Scott Westby try to collect the balance of his judgment by judicial sale. That could spell the end of Harrington Industries. I'll do anything to keep that from happening.*

He knew this was the most catastrophic and potentially devastating situation he'd faced in his career. He clenched his fist as he uttered under his breath, "It's time to play hardball."

Clevis had become totally immersed in the financial challenges he faced. His relationship with Veronica had suffered significantly. The demands on his time dealing with the problems at the company were all-consuming. The time they had to spend together had been reduced to almost nothing.

The stress between the couple was becoming apparent. They were drifting apart. Veronica hoped to remedy the situation. But she wasn't certain how that could be done.

She always had a persistent romantic perspective on life. In many ways, she was the opposite of Clevis. She saw life in a much softer light. Veronica believed there was good in everyone. She wanted to draw that goodness out of Clevis. She yearned for the Clevis she remembered from their early days together.

Veronica's thoughts drifted back to the nascent years when Clevis and Veronica were inseparable and truly in love.

I need to do something that would be a surprise. Finding a little love note in his dresser drawer should touch his heart.

The note read-

"Clevis, I can't tell you how much you mean to me. We have been together for many years. I loved every minute. We don't get to spend as much time with each other now. Life has become so complicated. I wish we could recapture the simplicity of the time when we met at Huntsville High. We wanted to be together every hour of the day. I hope we can rekindle what we once cherished. Your love and life partner forever, Veronica"

Veronica was convinced this was exactly what their relationship needed. She opened the top drawer of his dresser to place the note next to his cufflinks. While placing the note, a small piece of paper partially hidden under his socks caught her attention.

Veronica knew she had no reason to pry. But the conspicuous scent of perfume on the note prompted her to read the contents. The note was from someone named Crystal. Veronica had no idea who she was. When she read the note, she quickly realized something untoward was happening.

The note was filled with affectionate references and intimate descriptions.

Her heart raced uncontrollably as she slowly sank into the chair next to the dresser. She didn't know whether to scream or to cry. She suddenly felt numb. *How could he do this? I had no idea this was going on. What have I done wrong?*

Veronica sat in the chair, staring at the note for what seemed like an eternity. As she read and reread the words, anger welled up inside.

Veronica had always been a strong person. Resolute in her values and resilient in the face of adversity.

What am I going to do? I can't pretend I didn't see this. I'd be a fool to let him have his fling.

As she processed this shocking development, she summoned the strength to confront Clevis with her discovery.

When Clevis arrived home from work, he immediately went into the den to pour a drink and relax in his favorite recliner. As he turned away from the bar, Veronica abruptly entered the room. She tossed the note in his direction. "What the hell is this?"

"What are you talking about?"

Veronica's chest heaved in and out as she stared intensely at Clevis. "The note I found in your dresser drawer this afternoon. What in the hell has been going on, Cleve? Who's Crystal?"

Clevis looked stunned. His expression became lifeless as the blood drained from his face.

"That's nothing. I can explain. The whole thing was supposed to be a joke."

"Cut the crap, Cleve. You don't write that kind of note as a prank. How damn stupid do you think I am? Tell me about Crystal. Is she some young super-hot hood ornament you picked up at a bar somewhere?"

Veronica glared at Clevis as he gazed down at the floor.

He clenched his jaw. He sat there expressionless, eventually looking up at Veronica.

The silence that fell upon the room was stifling. It seemed that all Clevis and Veronica ever had together, and all each meant to the other, had suddenly disintegrated in a single instant.

Veronica realized at that moment as enormous as their stately mansion was, it was not big enough for the two of them.

CHAPTER 4

The following morning, Veronica packed her belongings and left behind the life that had been her entire world for decades.

From an emotional perspective, Veronica felt mortally wounded. She was consumed by nervous anxiety and overwhelmed by pervasive uncertainty. She wasn't at all sure where she was going. She'd never been in this situation.

As she exited the entry gate of the Harrington estate, she decided to stop long enough to call her sister, Carol Morgan, in Memphis. The two had not been particularly close in their adult years. Veronica and Carol routinely exchanged Christmas cards and called each other on their birthdays. For the most part, they both had evolved into separate lives. They had been on separate tracks for many years.

Compared to Veronica, Carol's life had been fairly rocky. She had been through two divorces and was currently living as a single person with two grown children living in different parts of the country.

Veronica was hesitant to call Carol abruptly but realized she had no choice. Veronica found Carol's number in her phone directory and placed the call. The phone rang for an extended period of time, then went to voicemail, "Hello, this is Carol Morgan, please leave a message."

"Hey, Carol. It's me, Veronica. Hope you're doing well. I just wanted to let you know I thought I would head up your way for a short visit. I hope we can get together. I should be there later today. I'll give you a call after I get into town. See you soon. Love you."

It wasn't more than twenty minutes until Veronica's cell phone rang. The caller ID read "Big Sister."

"Hi, Carol. Thanks for calling me back. I guess you got my message."

Carol replied, "Yes. It's good to hear from you. It's a bit unexpected, though. Is everything all right in Huntsville?"

Veronica hesitated. "Sure. I just wanted to get away for a brief respite from all the daily grind in my life. Thought it would be nice to see you again. It's been so long."

Carol's voice was etched with apprehension and surprise. "That would be great. I work full-time at a law office, Davis and McGill, here in Memphis. I went to night school and got my paralegal license. I guess I never got a chance to tell you about that. Our lives get so busy we never really talk to each other very often."

"I know. I should have called sooner. I just never got around to it. I feel awful about that." Veronica's heart clenched. She knew she should have called her sister a long time ago. "We'll have to catch up on everything after I get there. I'll get a place to stay. I'll call you after I settle in. Maybe we can go out for dinner tonight?"

"That sounds great. It's Friday, so I won't have to worry about getting up early to go to work the next day. Talk to you later."

Veronica had not driven the route to Memphis in decades. She was not familiar with the highway system leading into town.

It was now the fall season of 2003. The brilliant colors of red oak and maple trees lining the highway were on full and glorious display. Each bend in the road introduced a magnificent vista of yellow, crimson, and gold colors swirled onto the natural pallet of forested hills visible at every turn.

Veronica was amazed at how much the Memphis area had grown. A cluster of name-brand hotels was nestled along I-22 on the city's eastern edge. She had no trouble finding accommodations in a safe part of town.

After checking in, Veronica took a few minutes to relax. This whole thing came on so fast. Like a car wreck. Veronica knew she was in shock. It would take some time for all this to sink in.

A few minutes before five p.m., Veronica's cell phone rang. It was Carol. "Hi. It's me again."

"Hi, Carol. I found a hotel. I'm at the Worley Inn and Suites on I-22 just east of downtown. Any suggestions on where to meet for dinner?"

"There's a nice restaurant just a couple of miles from where you are. It's called Ladondo's. It's an Italian restaurant right off of I-22 at the interchange with I-90. I can meet you there at around six p.m. Will that work?"

"That's perfect. See you then."

Veronica had no trouble navigating through Memphis despite all the traffic. The trip to the restaurant was a short drive.

Carol arrived early and secured a booth near the bar. As Veronica entered the small, dimly lit restaurant, Carol waved to get her attention. Veronica walked briskly over to greet her.

"Carol, it's so good to see you again. You look great. Life must be treating you well."

"Thanks. You look as young as ever."

After placing their orders for dinner, followed by some chatty small talk, the conversation gravitated to the obvious.

"It's great you could come to Memphis. I have a feeling there's something more to the story than what you've told me."

Veronica's breathing became shallow and rapid. She repeatedly ran her index finger around the rim of her drinking glass. "Yes, there is. I didn't want to jump into the details on our phone call."

Carol raised her eyebrows. "Well, tell me what's going on. Is everything still good between you and Clevis? Is he doing okay?"

Veronica shook her head. "The truth is everything seemed great up until a couple of days ago. That's when I stumbled across a note in Cleve's dresser drawer."

Carol frowned. "What note? What's that all about?"

Veronica took a deep breath and sighed. "It's kind of a long story. I felt like Clevis and I were getting too busy with our lives. We seemed to be doing everything separately. He was constantly either at his office or on a business trip. We never took the time to get away, just the two of us. Not even for a weekend. After a while, we began to grow apart. We were still a strong, committed couple, but we never did anything together."

Carol nodded in agreement. "I certainly know how that can happen. As you know, I've been through two divorces. In both cases, we drifted apart as time went on."

Veronica twisted her mouth to the side, biting nervously on her upper lip. "There's actually more to it. I got the idea to surprise him by writing a love note, which he'd find when he got dressed in the morning. When I placed the note in the drawer, I ran across a piece of paper sticking out from under his socks. I didn't think anything of it until I noticed a perfume scent. I don't wear perfume as a general rule."

Carol interrupted, "I think I know where this is going."

Veronica continued, "The note was written by a woman named Crystal. I don't have her last name. The message in the note was unmistakable. Clevis was having an affair with this woman."

Carol cocked her head and looked askance at Veronica. "It's an age-old story. When a guy gets some success under his belt and sees he's not getting any younger, he latches onto some young hardbody he met at a bar or a business meeting."

Veronica cupped her chin in her hand. "You got that right. I don't have any details, but I would imagine Clevis met this woman while he was at some business function."

Carol furrowed her brow. "The obvious question is what are you planning to do?"

"I'm not sure. It all happened so fast."

"You can stay with me if you want until you get things under control. It's just me at my house. I've got plenty of room."

"I'm okay at the hotel for now, at least until I figure out what I'm going to do."

"Okay. Let me know what I can do to help."

As the evening ended, Veronica returned to the hotel to get some rest.

The next morning, Carol called. "I've been thinking about what you said last night. You should plan on staying in Memphis for the foreseeable future. I can help you find a job if that's what you want."

After an extended silence, Veronica reluctantly agreed. "I guess that does make sense. I definitely don't want to go running back to Huntsville."

Carol nodded.

Veronica's voice was choked with emotion. "I hardly slept last night. I couldn't get my mind to shut off. Around two this morning, I had an epiphany. A little voice told me I'm not sure I want to stay married to Clevis. He's become someone I don't know. It's a shame."

"I'll tell you what. I'll check at the office to see if anyone knows of a good job opportunity for you. I bet we can come up with something which will work well for you."

Veronica shook her head. "It's been a long time since I was in the workplace. I'm kind of rusty. The technology has changed so much since I was working."

"Oh, you'll do fine."

As Veronica made her best effort to reconstruct her life, Clevis sought solace in his relationship with Crystal. She was sixteen years younger than him. The attraction was purely physical at first. By any standard, Crystal was a knockout. She was relatively young, full of energy, and had a slender body with flowing auburn hair down to her shoulders. To any male, she was pure eye candy.

Clevis first met Crystal during a business lunch at a local restaurant in Huntsville. She worked there as a part of the wait staff. Her smile and flirtatious manner particularly attracted Cleve. She was a refreshing change from the more mature and staid attributes of Veronica's personality. One thing led to another. In a short time, Cleve and Crystal were immersed in a full-blown affair.

A few days after Veronica left for Memphis, Cleve called Crystal. "Hey babe, it's me. How are you doing?"

Crystal responded tentatively, "Okay. How have you been? I haven't heard from you lately. Are you mad at me or just too busy for anything but work?"

Cleve exhaled audibly. "It's been a hell of a week. Veronica found the note. She was livid, to say the least."

"What did she do?"

"I was kind of surprised at her response. I thought she would ask a lot of questions. That wasn't the case. She cussed me out and then just packed up and left. I think she was in shock. I found out later she went to Memphis. That's where her sister lives."

Crystal replied with a facetious tone, "Ah, I feel bad about that. I guess I'm the classic homewrecker."

"It damned sure turned out that way. I'm kind of pissed. She felt she could just walk out on me. I've done so much for her over the years. She'd be nobody if it weren't for me and all my success."

"Seriously, I don't like the idea of your marriage falling apart. That's not what I want."

"Well, at this point, I don't know if my marriage will survive. I didn't expect Veronica to react the way she did. I thought she would be more understanding and forgiving. I guess I was wrong about that."

"What do you plan to do now?"

"I'll just take it one day at a time."

The affair with Crystal had started as a mere fling. Over time, she became his sounding board and psychological support mechanism. She was a counterforce to his inherent diabolical, over-the-top personality. She tended to be caring and altruistic. By contrast, when Cleve reached adulthood, he had become arrogant and self-indulgent.

As odd as it seemed, Crystal tried to be Cleve's north star. To get him to put people ahead of money and success. She wanted him to reconcile and strengthen his relationship with Jarod.

Before Veronica stumbled onto the love note, Cleve had gone out of his way to keep his relationship with Crystal secret from Jarod. He knew Jarod was very close to his mother. If Jarod found out about Crystal, it would have been only a matter of time before Veronica learned of the affair.

Veronica did her best in Memphis to settle into a more predictable and independent lifestyle. Soon after Veronica arrived, Carol checked for opportunities at the law office. She was able to find an opening at the firm for an entry-level file clerk.

Carol told Veronica about the job. "I think it would be a good start for you. You would have the chance to learn how everything operates at the office. Law work can be stressful, but I'm sure you'll catch on fast."

The following week, Veronica interviewed for the job. She was offered the position on the spot. She had no hesitancy in deciding. She took the job. She really wanted to find herself and prove she could be independent. Working in law was all new to her. The opportunity to work for such a prestigious firm as Davis and McGill was the chance of a lifetime.

Shortly after taking the job, Veronica discovered she liked getting up each day to go to work. She especially enjoyed the interaction with the people in the office. For the most part, the attorneys had shown a lot of patience. The office manager, Kathy Sloan, quickly became her mentor.

Veronica was told she had to learn the workflow of the office to do her job. Her official title was file clerk, but it was not long until she was asked to do a wide variety of duties. After a couple of weeks, Ms. Sloan had Veronica delivering court documents to the court clerk's office for filing. This was an education in and of itself. As she sorted through the filings, Veronica couldn't help reading some of the petitions and answers for the various court actions handled by the firm. It was a case study of human nature, sometimes at its worst.

At the end of the first week, Carol invited Veronica to go to lunch. Carol was anxious to hear how things were going. "It's been so busy. I haven't had time to ask you how you like your work."

"My head's kind of spinning. There's so much to learn. Everything they gave me to do is new to me. I guess I'm doing okay. No one has cussed me out or fired me. At least, not yet. I really like the litigation part of the practice. I should have gone to law school after I graduated from the University of Alabama."

Carol responded confidently, "I knew you'd like this. It's very fast-paced and intense at times. Overall, it's very exciting to see all the moving parts of a big law firm. But I should warn you, there are some players and gamers practicing law here. Just be aware."

It wasn't long until one of the senior partners in the firm, Ainslie "Buddy" Howell, III, noticed the diligent work ethic Veronica routinely displayed. He could tell Veronica was one of those "all business" kind of workers. Mr. Howell was a local celebrity in the firm and within the larger legal community in and around Memphis. He was better known to his friends and colleagues as "Buddy." A cherubic-looking Irishman of average stature, graying temples, and the traditional bulging Irish paunch, he possessed all the traits of his Celtic ancestry.

Howell's courtroom antics and melodramatic style branded him as a showman. Buddy's trademark characteristic was his ready smile and uncanny ability to instantly turn a discussion or debate in his favor.

He had an unsettling propensity to speak as an affable, good old boy with a slow deliberate cadence. Then suddenly, he'd turn deadly serious with a scowling facial expression and a piercing, almost hypnotic stare whenever such tactic suited his purpose.

With appropriate admiration, Buddy observed Veronica's intense interest in learning all she could about the law. He could see she was a quick study. In the beginning, he asked Veronica to pull case decisions when the paralegals were unavailable. Later, as her confidence and capability grew, he assigned basic legal research projects to her to see if she had what it took to get the job done.

Veronica took to the law like a natural. She was intrigued by the analytical approach to the practice of law and admired the collective intellect of the attorneys at the firm. After a few weeks, Buddy Howell began to refer to Veronica as 'Ms. V'.

Some of the members of the firm were surprised that Howell had given Veronica a nickname. He wasn't known for being particularly warm and cordial toward other colleagues in the firm. He obviously admired Veronica's drive and self-confidence in her job performance.

The days flew by as Veronica delved into her new job and the opportunities it offered for personal and professional development. For the first time in many years, she felt a sense of liberation and independence. After a couple of weeks, she realized she hadn't heard from Clevis. She didn't really know what to make of that. She was surprised he would just ignore her entirely, especially after his betrayal of their marriage.

Veronica knew Cleve was a strong-willed man. A proud man who never liked to admit a mistake. Over the years, Veronica noticed Clevis never apologized for anything. He once told her an apology was just an excuse for poor performance or personal failure. Veronica knew, from Cleve's perspective, he had never been guilty of either.

In the back of her mind and in her heart, Veronica hoped Clevis would call. She had talked with Jarod at least three or four times since leaving Huntsville.

Veronica felt relieved that Jarod was no longer a child. This whole matter was hard enough for him but would have been doubly difficult if he had been a vulnerable teenager at the time of her departure for Memphis.

In any event, Veronica knew Jarod was very upset about the whole thing. He'd mentioned to her that Clevis hadn't shared any details about the separation. From the early years of Jarod's adolescence and into adulthood, Clevis had always played the hardass, tough-guy role.

On the most recent phone call to Veronica, Jarod mentioned he planned to come to Memphis for a visit that next weekend. Veronica was looking forward to seeing him.

Finally, it was Friday afternoon. It had been a long week. His dad had been in a perpetually bad mood ever since Veronica's departure.

At about seven-thirty p.m., Jarod arrived at Veronica's hotel. She had anxiously watched for him from her second-floor room overlooking the front entry. As Jarod entered the parking lot, she spotted his car and hurried down to the lobby to greet him. "Jarod, it's so good to see you. I missed you."

Jarod hugged his mother. "I've missed you too. It seemed very weird not to have you around."

"I have to admit, I don't miss Huntsville. It was such a cold life in that big house." Veronica motioned toward the rear of the lobby. "Let's go into the coffee shop so we can talk."

Jarod and Veronica found an empty table near the kitchen. The waitress arrived as soon as they sat down. "Would you like to see a menu?"

"No, I just want some coffee," Veronica responded.

"That sounds good. Same for me."

"So, what's been happening with you?"

Jarod pursed his lips and shrugged. "The usual. Work at the office every day. Back to the apartment each evening. Same old grind, I guess you could say."

"Are you getting along with your father?"

Jarod looked down at the table. "About the same as always, which isn't saying much. He's acting like a big baby. He can be such a prick. He never misses a chance to let me know that I don't measure up to his expectations. He keeps bringing up the financial problems of the company. He blames most of that on me because of that damn crane accident. As if he didn't already have serious cash flow problems."

"Sounds like he hasn't changed a bit."

"It probably comes as no surprise to you. After all this time, he hasn't been able to come up with the funds to pay off the balance of the settlement with Scott Westby. I wished he would lighten up a bit. It would make everybody's life a lot nicer. I don't know about you, but I feel much more relaxed being out of Huntsville."

Veronica gently stroked Jarod's hand. "Me too. I've been here for a few short weeks now and feel much more at ease. I'm beginning to feel like I've finally found myself. When you're living in Huntsville day to day, you don't realize how destructive it is to be in the toxic and oppressive atmosphere created by Clevis."

Jarod nodded. "I know for a fact I'm not going to be excited about heading back home on Sunday."

Veronica hesitated briefly. "Jarod, I want to let you know. I'm so sorry I couldn't attend your graduation at the university last month. When I called you to let you know I wouldn't attend, I didn't explain appropriately. I wanted to be there more than anything in the world, but I was afraid your father would show up. I didn't want to face him. Not now. Not yet."

Jarod leaned toward his mother. "That's okay. No big deal. I understand."

After several hours of conversation, Veronica and Jarod left the coffee shop to return to Veronica's room.

Jarod asked, "How's Carol doing?"

"She's doing great. I'm so glad I contacted her after I left Huntsville. You know, she's working for a law firm here in town. I mentioned to you that she got me a job at the firm. I love the job. It's a whole new world."

Jarod paused. "I'd like to see her while I'm here. Do you have her address?"

Veronica reached for her purse to retrieve the address. "It's 1136 E. Hollandale Road. I've been over there a couple of times. I think I remember how to get there. She said we could drop by anytime while you're in town. I'll give her a quick call to let her know we're coming."

As they drove toward Hollandale Road, Veronica mentioned

that the area was rich with the history of Memphis. It had been designated as a historical preservation district many years prior.

The well-maintained cottage-style homes were neatly arranged in straight rows along the tree-lined boulevard. Carol's house was a stand-out on the block. An immaculate 1930s-era cedar shingled bungalow featuring an arched porch canopy over-looking a deep crimson mahogany-paneled front door.

Carol was standing on her porch as they pulled into the drive-way. She greeted them enthusiastically. "Come in, please."

As they entered the house, Carol reached out to hug Jarod. "Hi Jarod. I haven't seen you for … how many years has it been?"

"At least five or six."

"Hope you didn't have any problem finding my house."

Veronica replied, "No. I remembered how to get here. It wasn't that hard. I'd stopped by a couple of times since I moved to Memphis."

"You guys come on in and have a seat. Jarod, tell me how you've been. Did you ever get married?"

"Nope. Still single. But I've been ----"

Veronica interrupted, "Carol, I would have told you if Jarod was getting married."

"Well, the right girl will come along someday. It always seems to work out that way. I guess that sounds kind of silly coming from a two-time divorced person. I guess I'm still waiting for the right guy to come along. He'd better hurry up, though, I'm not getting any younger!"

Carol closed the front door and sat down on the sofa. "Jarod, I know you work at the company. Veronica told me you're now Vice-President of Operations. I'm impressed."

"Yeah. It helps if your dad owns the company. I still get teased by my friends about that. Jarod paused. "Oh well, it is what it is, I guess."

"Well, Jarod, what's been going on in your life?"

"There's not much to tell. I'm sure you know I graduated from high school in 1998. Went on to the University of Alabama. Dad insisted I go to his old alma mater. I majored in business administration. Graduated from U of A just last month."

"That's great. When did you go to work at the company?"

"I started full-time right after graduation. Got my own apartment. It's a short drive to the plant from where I live."

Veronica emerged from the kitchen area holding a fresh-brewed cup of tea and exclaimed, "Carol, I've got some exciting news. I've decided to go to night school to learn to become a paralegal. I guess my big sister influenced me once again. I can tell you really like what you do. I've enjoyed learning all I can at the firm. But I need my paralegal license to really advance."

"That's great. I think you'll do fine. You seem to have a knack for the law."

Jarod furrowed his brow. "But how will that work with Dad in Huntsville? Doesn't the paralegal curriculum take a couple of years to complete?"

Veronica replied, "I know. I'm going to take this one day at a time. I can't just sit around waiting for your father to have a change of heart and come 'rescue' me. Besides, I don't feel like I need to be rescued. I like what I'm doing. I plan to push ahead with this."

"I don't quite know what to say, Veronica. I'm thrilled you want to do this," Carol declared.

At the end of the weekend, Jarod reluctantly loaded his suitcase and headed back to Huntsville. As he approached the city limits, he couldn't shake that all-too-familiar sense of tension and dread that had plagued his daily life for several years.

I don't know why I continue to do this. Dad doesn't know how to let up. He's way too intense. He just needs to learn how to live in the moment. He's driving me crazy.

CHAPTER 5

Veronica and Carol returned to their regular jobs at the firm. Shortly thereafter, Veronica moved in with Carol to save money and to rideshare to work on days when Veronica didn't have to work late.

Veronica enrolled in night classes for paralegal training at Caledonia Community College in Memphis. The rigorous schedule was daunting. The demands of working full-time and attending night classes were almost more than she could handle.

The class assignments required time to study and do research. She adopted a schedule using her lunch hour to do research assignments in the firm's law library. Veronica routinely reminded herself that she was not the first person to work full-time and attend night classes.

One of the more challenging assignments for Veronica was serving as the first assistant to Steven Gaither. Gaither was in his mid-forties. He had been a partner in the firm for six years. Veronica could not help but notice. He was tall and handsome. Filled with confidence. A truly smooth operator.

Steven was the lead counsel on a multimillion-dollar international corporate conglomerate case. The case dealt with multiple issues, including theft of intellectual property and potential tax fraud.

The firm was acting as defense counsel in the action. The plaintiff alleged that the firm's client had swindled the plaintiff out of millions of dollars through an elaborate scheme designed to disguise the actual financial picture of the corporation. Veronica felt very fortunate to have been asked to participate in such a high-stakes case. She was extremely excited to be able to assist in the legal research for this epic matter.

The trial for the case had been tentatively scheduled for later in the year. Mr. Gaither knew he had a lot of work to do to properly prepare for trial.

The court had ordered each of the parties to prepare a trial brief outlining the key issues and applicable case law for the matter. The demands of the case required Veronica to spend the majority of her office hours in the firm's law library searching for and printing copies of relevant case law for Gaither's review.

During the project, Steven suggested he and Veronica have a working lunch at The Eatery, a small soup and sandwich shop located a block away from the firm's downtown office.

The two packed up a file folder of documents for discussion and headed out, arriving just as the noon crowd began to flow into the small establishment. A table for two remained open against the east wall near the front entrance.

Steven commented, "Grab that table. I'll get a couple of menus."

Veronica quickly secured the table and waited for Steven.

As Steven sat down at their table, Veronica said, "This was a good idea to break away for lunch. There are a lot of interruptions at the office."

Steven confirmed, "We've got a lot to get done. The trial brief submission deadline is coming up very soon."

While waiting, the two ordered their food and began to review some of the critical issues related to the case.

Near the end of lunch, Steven asked, "Do you like working at the firm?"

"Sure. It was a bit scary at first. But I think I'm slowly beginning to understand enough to not screw things up."

"You know, I asked for you to be assigned to my project because I could tell you're on the ball. You've acquired a damn good reputation at the office. Especially for someone who's not yet a paralegal. Some of the partners have described you as a fireball. That's damn high praise coming from lawyers who've been around a long time and seen a lot."

"I have had a lot of help along the way."

"That's true, but new hires either have the drive to succeed or they don't. The ones who don't have it end up getting their ass kicked by the senior partners. The ones who have what it takes get worked like slaves. I've seen quite a few newbies who didn't survive the process."

"My sister warned me about that when I took the job. She said the firm used an attrition system to weed out the mediocre people and to encourage the performers. I understand they call it 'the meat grinder'. After being here for a while, I can see what she meant." Steve hesitated. "One last thing. I know it's really none of my business, but I've heard you came to Memphis to escape a difficult situation in Huntsville."

Veronica looked startled by his forwardness. "Yeah, that's true. I don't particularly like to discuss my personal life. But I have to say I never expected to be living away from what had been my home for decades. Life can be tough."

"Well, I just want you to know, I admire you."

The days leading up to the trial passed at lightning speed. The pace of the trial prep was intense. Two weeks of hard work flew by. That time seemed like mere hours. The trial brief deadline was looming. Steven and Veronica worked tirelessly and continuously on this one big case.

At the end of an exhausting week of mind-numbing work, Steve asked, "Why don't we take a break? I'd like to have dinner with you sometime."

"Well, that's nice of you to ask. I'll have to check my schedule."

"How about tonight?"

Steve could see that Veronica was caught off guard.

"I was thinking I would just go home. It's kind of short notice."

"I know, but you deserve a break. I'll call ahead and get a reservation. I know a little restaurant and bar not too far from here. I'll make it for six p.m. We can go over in my car."

Veronica was not at all thrilled about the spontaneous dinner invitation. It seemed thoughtless and selfish to assume that she had no plans on a Friday evening.

On the other hand, she understood the political dynamics of a large law firm. You get along to go along. Steve had become a second mentor to her. She felt indebted to him.

Veronica needed that kind of connection to really achieve success in her legal career. Besides, Steven was a very personable and friendly guy. Although she hated to admit it, she had actually become very fond of him. His casual manner and agreeable personality were a refreshing respite from her experience with Clevis.

Veronica noticed that Steven had become exceptionally complimentary at a personal level in the weeks leading up to the trial. It was obvious he liked her. She could see it in his eyes.

In the end, she knew she couldn't say no to the dinner invitation from a partner in the firm. She had to admit it: She did enjoy his company.

At five-thirty, Steven and Veronica drove the short distance to Colby's Seafood and Steakhouse. Located off of the main highway at the edge of a residential district, it appeared to be a genuine out-of-the-way venue. Veronica noticed that the exterior of the building resembled a Swiss chalet.

As they entered the restaurant, the manager escorted them to their table. The interior of the restaurant was quaint and charming. The décor was rustic, filled with knotty pine paneling, giant wrought iron chandeliers, and massive oak beams soaring to the peak of the cathedral ceiling, creating a uniquely homey atmosphere

Steve remarked, "They've got some great food here. I've been coming to this place for years. Do you like seafood?"

Veronica shrugged. "It depends. I grew up in Huntsville. We ate catfish and frozen shrimp. My family was more the meat and potatoes crowd."

Steven grinned broadly. "Well, then, I won't suggest the calamari. I think I know what I'll have. The blackened sea bass with almondine sauce."

Veronica carefully studied the menu. "I guess I'll try the grouper."

"That's a great choice. It's really good here." Steve raised his hand to summon the waiter. "I'll get the wine list. They have some great varieties."

The evening flowed steadily into the night. The conversation was easy and interesting. Steve didn't mention the office project at all. He described his diverse life experiences, which included everything from deep-sea diving to mountain hiking. His athletic activities starkly belied his relatively sedate daily routine at the law firm.

As the conversation evolved, Steve began to ask more intimate questions. He hoped to pull Veronica out of her protective bubble. He sensed that Veronica was somewhat uncomfortable with his questions. She appeared to be very reluctant to delve into her life prior to coming to Memphis.

After dinner, including multiple glasses of wine and a decadent dessert consisting of blueberry lemon trifle and German apple strudel, the conversation continued to evolve to a more personal level.

"It's a shame your relationship with your husband has soured. I assume the two of you are technically separated since you are now living in Memphis."

Veronica looked askance at Steven. "We aren't divorced, if that's what you mean."

"I guess I'm asking if your arrangement with him would be described as estranged."

"That's a fair description."

"It must be a lonely existence being here in Memphis when your family is in Huntsville."

Veronica quickly replied, "My son comes to visit on a regular basis. And I live with my sister, Carol."

"No, what I meant was you don't have anyone to tuck you in at night. A woman like you shouldn't have to be alone. The worst thing in the world is to feel lonely. You know, I can help with that."

Veronica suddenly felt the cool sensation of sweat emerging from her torso. Her heart pounded in her chest. She never expected Steve to come on to her. She was truly lonely. But she was well aware of the fact she was still married to Clevis. She knew she needed to keep her job. Carol had warned her to do her best not to offend the power brokers at the firm. But, at the same time, she didn't want to acquire a reputation as part of Davis and McGill's "meat market".

With some lawyerly persuasion, Steve convinced Veronica to come with him to his place. He was living alone as a recent divorcee. As they approached Steven's home, Veronica was surprised to see his house was relatively ordinary for a partner in the firm. The three-bedroom ranch-style house looked more like a starter home than the residence of an accomplished lawyer.

Steve swerved sharply into the driveway, stopping within inches of the garage door.

"Well, this is it. The humble abode of a newly divorced trial lawyer. As they say back home, 'It ain't much, but it's all mine.' Come on in. I've set up a cozy little bar in the basement. I've got all the top-shelf labels. Just name it, and I can serve it."

Steven invited Veronica to make herself comfortable as he opened a bottle of Merlot and poured ample servings into two crystal goblet glasses.

Steve placed the wine goblets on the small end table next to the sofa and sat down uncomfortably close to Veronica. Without saying a word, he thrust his right arm around her neck and shoulder as he abruptly slipped his left hand under her skirt onto her bare left thigh.

At that point, Veronica realized this was not merely a social visit. She didn't want to offend Steven, but she definitely wasn't interested in spending the night with him. Veronica reflexively lurched backward.

"Look, Steve, I need to get home. It's late. My sister would be expecting me to be home by now."

Steve looked puzzled. "I thought you wanted to be with me for the evening. I promise you, this will be a night you won't soon forget."

As he uttered those words, Steve aggressively pressed his body firmly against her torso, forcing her down against the seat of the couch. His right hand methodically searched for the upper waistband of her panties. Veronica struggled desperately to wrest her body free of the oppressive weight of his bulky frame.

With uncharacteristic physical strength, she was finally able to push Steve off of her. With one herculean thrust, Veronica was free of his unwelcome advance.

She quickly stood up and backed away. "I may get fired for this, but I can't justify a spontaneous fling with you just because my marriage is in trouble. That's not the way I operate. It may not be a good marriage, but I'm still married. Call me a damn fool or old-fashioned, but that's the way I am."

Steve looked up at her. Veronica could see his clenched jaw and angry expression.

"It does disappoint me. You disappoint me." He shrugged. "But, if that's the way it is, so be it."

Steve left the room for a brief period to relieve himself in the bathroom. Shortly thereafter, he drove Veronica back to the office parking garage to retrieve her car. The chatty, cheerful conversation and witty charm were gone. The silence was palpable.

After he dropped her off, she drove home thinking this whole evening was a big mistake. She wasn't sure how this experience would affect her work at the firm, especially her working relationship with Steve. Only time would tell.

That next Monday at the office, Steve conducted himself as if nothing had occurred. The charm offensive had evaporated. From that day forward, he was strictly business. Veronica chalked the whole experience up to a life lesson well learned.

She remained conflicted by the whole experience. In her heart, she knew she had a certain level of attraction for him, but he was out of bounds with his unwelcome come-on.

To Veronica, there was no doubt. Steve was a great lawyer and an outwardly friendly person. After the experience on Friday evening, she knew he was one of those guys who can't keep his pants zipped. Obviously, he knew how to use his charm to get what he wanted. Veronica wondered if Steve's predatory approach to women was the main reason he was no longer married.

In the days following that fateful dinner debacle, Veronica was pleasantly surprised. Everything seemed fairly normal in her work world. She soon learned through the office grapevine that Steve was a notorious perennial womanizer who saw every available female as his prey. She quickly realized he had simply written off the whole experience as a missed opportunity and a waste of his time. By his standards, you win some, and you lose some.

In the following weeks, life went on for Veronica with a certain routine predictability. Toward the end of the first semester of the two-year associate degree paralegal program, Veronica received an unforgettable phone call.

Her cell phone rang just as she entered her bedroom. It was Clevis.

"Veronica, how're you doing? I've thought about you a lot, and I've been concerned about you."

Veronica impatiently interrupted, "Why are you calling me? Are you running out of clean laundry? Did your little girlfriend find someone else? Is that why you called? What do you want, Clevis?"

Cleve hesitated, then spoke in a soft and deliberate tone. "I understand why you're angry with me. I don't blame you. I've been a real horse's ass, I know that."

Trying to control her anger, Veronica blurted out, "You really don't get it, do you? You betrayed me. For that matter, you betrayed Jarod as well. I trusted you. We trusted you! Do you think you can just waltz back into my life and say you're sorry? I've got to go, Cleve. I'm busy right now. Goodbye."

Veronica hung up the phone and spontaneously collapsed onto the bed. She wasn't one to cry, but this whole thing was just too much. She lay motionless for twenty minutes, staring at the ceiling as the tears streamed down her face. She pondered, *Whatever happened to honesty and dedication in a relationship?*

As Veronica slowly regained her composure, her body began to relax. Her head sank back into the pillows lining the upper portion of the bed. Within minutes, she fell into a dream-like state, thinking back on the early years of life when she first met Clevis at Huntsville High.

Her thoughts danced through the cardinal events of her life with Cleve. How young Clevis developed into the person she now knew was a total mystery. She recalled the stories Cleve told about growing up in the little hamlet of Brecksville, Alabama. About the childhood adventures he and his friend, Loren, experienced while playing and exploring down on the Chenawa River.

As she drifted back through the passage of time from her high school days to the present, she could see the transformation of Cleve's personality from a considerate and athletic straight-shooter high school kid to the obsessive win-at-any-cost industrialist he had become. The evolution of his personality was unsettling for Veronica. The haunting image of his diabolical transformation rocked her to her core.

She recalled Cleve had told her more than once that he didn't want to end up like his dad. Working forty years at a dead-end job. Nothing to show for all the hard work when it was all over.

She remembered the story Clevis liked to tell about buying a motor scooter with his own money. "The thing that stuck with me was my dad telling me he couldn't buy the scooter for me on the money he made as a rural mail carrier. I knew right then that money meant power and opportunity. Without money, you're nobody."

Looking back, Veronica could see that those early formative

years for Clevis and the experience of relative material depriva-
tion sparked his desire to prove something to the world. From
Veronica's perspective, Clevis viewed life as a binary choice. You
either went full speed toward unlimited professional and financial
success, or you ended up mired in mediocrity and relative
obscurity.

CHAPTER 6

After the unpleasant encounter with Clevis, Veronica settled into a consistent routine in Memphis. Working at the firm during the day. Attending night classes after work four days a week. The schedule was grueling. She knew she was extending herself beyond healthy limits. She was totally exhausted, both mentally and physically.

On a Thursday evening after class, while driving south toward home on Lamar Avenue, Veronica approached the intersection of Shelby Drive and Lamar just as the traffic light on Lamar Avenue turned green. An oversized pickup truck with rear dually wheels traveling westbound at a high rate of speed on Shelby Drive ran the red light and blew through the intersection. In the next millisecond, the giant truck violently struck the driver's side of Veronica's car. The unmistakable deafening sound of instantaneous compression of crushing steel and shattering glass echoed through the warm night air. The explosive force of the crash left an aftermath of utter destruction.

The momentum of the impact spun the two vehicles in a clockwise spiral, collapsed the driver's door of Veronica's car into a U shape and propelled both vehicles approximately one hundred feet past the intersection.

After the initial impact, the pickup truck careened off the right-of-way into the drainage causeway bordering the street. The severe force of the collision compressed the front end of the truck, driving it into the midsection of the engine compartment. Both vehicles came to rest at different points in or near the intersection approximately thirty feet apart.

The constant hissing sound of escaping steam from the punctured radiator of the truck could be heard over the dull hum of traffic on the adjacent interstate highway. A passing motorist frantically called 911 on her cell phone to summon emergency services. In a matter of minutes, the crash site came alive as ambulance, fire rescue, and police units converged on the scene. Veronica's vehicle was a mangled mass of twisted steel bearing little resemblance to the car it had once been.

Due to the massive size of the truck and the deployment of airbags, the driver of the truck escaped with only minor cuts and abrasions. Veronica's fate was a starkly different story. The fire rescue unit immediately utilized the hydraulic jacking system, commonly called the jaws of life to force open the driver's side door of Veronica's car to gain access to the interior.

After twenty minutes of intense effort, the fire rescue crew was finally successful in extracting Veronica from the contorted mass of steel in which she had been imprisoned. The EMTs administered first aid at the scene to minimize any bleeding and to stabilize the multiple bone fractures in Veronica's lower extremities.

Following stabilization, the paramedic crew carefully loaded Veronica into the ambulance and transported her to the nearest emergency trauma facility at Parkside Memorial Hospital. The investigating police officer noted that the collision was a classic T-bone configuration resulting from excessive speed and failure to obey a red traffic signal.

The medical team at the trauma center quickly began to assess Veronica's injuries. After a complete examination and medical workup, Veronica was admitted to the intensive care unit in serious condition. She had sustained multiple bone fractures. The x-rays revealed compound fractures of her femur and tibia bones in her left leg. She also suffered a ruptured spleen, a collapsed lung, and multiple abrasions and contusions.

Upon learning of the accident, Carol dropped what she was doing and immediately rushed to the hospital to check on Veronica. Carol was totally frustrated to learn that, due to privacy issues, the information desk was unable to provide any details regarding Veronica's injuries.

She asked emphatically, "My sister was just brought in from a bad car wreck. Where can I get information on her? I need to know how she's doing."

The information desk attendant replied nonchalantly, "You might try the admitting department on the second floor."

Carol ran frantically down the hallway to the elevators to make her way to the second floor. Trying to contain herself, she asked the woman in the admitting department, "My sister was in a car wreck and was transported to this hospital. I need details regarding her condition. Can someone please tell me about my sister?"

With an expression of matter-of-fact indifference, the woman replied, "I can page the charge nurse on duty."

"Oh, thank you. I'm beside myself worrying about her."

"Uh-huh," the woman responded.

The page blared out over the intercom system, echoing through the granite hallways of the hospital, "Nurse Johnson to Admitting. Nurse Johnson to Admitting, please."

Shortly thereafter, Margaret Johnson, the charge nurse on duty greeted Carol in the main lobby. Her warm smile provided a modest level of reassurance to Carol.

"Hello. I'm Margaret. The admitting department told me your sister had been processed into the emergency room and ICU. I understand you have some questions. I think I can help with that."

Carol nervously inquired, "I just want to know that she's going to be okay. How badly was she injured?"

"Well, she was in shock when she arrived. We've been able to stabilize her. We took her into emergency surgery shortly after her arrival to repair the internal injuries caused by the impact of the collision. After she's had a brief period of recovery, probably in a couple of days, we'll set the broken bones in her left leg."

"Is she out of surgery?"

"Yes. She's back in the ICU."

"When can I see her?"

Johnson quickly responded, "Not yet. She's heavily sedated. I'd suggest you wait until sometime tomorrow afternoon to visit her. I think she'll be alert enough to talk to you then."

Carol fidgeted with her car keys. "Okay. I guess I don't have any choice. I'll be back tomorrow after work. Thanks for the information."

Carol left the hospital, consumed by the dilemma of what she should do for her sister. This all happened with lightning speed. She realized the best approach would be to monitor Veronica's progress through daily visits to the hospital.

As she drove toward home, Carol called Jarod to let him know about the wreck.

The next day at the office, all of Veronica's friends and colleagues were anxious to know how she was doing.

Within minutes after Carol's arrival at work, Buddy Howell walked into her office.

"I just heard about Veronica. That sounds like a bad wreck. How's she doing?"

Carol looked up from her desk. "I stopped by the hospital last night. She's doing as well as can be expected. She suffered a lot of injuries. She had surgery for a ruptured spleen and a collapsed lung. They said they'll set the bone fractures in her leg sometime today."

Howell shook his head. "My God, that poor girl. That must have been a hellaciously traumatic experience. Keep me posted on her condition."

In the days that followed, Carol developed a regular routine.

She would stop by the hospital each day after work to visit Veronica. In a short period of time, she could see the progress.

Five days after the wreck, while still in the hospital, Veronica began preliminary physical therapy. She had great difficulty walking, even for a short distance.

For the most part, Veronica was confined to a wheelchair. After two weeks, she was released from the hospital. To regain the use of her legs, Veronica was instructed to obtain advanced physical therapy.

Two and a half months had elapsed since the accident. Since her dismissal from the hospital, Veronica had undergone extensive physical therapy involving hour-long sessions several times a week. Eventually, Veronica was released by the doctor to return to work.

On her first day back at the office, Veronica was inundated by well-wishes and inquiries as to how she was doing. She was very happy to return to the office. But she still had a long way to go to regain her full stamina for the challenging work at the firm.

Toward the end of the first day back, Carol stuck her head into Veronica's office. "Hey, I just want to tell you. About a dozen people stopped by to ask me how you're doing. You've got a lot of people routing for you."

"Same here. I couldn't believe all the attention. It's nice to know people really care."

"Well, I don't want to rain on your parade, but I guess you noticed Clevis never visited you in the hospital. As far as I know, he didn't even bother to call to see how you were doing."

"Yeah. I did notice. He probably doesn't know about the wreck. No surprise, I guess. Cleve's never been a touchy-feely kind of guy."

In Veronica's absence, the pace of work had definitely not slowed. Despite her disability, she was able to maintain a satisfactory level of productivity. However, her mobility was compromised by the injuries she'd sustained. The doctors at the hospital had implanted a pin in her left leg to reestablish the structural support of the femur bone destroyed by the crushing effect of the collision. Veronica now walked with a slow, stiff, and deliberate gait, slightly dragging her left leg forward with each step. The limp in her leg was now a prominent feature of her stride.

In the second week following her return to work, she passed Buddy Howell in the hallway.

"Hey Veronica, stop by my office when you have a minute. I need to talk to you."

"Will do," Veronica dutifully replied.

Veronica was somewhat uneasy as she walked into Howell's spacious and immaculately decorated corner office, not knowing what Howell had on his mind.

As she entered, he glanced up from his computer keyboard. "Oh, come in. Have a seat. I got to thinking about your car wreck. I don't have any of the details, but I assume you haven't settled your damages or signed anything with an insurance company."

"That's right. I've not had time to deal with it. I did get a phone call from some guy who said he was an adjuster with the truck driver's insurance company."

"But you didn't sign anything, right?"

"That's correct."

"Well, I don't want to try to tell you what to do, but we would be happy to represent you to get a decent and fair recovery for your injuries and property damage."

Veronica was somewhat taken aback by Howell's assertiveness. "I hadn't thought about that. I guess it makes sense to use the firm."

Howell emphasized, "Mind you, we don't normally take personal injury cases. As you know, we focus on corporate law and insurance defense work for the most part. But I think we can get you a good judgment or settlement. Just let me know how you want to handle this. It's totally up to you."

Veronica hesitated momentarily. She stroked the side of her mouth with her index finger as she contemplated her options. "I guess I'd prefer to use the firm. That way, I don't have to go out and find a lawyer on my own."

"Good. I'll have someone draft a petition and an engagement

letter for our services for your review. I will need the truck driver's name and any other information you can obtain on this guy."

The following week, the personal injury lawsuit was filed in district court in Madison County. The action sought actual and punitive damages for her injuries. Veronica had never been involved in litigation in her life. Buddy Howell was convinced he was in the cat bird's seat on this one. He was certain he would have no trouble proving gross negligence on the truck driver's part.

In their discussion of the case, Howell told Veronica, "The speeding and blatant disregard for a traffic control device was prima facie evidence of gross negligence."

He said it was a textbook case. Howell predicted that, after some initial discovery through depositions, the defendant would likely be inclined to tender a decent settlement offer.

In time, Howell's prediction proved to be correct. The defense legal team tendered an offer of settlement, which was countered by the plaintiff's counsel. After several offers and counteroffers, an agreement was reached.

The total for all monetary damages was three million dollars, payable in annual installments over a period of fifteen years. In exchange for the money, Veronica agreed to sign a non-disclosure agreement to conceal the details. The agreement contained the usual language prohibiting any discussion of the settlement with anyone except her spouse.

Despite the trauma of the car wreck and her substantial injuries, life went on for Veronica. It had been several months since Clevis made a run at her, trying to convince her to return to Huntsville. Her obstinance about his proposal remained unmitigated. She had no real desire to return to her old life with Clevis. After all, Jarod was making regular visits to Memphis to see her. Veronica had what she wanted in life, at least for now.

Eventually, Clevis heard about Veronica's car wreck. He mentioned to Jarod that he was concerned about her condition. He asked Jarod to provide regular updates regarding Veronica's path to recovery. In one of the conversations, Jarod mentioned that Veronica's law firm was representing her in a personal injury action against the other driver.

Shortly thereafter, Clevis discovered that Veronica had obtained a sizeable amount of money for her injuries. After learning of this, he stopped by Jarod's office at the plant.

"Jarod, you'd mentioned that your mother was able to get a settlement for her car wreck, but you didn't say how much she got."

"I don't know. Mom said she couldn't say. She signed some kind of agreement not to tell anyone about the details. I think she said the only person who she can discuss the settlement with is you."

Clevis nodded his head. "That makes sense."

The following Wednesday, Clevis called Veronica to see how she was doing. "Hello?"

"Hey Veronica, it's me. How've you been?"

"I'm doing pretty good, considering what I've been through."

"Yeah. I heard about your wreck. I wish Carol had called me to let me know. I could have come to Memphis to help out."

"Never mind Clevis. We got along just fine."

"I've been thinking about you. I wish we could get back together. Why don't I come to Memphis so we can talk? We can go out for dinner, someplace nice."

Veronica abruptly interjected, "Clevis, I like my life here in Memphis. I don't see any reason to return to Huntsville."

"There's no hurry about that. I thought it would be nice to have dinner together. I miss you. I can come to Memphis next weekend. How about it?"

Veronica intuitively sensed that Clevis undoubtedly had some undisclosed ulterior motive disguised by his overt concern for her welfare. She knew he had never been an empathetic kind of guy.

"I don't know, Cleve. I don't see the point."

"Just say yes. It's just dinner. It will be good for both of us."

Veronica remained silent momentarily. She was truly conflicted. She wanted to trust Clevis, but her instinct told her otherwise.

She reluctantly agreed. "Okay. Let me know where you want to go, and I'll meet you there."

"I've already checked it out. There's a place where we can have a little privacy. How about next Saturday at the Fontainebleau Steakhouse on North Alecote Drive? I heard it has good food and is kind of quiet. Let's plan to meet there at six p.m."

Veronica still hadn't learned how to say no to Clevis. At some deep psychological level, she was still that young, starry-eyed college girl infatuated with the tall handsome ex-Marine football hero.

Over the last few months, Carol had repeatedly warned Veronica about Clevis.

"I don't think it's a good idea to have contact with Cleve. He can't be trusted. He's a master manipulator, and you're his target."

Despite the indisputable evidence of his extramarital affair with Crystal, Veronica didn't want to believe what Carol was saying. By nature, Veronica was a forgiving person. And a bit naive.

The balance of Veronica's week was filled with nervous antici-pation of her upcoming dinner engagement with Clevis. She was definitely conflicted about seeing him again. At some point, she would have to decide about the future of their relationship. She had intentionally immersed herself in her work and paralegal classes to escape any thought of a renewed life back in Huntsville.

For Veronica, this may be her seminal moment. Her head and her sister told her to continue down her current path of financial and professional independence from Clevis. But yet, her heart spoke to her in ways that defied logic and reason. She was aware that she could have declined Cleve's dinner invitation. But, for some reason, she had a lingering need to preserve the relationship.

On Saturday, Cleve left Huntsville shortly after noon. He wanted to be the first to arrive at the restaurant in Memphis. He had no idea how the evening would go. He felt confident that, given a chance, he could persuade Veronica to at least consider returning to Huntsville.

Clevis pulled his black Mercedes into the restaurant parking lot a full half-hour before their scheduled six p.m. meeting time. The dining area was already filled with customers. The maître d' inquired, "Good Evening, sir. Do you have a reservation?"

"Yes. It's under Harrington."

"Of course, sir. Right this way."

Cleve was escorted to a small table near the rear of the restaurant. He sat anxiously awaiting Veronica's arrival. Finally, he spotted her entering through the front door. He briskly walked to the front of the restaurant to escort her to their table.

"Veronica, thanks for coming. It's great to see you again. You look really good."

Veronica's breathing became more rapid. She could feel the muscles in her back tighten. There was noticeable tension in her voice.

"Nice to see you too, Cleve."

As they sat down at their table, a brief period of awkward silence overshadowed the moment. Clevis finally began to speak, "First of all, tell me how you're doing. How's your leg? Are you getting around okay?"

"Oh, sure. I can go wherever I want. I have a limp I can't seem to get rid of. Sometimes, my left leg aches at night, and occasionally, I get numbness. Other than that, I'd say I'm doing pretty good."

The two ordered dinner. Clevis selected a bottle of vintage Cabernet Sauvignon.

As the evening progressed, the conversation evolved to the seminal question.

"I know you and I have talked about this before. I would like you to consider returning to Huntsville." Clevis nervously twirled his index finger around the top of his drinking glass. "I'm sorry for what happened. It was a mistake in judgment on my part. I don't know what I was thinking when I got involved with Crystal. I want you to know Jarod and I miss you."

"I told you already, I have my job here, and I'm in the middle of my training to be a paralegal."

Clevis reached out and softly touched the top of her hand. "I understand that. I was going to suggest you get your paralegal certificate in Huntsville. Then, if you want, you can find a job with a law firm there. I can help you with that."

Veronica queried, "How's that any better than what I have now in Memphis?"

"Well, for one thing, you would have Jarod and me back in your life. You would be living in our spacious home rather than in a spare bedroom at Carol's house."

Veronica quickly interjected, "I don't mind living with Carol for now. The spare bedroom at Carol's has plenty of room. Besides, I see Jarod fairly often. He's been coming to Memphis to visit me on a regular basis. You probably don't know this, but Jarod was extremely upset by all of this. He told me he's ashamed of the way you behaved."

Clevis shifted in his chair.

"He was particularly hurt when he learned of the affair. He's a sensitive young man. To him, your affair was a betrayal of his relationship with you as his father."

Clevis took a sharp breath. He paused before he spoke. "I know I've not been a world-class dad for Jarod. He's a complicated guy. I don't have the time to deal with his issues every day."

Veronica shook her head in frustration. "I just want you to know the law firm has been very fair with me. They have supported my efforts to get my paralegal training to advance in the firm. I don't want to pull up stakes here and come back to a life filled with stress. Cleve, you know better than anyone that you are a driven man. You can be hard to live with. Damn hard! You devote all your free time to your work and the company. Jarod told me he's stressed to the max working with you. Here in Memphis, I get respect and encouragement from my work colleagues."

Following that exchange, the two sat silently for what seemed like an eternity. Although Clevis was staring directly at Veronica, she suddenly found it very difficult to make eye contact with him. The pain she felt ran very deep. She could not ignore the blatant betrayal of the affair.

Her clenched fist revealed the disgust she felt toward Clevis and her sheer determination to pull her life together in her own way.

"Clevis, I am no longer the same person I was before your affair. I've found new self-confidence. For the first time in my life, I have a genuinely positive outlook. The life I have now is truly fulfilling. When I was in Huntsville, I didn't realize how empty and superficial life was with you."

Clevis furrowed his brow. "I know you've changed. I'm not asking you to give up anything. I just want you to consider returning to Huntsville so we can be a family again."

Veronica was no longer looking down at the table. She leaned forward with a piercing stare, her elbows planted firmly on the table. "You really don't get it, do you? You have an affair behind my back and now expect me to come crawling back so you can have the life you found so easy to betray? That says a lot about what you thought of our relationship. Am I not good enough? Damn it, Cleve! You haven't said one word about what's going on between you and Crystal. Are you still seeing her? It's pretty damn selfish for you to think you don't have to explain these things."

Seemingly unphased by her emotional response, Clevis replied, "I know you would be happy back in Huntsville. We can take some trips together, just the two of us."

Veronica sat silently in contemplation, her chin resting in the palm of her hand. Her eyes locked directly onto Cleve's face as if searching for the truth in his words.

"I can see you're not ready to decide. Give it some thought. I'll check back with you soon."

The evening eventually ended in an awkward and uncomfortable way. An uneasy truce had been reached.

CHAPTER 7

The next morning, Clevis returned to Huntsville. Five days later, he called Veronica to continue his pitch for her return. "I've given this a lot of thought. I know I made a mistake getting involved with Crystal. The affair is over. The whole experience made me realize how important our relationship is for both of us."

Veronica remained deathly silent.

"Are you still there?"

Veronica finally responded. "Cleve, I don't intend to return to Huntsville. At least not at this point. Why should I? As I told you at dinner the other day, I have a new and rewarding life in Memphis."

"I know that. I was hoping you'd reconsider. Life could be good again for us. Damn good."

Veronica replied with an unmistakable sternness in her voice. "The truth is, Cleve, I may file for divorce. It's something I've considered."

Silence ensued. Cleve was speechless.

The phone call abruptly ended. Veronica had hung up.

In the days that followed, Veronica continued her paralegal training at night while working days at the law firm. She rarely allowed her thoughts to linger on Cleve's offer of a renewed life in Huntsville. But as time passed, the rawness of the betrayal began to diminish. Clevis continued to call on a regular basis. He doggedly pursued her to return to her former life.

After many phone calls initiated by Cleve and innumerable sleepless nights thinking about her options, Veronica's resolve began to wane. Cleve's reassuring and flirtatious comments during the phone calls had elicited a renewed romantic feeling toward Clevis which Veronica had not felt in years.

With a notable amount of unshakeable reticence, Veronica reluctantly decided to return home to Clevis. After considerable soul searching, she was resolved to do her part to try to restore the life the two had known in happier times.

Carol quickly learned of Veronica's decision to return to Clevis and was adamantly opposed. She pleaded with Veronica to open her eyes to see what Clevis was up to. Carol urged Veronica, "Once you're back in Huntsville, it's going to be no better than before. Clevis is going to do whatever he damned well pleases. You must know by now. To him, it's all about Clevis and his career success."

"Oh, I don't know about that. I think he's seen the light. He deserves another chance. He sounded so sincere on the phone."

"Listen to me, Veronica. Have I ever misled you? Open your eyes. I can see what's happening. He's a damn snake. He may have been a good guy, but the taste of success has destroyed his moral compass. You have to hear what I'm saying before it's too late."

"I appreciate your concern, but my heart tells me it's going to be okay. People make mistakes. We all make mistakes. I've already told Cleve I'm going home. I can't back out now."

Veronica had given this a lot of thought. She continued to have reservations about her decision. But she had made up her mind. She was not going to go back on her word. She wanted to believe that Clevis was sincere in his comments. After all, he had apologized to her. Everyone knew Clevis Harrington never uttered the words "I'm sorry" to anyone. Veronica took that as a subtle sign of his abject sincerity.

Over the years, Carol had always been a devoted sister to Veronica. She was not giving up on her effort to thwart Clevis' plan to get Veronica to return to Huntsville.

The day after Cleve's visit to Memphis, Carol called him.

"I want to talk to you about what you're trying to do to Veronica. Do you think I don't know what's going on? She's too blind to see what you're up to. I know you too well, Cleve. It's always all about you."

Clevis responded with a contrived tone of indignation. "I don't know what you are talking about."

Carol shot back, "The hell you don't! Cut the crap, Clevis. I'm not naïve. I've seen you in action. I'm sure you promised the world to Veronica to convince her to come back to you."

"All I did was talk to her. I stated my case, and she made her decision."

"Bullshit, Cleve. You're a damn liar, and you know it." Carol hesitated momentarily to collect her thoughts. "I'll promise you this, Clevis Harrington, if anything, and I mean anything, ever happens to my sister, or if I find out you mistreated her in any way, I will personally come to Huntsville and have you thrown in jail!"

Cleve rebutted indignantly, "You can threaten me all you want. I know what I'm doing. It has nothing to do with you. I'd suggest it would be advisable for you to keep out of this."

"You wish I'd keep out of this!" Carol replied sharply. "Not on your life."

In a dismissive tone, Clevis said, "It was really nice to talk to you, Carol. I've got to go. I'm extremely busy right now. Goodbye."

Veronica remained in Memphis until the end of the current semester. She gave notice to the firm that she would be leaving at the end of the third week in May.

When her mentor and friend, Buddy Howell, received word of her impending departure, he asked her to stop by his office. Veronica dutifully reported to his spacious corner suite, knocking hesitantly on the partially open door to draw his attention.

Howell looked up over the top of his reading glasses. "Oh, Veronica, Come in, please. What's this I hear about you leaving? Someone told me you plan to go back to Huntsville."

Veronica took two tentative steps into Howell's wood-paneled oasis. "Yes. I hate to leave. I really enjoyed working in the firm."

Howell paused, took a deep breath, then gestured for Veronica to sit in one of the leather chairs in front of his desk. "Are you going to finish paralegal training?"

"I plan to. I want to go to work for one of the law firms in Huntsville."

Howell nodded his head with conspicuous approval. "Let me know when you graduate. I can make some phone calls to try to get you into a good firm. I know quite a few of the senior partners in a couple of the bigger firms in Huntsville. It shouldn't be any problem getting you well placed."

"I appreciate all that you've done for me. I'll miss this place."

At the end of the spring semester, Veronica packed up to head back to Huntsville. As she loaded her personal belongings into the car, she turned to give Carol a hug. "Thanks for all your help. You've been a lifesaver, especially when I was recuperating from the wreck."

Veronica could see that Carol's expression revealed great concern and doubt.

"I hope it all goes well for you. Let me know. I look forward to seeing my little sister become a paralegal just like her big sister. We'll be quite the pair."

The drive back to Huntsville was unsettling. Veronica's thoughts swung wildly from confidence about her decision to haunting moments of self-doubt. She could not shake the gnawing feeling that this may not go well. She was gripped by apprehension. She had made a commitment to return to Cleve. There was no obvious way to turn back.

After arriving in Huntsville, Veronica and Cleve quickly resumed their lives together. In the beginning, Cleve was noticeably more compassionate and attentive toward Veronica. She was encouraged and somewhat taken aback by his overt tenderness and uncharacteristic thoughtfulness. Jarod was very happy to be able to see his mother whenever he wanted. It seemed life was good once again in the Harrington household.

The newfound tranquility at home was soon overshadowed by the reality of the pressures Clevis faced to reconcile the financial problems at the office. Total sales at the company had dipped significantly. A substantial balance remained unpaid for Jarod's unfortunate crane accident at the plant.

Things were far from ideal, despite the scenario Clevis had described to Veronica in his pitch to lure her back home. After three months, Cleve decided to ask Veronica about her car wreck.

Based on what Jarod had said, he knew the lawsuit against the truck driver had been resolved. But only Veronica and her lawyers knew the amount of the settlement.

It was Saturday morning. Clevis and Veronica were having breakfast together. It was a tradition for the two of them. A rare opportunity in their busy lives to have a meaningful conversation without the distraction and pressure of the weekday grind.

In the midst of their meal together, Clevis casually asked, "Jarod mentioned that you were able to settle your lawsuit for the wreck. Do you think the amount was fair?"

"Yes. The firm did a good job representing my interests."

Clevis sat silently for a moment. "How much did you get?"

Veronica's brow lowered in a scowl.

Why would he be so interested in the details of the settlement?

A niggle of apprehension worked its way through her.

"I'm not allowed to talk about it."

Cleve quickly replied, "Jarod told me your non-disclosure agreement said you could discuss the details with your spouse. That's me."

Veronica took a deep breath. "I guess it's okay to tell you the details. The total was three million dollars. I had to deduct legal fees from that. I don't get the money all at once. It's a structured settlement, paid out over fifteen years. It sounds like a lot, but it's not as much as you'd think."

"What do you mean?"

"Three million dollars, less about a million in legal fees, the remainder paid out over fifteen years. Do the math."

"Okay. I get what you're saying."

"My lawyers told me I was lucky. The truck driver had substantial personal assets and carried a sizeable amount of liability insurance. They said that was very unusual."

A subtle smile emerged on Cleve's face. "The settlement seems very appropriate, considering your long-term disability from the accident."

Veronica commented in a matter-of-fact tone, "I think so. I was just glad to get it behind me."

Shortly after breakfast, Clevis and Veronica relaxed in their den, enjoying the warming rays of the morning sun.

Cleve moved closer to her. "I don't have to tell you, Veronica, it has been really tough lately. We've all been under tremendous pressure with the demands of the company and the tragic accident at the plant. It's easy to see the car wreck in Memphis has taken its toll on you." Clevis paused. "You know what? I think we need a respite from all this. Why don't we plan a family retreat? We can spend a few days on our boat down on Mobile Bay."

Veronica's face erupted with a broad smile. "That's a great idea. It will be just the three of us as a family. Oh, Cleve, you don't know how much it means to me to get away to relax and enjoy each other's company. You know, it's 2005 already. Do you realize we haven't spent any time together in several years? I know this is exactly what we need."

CHAPTER 8

I t had been quite some time since Cleve and Veronica had an opportunity to use the boat. Cleve spared no expense in purchasing his toys. From his perspective, his cars and the boat were symbols of extraordinary success. Even though the craft was rarely used, it was one of the finest mid-size seaworthy marine crafts available.

The sleek V55 Phantom yacht was a beautiful vessel. He had named her "Alpha One." Cleve fell in love with the stylistic lines of the bow of the ship the minute he saw her at the marine show. The craft has two deck levels, two living areas, twin inboard Valera Magnum engines, a master stateroom, three guest cabins, and a large L-shaped seating area next to the teak wood wet bar.

Since the early years when Cleve set out on his own in the aeronautical and aerospace business, Cleve's motto had been 'Nothing's too good for a Harrington.' His high-end boat was the perfect example of that philosophy.

The trip down to Mobile took a little less than five hours, not including the stop for lunch at Dixieland Barbeque along the way. On arrival at Mobile Bay Marina, Cleve told Veronica, "I'll stop by the boat house before we head out onto the water. I need to check with the boat master to be sure everything is ready to go."

As Clevis walked down the wooden ramp toward the water's edge, his heart began to pound as his pride and joy came into view. The vessel was sparkling clean. She looked as if she'd just come out of the dealership showroom.

The management at Mobile Bay Marina had always done a great job maintaining the moored vessels. Billy Williams, the marina general manager, never passed up an opportunity to tell his customers, "We like to protect these babies from deterioration. The summer's blazing sunlight, and the bay's caustic saltwater can really screw up a boat's finish."

"Let me help you with that case," Cleve told Veronica as the three quickly loaded all their gear and supplies onto the vessel. "I want to get out on the water early enough in the afternoon to have some time to relax before it gets dark."

Cleve loved to pilot his boat. He bounded up the short run of steps into the cabin and sat down in the captain's chair. As he firmly gripped the steering wheel, he gingerly turned the ignition key. In an instant, the engines roared to life. Cleve loved the throaty rhythmic growl emanating from the rear of the craft as she slowly emerged from the mooring.

After the boat cleared the no-wake zone, Cleve gunned the engines to full throttle. The bow of the sleek craft suddenly surged upward as the vessel hurled through the water, resembling a shiny rock skipping across the glistening surface of a sprawling mountain lake.

He quickly accelerated to just shy of the craft's maximum speed of thirty-seven knots. Cleve had always been a speed junkie. He couldn't get enough of fast boats and high-dollar sports cars.

After a short sprint across the bay, the boat approached Cleve's favorite fishing spot, a secluded cove near a remote outcropping of land about a mile out from the marina. As the boat pulled into the cove, the afternoon sun began to gently sink into the western sky, creating tiny glistening stars of sunlight reflecting off the rolling swells of deep azure blue water.

"This is it- paradise lost," Cleve remarked to Veronica and Jarod. "It's still early enough for us to do a little fishing. I'll round up the gear from the back of the boat."

Cleve and Jarod sat down in the fighting chairs at the rear of the boat and cast their lines into the calm waters of the protected cove. "I don't mind if we don't even get a nibble. I just want to relax and enjoy the fresh air and sunshine."

As the sun slowly set on the distant horizon, Veronica began to prep the evening meal. The delicate aromas wafted through the galley and onto the gentle breeze.

"Hey, Mom. Something smells really good. What's for dinner?"

"I'm fixing a special meal for you and your father. We're having Delmonico ribeye steaks, albino asparagus spears, and double-baked potatoes."

Veronica loved to cook. Most of all, she enjoyed cooking for her two favorite guys. She was ecstatic simply to be away from the pressures of life back in Huntsville. To live in the moment with her family.

As the afternoon progressed into evening, the last rays of sunlight gave way to the inky darkness of the night sky. The stars emerged shining radiantly in the celestial sea of black as if millions of tiny twinkling fireflies hovered overhead in a cosmic stellar light show.

After dinner, Cleve selected his favorite easy-listening music and prepared cocktails for the two of them. "I made your favorite drink. A Manhattan straight up."

"Thanks, honey. You take such good care of me. Where's Jarod?"

"He's down on the lower deck watching TV in one of the guest cabins."

Veronica embraced the comforting warmth of the evening summer breeze as she stretched out in her chase lounge chair. The rhythmic sound of the water lapping against the bow of the boat created a hypnotic atmosphere as she gazed wistfully into the night sky.

"Do you remember when we first met at Huntsville High? You were so handsome in your letter jacket. I couldn't take my eyes off you. Those were the best days of our lives, Cleve. Do you ever stop to think about how much our lives have changed? We get so busy nowadays, we don't seem to have time for each other. You probably don't realize it, but you've changed over the years. You were so easygoing back when we first met. Now, you're all business. Success is all you think about. I want to get back to devoting more time for the two of us. I really miss that. I wish we could get back to that kind of time. We really need to rediscover the relationship we had together back in high school."

As Veronica spoke, Clevis sat silently staring into the night sky. She had an uneasy feeling his mind was off in some distant unknown place. She was truly rattled by the thought that he didn't hear a word she said. She wanted this outing to be special. A chance to reconnect with the Clevis she grew to love so many years ago.

The evening quickly progressed into the night. The breeze emerging from the clearing in the trees lining the shore subsided into a subtle calmness. The water in the cove became as smooth as glass.

After several drinks, Clevis and Veronica sat on the foredeck watching the sky, trying to identify celestial bodies just as they did when they were young high school lovers.

"My lord, look at the time, Clevis. It's almost midnight. We probably ought to get some sleep."

Veronica attempted to stand. She stumbled slightly and grabbed the edge of the chair. "I think I've had enough cocktails for one evening. You do know how to make a stout drink, my dear."

Clevis watched as Veronica struggled to maintain her balance. He couldn't help but notice. Her unsteady gait caused by the car wreck was exaggerated by the alcohol she had consumed.

As Veronica made her way toward the master stateroom to prepare for bed, Cleve walked toward the bow of the boat. He stopped midway to look out across the shimmering ebony surface of the cove. In the distance, the faint image of lights twinkled along the far shore.

The water's pretty calm right now. Just to be safe, I'll drop the anchor. The wind might pick up before dawn.

For the entire evening, Jarod had been down in one of the guest cabins. At his age, he'd rather watch TV or play video games than sit around with his parents.

At ten minutes past midnight, before retiring for the evening, Veronica stuck her head into Jarod's cabin to say good night.

It was now five a.m. the next morning. The first rays of sunlight were yet to appear in the eastern sky. Clevis frantically ran into Jarod's cabin, shook him violently, and screamed, "Where's your mother? She's not in our cabin and I've searched all around the boat. No sign of her anywhere. Where the hell is she?"

Jarod quickly emerged from his deep sleep and bolted to his feet. The shocked look on his face said it all. "What do you mean she's not here? I saw her getting ready for bed just a few hours ago."

He sprinted around the boat, checking all the cabin rooms and both decks. No sign of her. Nothing seemed amiss, except his mother was gone.

Jarod lamented, "I don't see her anywhere! Oh my God, where is she?"

Clevis quickly pulled anchor and sped back to Mobile Bay Marina to call the police. The speed of the large boat approaching the marina created whitecap waves that slapped against the massive piers along the dock.

Clevis abruptly reversed the engines to slow the vessel's rapid approach. The boat had barely stopped its forward motion when Cleve jumped onto the dock and hastily tied the vessel to the pier walkway.

Cleve hollered back as he ran toward the door, "Jarod, stay with the boat to be sure she doesn't come loose."

The marina had just opened for the day when Cleve burst

through the entrance. "I need to use the phone. It's an emergency!"

The manager, shocked by the abruptness of Cleve's explosive entry into the marina office, replied, "It's over there, on the counter."

Cleve frantically keyed in the number.

"911, what's your emergency?"

"My wife. My God, she's missing. I don't know what happened. We were out on Mobile Bay overnight on our boat. When I woke up this morning, she was gone."

The dispatcher inquired, "Did she fall overboard?"

"Well, I guess so. What else could it be? I don't know what could have happened to her otherwise. Can you send someone out here right away to try to find her?"

The dispatcher replied, "Now calm down sir. We need to get some information."

"Please do something quick! She may be trying to swim. She's not a good swimmer at all. I need your help. Oh my God, I can't believe this is happening."

The dispatcher calmly asked, "Where were you when your wife went missing?"

"We were in a small cove area on the east side of the tidal channel. Near the outcropping about a mile offshore."

"We'll contact the Coast Guard. They'll have a search and rescue team scour the area. They'll find your wife if it's at all possible."

"Please hurry. Please."

As Clevis returned to the boat, Jarod shouted, "Dad, we've got to go back. We can't just wait around for the rescue boat. She's out there somewhere. She may be struggling to hang on. I don't want her to drown!"

Clevis reached out and placed his hand on Jarod's shoulder. "We both want to find your mother, but it's still too dark. We wouldn't be able to see anything. We'll have to wait for the Coast Guard. They'll find her."

After receiving the call, a Coast Guard UTB rescue boat sped to the location provided by Cleve's description of the area. The unit made a quick grid pattern search, shining a massive cabin spotlight from side to side as the vessel moved back and forth across the water. The muffled sound of the engine of the Coast Guard craft rose and fell as the boat accelerated across the search zone, slowing at the end of each pass to negotiate a sharp turn to repeat the process.

Nothing was found. The rescue diver on board donned her wet suit to check for any indication that someone had entered the water. After several dives, there was no sign of Veronica or any of her clothing. The coast guard crew eventually determined that there was nothing more they could do until a search team could be deployed to comb the shoreline for evidence of a drowning victim.

The Coast Guard cutter boat made a tight turn in the water and headed back to the station to file a report. The search and rescue unit had done all they could that morning to find Veronica. It now appeared the effort had transformed from a rescue operation to one of recovery.

The Coast Guard commander on duty sent the report to Sergeant Brent Palmer, an eleven-year veteran of the Mobile metropolitan police department. Sergeant Palmer was familiar with the area in Mobile Bay where the boat had been anchored at the time of the incident. He'd lived in southern Alabama all his life. As an avid fisherman, he spent many weekends navigating the nooks and crannies of the bay. He knew his way around the cove and the outer reaches of the waters surrounding the area where the tragic incident occurred.

CHAPTER 9

The next day, Sergeant Palmer called Clevis regarding the disappearance of his wife.

"Mr. Harrington, we'd like for you to come down to the precinct headquarters to tell us what you know about the events last night on Mobile Bay."

Clevis replied, "What time? You know we want to cooperate, but we have to get back to Huntsville as soon as possible. I'm expected to be at my office for some meetings later today."

"Under the circumstances, I would suggest you plan on spending several days here in Mobile. We want to talk to you and to your son to get the full picture of what transpired out there. I would think that you would at least want to stick around until your wife is located. Why don't you be down here at headquarters around eleven a.m. today?"

"I can do that. Do you want both of us to come?"

"Yes, we want to talk to the two of you."

Upon arriving at police headquarters, Clevis was escorted into an interview room in the west wing of the building. The room was stark by any standard. Not exactly luxury accommodations. A small dinged-up rectangular table sat against the easterly wall with three stiff back chairs haphazardly strewn around the room.

An antique-looking phone was positioned on the table with the cord dangling off the far end as if inviting the interrogated party to request permission to make a call. A dark-tinged mirror was mounted to the wall directly across from the table. Clevis knew from watching detective stories on TV that this was likely a two-way mirror to allow others to anonymously monitor the proceedings. A camera was mounted to the upper corner of one wall, with the lens conspicuously positioned to record the activities occurring at or near the table.

As Clevis sat uncomfortably in one of the small metallic chairs, Sergeant Palmer entered the room. Palmer had an imposing appearance. A semi-portly man with a neatly trimmed mustache and a partially bald bulbous head surrounded by closely-cropped salt and pepper hair forming a horseshoe shape resembling a fuzzy headband hugging the back of his skull.

Palmer began, "My name is Sergeant Brent Palmer. I'm part of the homicide unit here at Mobile Metropolitan Police. I'll be asking several questions here today. First of all, is your son with you?"

"Yes, he is out in the waiting room. Do you want him to join us?"

"No, that won't be necessary. We'll talk to him after we discuss the situation with you."

Palmer pulled up one of the chairs and sat with his legs straddling the chair seat and his arms resting on the chair back. "Let's start at the beginning. You're from Huntsville, is that correct?"

"Yes, we decided to come down to Mobile to spend a few days on our boat. Just to get away for a while."

"To get away from what?"

Clevis fidgeted nervously with the phone cord. "Well, it's kind of a long story. I'll try to be brief. We have a company in Huntsville- Harrington Industries. We are involved in the design and manufacturing of all types of component parts for both the aerospace and aeronautical industries. Without getting into too much detail ----"

Palmer interrupted, "No, go ahead. We want all the details you can provide. Tell us the whole story. Please continue."

"Well, it's been very challenging lately at the company. That's the reason my wife and I decided to take a little time off to come down here with our son, Jarod. We just wanted to spend some time together to relax and unwind."

As Clevis spoke, Sergeant Palmer was taking notes in a dog-eared flip notebook. "Tell me in your own words what transpired on the evening your wife disappeared." Palmer reached over to retrieve some papers stacked on the corner of the table. "The incident report states that her name is Veronica. Do we have that correct?"

"Yes, that's correct. Veronica. I'll start at the beginning. We arrived at Mobile Bay Marina where our boat was moored in a wet slip storage unit. After we arrived, I asked the boat master to have our vessel topped off with gas. We then headed out into Mobile Bay to find a spot in a cove area where we like to visit. It's about a mile out near a channel outcropping."

"Yes, I'm familiar with the area. I've done quite a bit of fishing in that same cove over the years. So, what happened next?"

"Once we found the spot we wanted, we tried our luck fishing. Didn't catch anything. After that, my wife prepared dinner."

Palmer prompted Cleve to elaborate.

"What did you do for the rest of the evening?"

"Our son went off to one of the guest cabins to watch TV and play video games. Veronica and I went up onto the foredeck of the boat to sit in the deck chairs. We enjoyed a couple of drinks and talked about old times. Just watched the night sky. Nothing all that extraordinary for us."

"What time did you and your wife go to bed that night?"

"It was about midnight. I remember Veronica had mentioned that the time had gotten away from us, and it was already close to midnight."

Palmer leaned forward, pressing his chest against the back of the chair. "Did both of you sleep through the night?"

"Yes, we did. We were both pretty tired and fell asleep right away."

Sergeant Palmer hesitated for a minute, resting his chin in the palm of his hand. "When did you first notice that your wife was missing?"

Cleve replied with an air of certainty, "It was the next morning when I woke up. I noticed that Veronica had gotten up before me. I assumed she was in the bathroom getting ready for the day. She tended to be a morning person most of the time. I didn't think anything was wrong at that point. I laid there for a little while and then got up to go to the bathroom. That was when I suddenly realized Veronica wasn't there. She wasn't getting ready. I could see she hadn't taken a shower. All of the towels were hanging on the rack just where they were the night before."

"What did you do at that point?"

"I got very concerned. I looked around the boat. I checked the upper deck and then went down to check each of the guest cabins and the bathroom on the lower deck. She was nowhere to be found. By then, I was in a panic. I went to the cabin where Jarod was sleeping. I woke him up and asked him where Veronica was. It turned out that he had no idea since he'd been asleep."

Palmer sat silently with his arms planted firmly on the back of the chair, his eyes locked on Cleve's face. He rocked forward and back, his face coming within inches of Clevis' head. After a long pause, he asked, "Did Jarod search the boat looking for his mother?"

"Yes, he ran out of the cabin and looked everywhere on the boat. And, of course, he didn't find her."

Palmer cocked his head to one side and pursed his lips. "What did you mean, 'of course, he didn't find her?'"

Cleve quickly responded, "That probably was not the best way to put it. What I meant was neither one of us could find out where she had gone."

Palmer rose abruptly from his chair and leaned over tightly

into Cleve's face. "Your wife mysteriously disappeared into thin air, and you don't try to search the immediate area? You weren't concerned that she may have attempted to swim to the little island outcropping? Or maybe she's still floating around in the water somewhere nearby. Seems a little odd to me."

Clevis looked shocked by the accusatory tone of the question. "No. We were very overwhelmed by the suddenness of her disappearance. We just did what came to us instinctively, I guess. Probably looks kind of bone-headed in hindsight."

Palmer slowly inhaled and exhaled with an audible sigh. He reached up and gently scratched the side of his forehead. "What happened next?"

"We pulled anchor and quickly headed back to the marina to call the police. You know, to get help."

"Why did you go to the marina to call? Didn't you have a cell phone on the boat?"

"Well, yes... I don't know why I didn't use the cell phone. I guess I wasn't thinking straight. My mind was scrambled at the thought Veronica had disappeared."

"Did you hear your wife get up during the night?"

Clevis shifted nervously in his chair. "No. I didn't, but I'm a fairly heavy sleeper. She may have gotten up to go to the bathroom and decided to get some air up on the foredeck. My guess is she walked along one of the side decks to get to the foredeck seating area and fell overboard along the side deck. The side decks are fairly narrow, and the railing slants outward. That area doesn't really give you a lot to hang on to. You know she was not all that stable on her feet. She was in a car wreck some time back. She walked with a limp."

Sergeant Palmer raised his eyebrows. He instinctively knew when someone volunteered a lot of collateral information without being specifically asked, they were often delivering a rehearsed explanation. "Wouldn't you have heard all that? As I understand your explanation of the layout of the boat, the side decks run right along the window area of the master stateroom."

Cleve quickly rebutted, "Nope. Didn't hear a thing. As I mentioned, I'm a heavy sleeper."

Palmer wrapped up his initial questioning of Clevis. "Okay. Thank you, Mr. Harrington. I want to visit with your son now for a few minutes to get his take on this. Oh, by the way, we'll be keeping the boat in a safekeeping location until the investigation is complete. At this point, the vessel is evidence and, until further notice, the boat will be considered to be a possible crime scene. You will no longer be able to access the boat or anything remaining on board until we're through. You're free to go, but it would be advisable for you and Jarod to stay in the Mobile area for a couple of days. Until we've completed the initial investigation."

Clevis promptly left the interview room as Jarod was escorted in. Jarod appeared exhausted and a little befuddled. He had that 'deer in the headlights' look in his eyes.

As a veteran detective, Palmer knew the first rule of a potential homicide investigation was that everyone present during the last moments of a victim's life was an automatic suspect. In Palmer's eyes, that would include Jarod. Palmer was old school. You ask the questions and let the facts lead you where they may.

After an hour of intense questioning, Jarod was allowed to join Clevis.

"Well, Jarod, it looks like we may be stuck here for a while. They've confiscated our boat for the time being. We'll have to get a hotel room for the night."

Palmer did not extract any new information from Jarod. He essentially confirmed Cleve's story that he didn't hear anything and was asleep from about midnight until about five a.m. when Clevis shook him awake to look for Veronica.

Two days later, Veronica's body was spotted a short distance from the cove by a group of fishermen. Jerry Brown, one of the fishermen, told authorities, "We saw something floatin' in the water just after dawn. At first, it looked like a piece of a wrecked boat fuselage or an old tire. When we got closer to check it out, turned out it was a dead body. The body had long dark hair.

Looked like a female to us. But it was all swelled up, so it was kind of hard to tell for sure. We figured we'd better head back to shore to let someone know so they could retrieve that person from the water. Looked to us like an alligator or something had been chewing on her arms. It was gruesome. Not something you want to see when you're out there doing some fishing for relaxation."

The following day, Sergeant Palmer met with Clevis to obtain additional information.

"We located your wife's body. She was floating in the bay. A group of early morning fishermen came upon her. It looked to us like she'd been in the water for a while. The coroner's office picked up the body. They'll conduct an autopsy to make a determination regarding the cause of death." Palmer paused as he checked his notes. "I have just a couple more questions for you. Have you and your wife had any marital difficulties? Any disputes or domestic disturbances?"

"Actually, not at all. We've been a very compatible couple since we met way back in our high school days."

Palmer queried, "Do you have any life insurance policies on her?"

Clevis hesitated for a moment. "I don't recall. If I bought any life insurance, it's been some time back. I'd have to check my records." Harrington reached up, nervously rubbing the palm of his hand on his brow. "I have to tell you, Sergeant Palmer, I can't really think straight right now. Just the other night, my wife and I were enjoying a pleasant evening on our boat. I wanted her to have some time to relax after her terrible car accident. Now she's dead. I can't believe it. I don't know how this happened. My God, this is a nightmare!"

"Car accident? Tell me about that."

"Veronica was in a bad car wreck when she was in Memphis. Hurt her leg really badly. She walked with a limp ever since."

"Okay. That's all for now. Please stick around the Mobile area so we can do a follow-up, if necessary."

The autopsy was scheduled for Friday at the Mobile County Medical Examiner's office. The senior pathologist, Dr. Mark

Webber, conducted the examination. Dr. Webber, a forensic pathologist with thirty-two years of experience, had acquired a national reputation as a renowned expert in the field of forensic review of suspicious deaths.

Upon completion of the autopsy, the report was forwarded to Sergeant Palmer. He quickly read the report and mentioned to John Dickinson, a rookie detective working in the homicide division, "This drowning case I'm working on is turning out to be quite fascinating. The autopsy report has some interesting comments."

Dickinson asked, "What do you mean?"

"Well, under the circumstances, I wasn't surprised to see her blood alcohol level was 0.10 percent. Mr. Harrington had mentioned they both had consumed several cocktails that evening. Also, I wasn't surprised to see the observation of the usual signs of drowning. However, Dr. Webber noted additional physical attributes on the body not typically found on a drowning victim. I'm not quite sure what to make of that."

Dickinson was hanging on Sergeant Palmer's every word. He had only been with the homicide division for two years. Being fairly young, he was anxious to learn all he could from Palmer.

Sergeant Palmer pointed out that the report noted the existence of frothing around the mouth and in the lungs. The lung histology profile indicated the presence of emphysema aquosum and alveolar edema. The report stated that this condition meant the lungs were hyperinflated and congested.

Palmer explained to Dickinson, "The pathologist observed bruising and numerous scratches and contusions on the outer or upper portion of her hands. The doctor mentioned this is not typical for a drowning victim and may be attributable to possible predator mutilation of the upper appendages during the time the body remained in the water."

The report further pointed out that, due to the aberrational nature of the injuries, x-ray studies were ordered of the victim's hands.

Detective Dickinson hovered anxiously over Palmer's shoulder as Palmer studied the report. Palmer casually leaned back in his chair with his right hand cradling his head, his eyes staring vacantly at the ceiling.

"Well, what do you think?" Dickinson asked.

Palmer looked down from the ceiling. "The x-ray report noted there were multiple fractures of the phalanges and the metacarpal bones in both hands. The examiner's comments did not provide a suspected cause of that condition. It stated that the observed injuries appeared to have occurred around the time of death. I'm not sure what this all means. It may be nothing, or it could later prove to be a relevant piece of information."

Sergeant Palmer determined he'd done about all he could in the initial investigation of the incident. A critical point for Palmer was the fact Huntsville was the hometown of the Harringtons.

It was time to coordinate with the Huntsville police department's detective division. Palmer called the central division and asked to speak with someone in the homicide division.

When the phone rang, Lieutenant Roy Mercer was sitting at his desk reviewing some crime scene photos of a recent homicide in preparation for testimony at a preliminary hearing.

"Lieutenant Mercer."

"This is Brent Palmer down in Mobile. I'm a detective in the homicide division."

"Yes, sir. What can I do for you?"

"We had a recent suspicious drowning on Mobile Bay. The reason I'm calling you is the victim is from Huntsville. The deceased's name is Veronica Harrington. I can send you more information later."

Mercer replied, "That name sounds familiar."

After a brief pause, Lieutenant Mercer said, "Oh yeah, Veronica Harrington. The wife of Clevis Harrington. I just saw a story on the news about her death."

"So, you know who she was?"

"Absolutely. The Harringtons are in the newspaper all the time. The family is well known in Huntsville. You might say they are Huntsville royalty. They own a huge manufacturing company here in town. What's the story about the drowning?"

Palmer replied, "It looked like a fairly routine accidental drowning at first glance. But the pieces just aren't fitting together for a run-of-the-mill accidental homicide. For one thing, Ms. Harrington allegedly fell overboard from their personal yacht in the pre-dawn hours on Thursday of last week. There's no apparent reason she would have been wandering around the boat at that hour of the night. From what they told us, both Mr. Harrington and their son, Jarod, were asleep in their cabins on the boat at the time of the incident. Harrington told me she probably had just gotten up briefly to go to the bathroom and fell overboard."

"Do you believe their story?"

"Well, I don't know. I suppose it sounds plausible, but it doesn't make sense she would then leave the lower deck area where the master stateroom is to walk to the aft deck and then, somehow, fall overboard. I realize it was a dark, moonless night. Damn difficult to see anything without turning on some deck lights. Hell, the boat was anchored at the time. It was going nowhere. It was a calm night. No wind at all. Harrington told me he'd dropped the anchor to stabilize the vessel in case the wind kicked up overnight. How do you fall overboard on a boat in calm water? Damn strange to me."

Mercer responded, "Sounds like there are a few loose ends on this one."

"Yeah, I'd say. Both Mr. Harrington and Jarod told me they didn't hear any splash. Their story is they didn't hear a damn thing. They both said they were sound asleep at the time. How can someone just walk off the backend of a boat and drown? Harrington told me his wife was not a very good swimmer. But it seems to me if she fell off, she could have grabbed ahold of the aft deck of the vessel and pulled herself back on board. When your life's at stake, a person can summon a lot of strength to save them-selves. If I'd fallen off of a boat at night, I'd be screaming my frig-ging head off to get someone's attention."

"That does sound strange, for sure."

After a brief pause, Palmer elaborated, "Another thing. The boat had night vision security cameras mounted around the vessel. I'm not sure why you would need security cameras on a boat. I guess to discourage theft and vandalism. As far as I could tell, the cameras covered all angles on the boat. However, when I went to look for the recording media in the central recorder unit for the system, I discovered the SD card was gone. I don't know if they just hadn't inserted a card or if someone pulled the thing so no one could see what was on it."

"Kind of odd. Do you have any reason to think someone was trying to hide something?"

"Don't know. Just a hunch. Nothing really makes any sense at this point. If the card was intentionally pulled, whoever pulled it probably threw it in the water. Based on what I know so far, I'd say this case is a jump ball as to whether it's a homicide or an accident. I asked Harrington about any domestic trouble. I also asked if he had any life insurance on his wife. He denied any marital problems. He was strangely vague about life insurance. The dots aren't lining up, Roy. That's where you come in."

"What do you need me to do?"

"You need to find all the dots. To connect this all together to get the real picture. We've got to figure out what came down out there that night. Did either Clevis Harrington or Jarod Harrington want Ms. Harrington dead? If so, why? They're from your town. You can sniff around to see if someone would benefit from the death of Veronica Harrington. At this point, I can't see what that benefit would be, but I don't know enough about Harrington's life back in Huntsville. I'll say this: I have a gut feeling the motive was not revenge or a crime of passion. It just doesn't have that feel. Anyway, you get the idea. Good luck, and let me know what you'll need from me during your investigation."

"Sure thing. This is going to be a challenge. I'll be back in touch as soon as I learn anything useful."

The day after Clevis and Jarod were told that the preliminary investigation in Mobile had been completed, they returned to

Huntsville. A week later, the coroner's office and the Mobile police authorized the release of Veronica's remains. Clevis quickly ordered her body cremated with no memorial service planned.

In the following weeks, due to the high-profile status of the Harrington family, *The Huntsville Tribune* carried a series of articles regarding Veronica's life as a social icon in the community and a philanthropist for many local charities.

Three weeks after the death, an investigative reporter published a series of articles delving into the details surrounding her death. The articles focused on the many unanswered questions vexing local authorities. The overt and ongoing publicity kept the matter in the public consciousness in and around Huntsville.

Several months had passed since Veronica's death. The ongoing interest in her demise was surprising to Clevis. He had assumed the news coverage of her death would subside shortly after the initial notice in the local newspaper.

The recent investigative articles cast a shadow over the family's reputation. Clevis had spent most of his adult life cultivating a positive reputation in the local community. Personal adversity was not good for business.

To stave off further negative publicity, Clevis reversed his original decision regarding a memorial service for Veronica. He decided a service at the family church might counteract negative news coverage and neutralize the ongoing interest in the mystery of her untimely death.

Cleve arranged for a memorial service to be held at the Crestwood Presbyterian Church in Huntsville. Crestwood Presbyterian was renowned for its iconic Gothic-style cathedral structure in the middle of the central business district of Huntsville. Crestwood was an old-line traditional church with a congregation consisting of the movers and shakers of Huntsville. Reverend Phillip W. Carter, the Senior Pastor, was in charge of the services.

Clevis wanted to ensure that attendance at the service would be significant. He placed announcements in both the Huntsville Tribune and the Memphis Gazette. Clevis chose a Saturday morning for the service to avoid conflicting with the usual church functions on a typical Sunday.

The weather was magnificent on the day of the service. A gentle breeze from the southwest accentuated the beautiful, crisp morning, with a majestic azure canopy of light emanating from a gloriously blue sky.

On arrival at the church, Clevis thought, *This weather is ideal. The Saturday morning schedule is perfect for a good turnout.*

The attendee list read like a Who's Who of Huntsville. The Harrington family's high-profile reputation in the community drew an auspicious collection of local dignitaries. Numerous business owners, executive directors of local charities, the mayor, and several leaders from the Chamber of Commerce were all in attendance.

Just minutes before the ten-a.m. commencement of services, Ainslie "Buddy" Howell, III slipped into one of the pews in the rear of the sanctuary. He had driven from Memphis to pay his respect to Veronica's memory.

At the appointed time, the mammoth seventy-year-old pipe organ, nestled in a balcony-level alcove off to the side of the altar, began to play 'You'll Never Walk Alone.'

The sound of the throaty bellowing bass notes of the arrangement reverberated throughout the facility, creating rhythmic vibrations that literally rattled the giant stained-glass windows perched above the elevated central pulpit of the epochal venue.

Reverend Carter began to speak in his thunderous baritone voice. "Please rise if you're able. We welcome all of you here on this glorious day. This is a day which the Lord hath made; let us be glad and rejoice in it."

At that moment, the organist began to play "Amazing Grace." The congregation stood in silence until the end of the composition.

"Please be seated. We gather here to honor the life and memory of one of our great servants of God, Veronica Harrington. I have known Veronica for more years than I care to admit. As I watched her carry out the duties and responsibilities of her life, she was a person of service. Service to her family, service to her community, service to her church, and, most of all, service to her God."

The memorial service continued with additional eulogies and musical selections, ending with the thunderous grandeur of the pipe organ performing the classic, "How Great Thou Art."

The massive sound of the mammoth thirty-two-foot bass pipes resonated throughout the sanctuary, echoing off of the highest point of the gothic dome ceiling of the iconic and gold-encrusted structure.

In the final portion of the service, Reverend Carter paused thoughtfully. He then commented that the family had asked him to include some personal anecdotal observations about Veronica.

Rev. Carter began, "Veronica's life was not free of adversity. She faced some difficult moments in her life. In those moments, she showed great resolve and determination. Not long ago, Veronica passed through some troubled waters. As some of you undoubtedly know, she lived for about a year in Memphis, Tennessee. In that time, she proved she was a resourceful and resilient person. While in Memphis, Veronica began a promising career in law. In addition to working full-time at a prestigious law firm, she was attending night school to complete her training to become a paralegal. Her career plans were cut short by her tragic and untimely death. Her ability to transform herself into a successful career person in her own right by pursuing a profes-sional career in law demonstrated she was much more than a social icon and charity fundraiser. She was a talented and ambi-tious person. More than capable of achieving any goal she set for herself. She was a unique and special person. She will be missed. May God accept her soul into his loving arms. Amen."

At the end of the service, Reverend Carter announced there would be a reception in the Davis meeting hall on the second level of the church. As the guests filed out of the sanctuary, Buddy Howell approached Clevis and Jarod to express his sympathy and condolences for the loss of Veronica.

"Mr. Harrington, I'm Buddy Howell. I had the privilege of

working with your wife at our firm in Memphis. I just wanted to let you know Veronica was a standout among the personnel we employ. She had an intellect and dedication which surpassed our expectations. She was a rising star. We felt privileged to have her working for us. Her future in the law was unlimited. It's a great shame this was all cut short by the tragic accident at Mobile Bay."

Clevis responded politely, "Thank you, Mr. Howell. We were all shocked and saddened by our loss. Veronica played an irreplaceable role in our lives. She will be sorely missed."

Cleve began walking toward the reception hall. He noticed Veronica's sister, Carol, standing near the door at the back of the sanctuary. "Hello, Carol. I didn't see you come in."

Carol glared at Clevis as she spoke in a hushed tone. "I cannot believe you had the unmitigated gall to put on this dog and pony show. You didn't give a damn about Veronica. This memorial service was not to honor her memory. It was to save your ass! You lured her back to Huntsville for your own selfish purposes."

Cleve, taken aback by Carol's abrupt verbal assault, replied, "Now, Carol, you know that's not true. Veronica wanted to return home. She cherished the life we had together. I know we had our problems. I admit it. But she told me she wanted to recapture the relationship we had in the good years. That's why she came back. Trust me. I knew Veronica better than anyone."

Carol's lips quivered. Her heart rate quickened. Her chest rose and fell as she drew quick, shallow breaths. "I warned Veronica not to fall for your scheme. She didn't listen. There's no doubt in my mind about Veronica's death. You're not going to get away with this."

Carol turned and walked out the back entrance of the church.

In the next moment, Reverend Carter walked toward Clevis. Carter instinctively reached out and cupped his hands around Cleve's right hand.

"Clevis, I want you to know how much we all admired Veronica and the entire Harrington family. We know it will be hard to adjust to the loss of such an extraordinary person. Our thoughts and prayers are with you and the family."

Clevis replied graciously, "Thank you, Reverend Carter." As Clevis transitioned to address the eulogy, he scowled. "Reverend, I'm a bit confused. What was the last part of the eulogy? I had given you the key points to express. Nobody asked you to mention Veronica's time in Memphis. That was not a pleasant period for any of us."

Carter tilted his head slightly, his eyebrows drawn tightly together. "You didn't want me to add those final comments? Jarod contacted me. He asked that I include them in the eulogy."

Clevis's teeth clenched, his eyes glaring at Carter. "Okay. Thanks for talking with me."

Clevis could see what had happened. In his own way, Jarod wanted to enhance his mother's image in Huntsville. Cleve realized his own son had double-crossed him. Jarod had sabotaged the intent and purpose of the memorial service.

The last thing Clevis wanted was to highlight the marital strife that plagued their domestic relationship prior to Veronica's death. Cleve had hoped for an upbeat memorial service for Veronica. That would have helped restore the Harrington image.

Cleve realized the bigger problem was the constant news coverage of her mysterious death. He pondered the best approach to reverse the negative press.

I've got to neutralize this ravenous ongoing interest of the local media. Their dogged pursuit of details regarding Veronica's death is hurting me... and it's hurting my company.

Despite Cleve's efforts, nothing seemed to hinder the heightened interest of the press and the police. Their ravenous appetite for information continued unabated. Lingering questions remained as to what really happened that night on Mobile Bay.

Jarod's actions at the memorial service marked the beginning of his effort to protect his mother's reputation and to resist his father's selfish agenda to preserve the Harrington's reputation at any cost.

Jarod was clearly resentful. His dad lived his life as if it was always all about Clevis. Jarod was determined to have the entire story told about his mother's strong will and self-reliant stubborn perseverance.

As Jarod left the church following the service, he thought, *I'll be damned if I'm going to let this pass. Dad expects me to just sit back and let him manipulate Mother's legacy for his own selfish interests.*

Within weeks following Veronica's death, Clevis filed a claim for payment on the life insurance policy insuring Veronica's life. The policy was for ten million dollars with a double indemnity clause paying twice the face amount of the policy in the event the insured died as a result of an accident.

Cleve had purchased the policy three years before the drowning. After reviewing the claim and an initial investigation of the circumstances of Veronica's death, the insurer placed a hold on payout of the policy proceeds.

The notice of refusal to pay under the policy stated the policy proceeds were being withheld pending a determination of the actual cause of death.

After Veronica's demise, the Harrington household became eerily quiet. Cleve and Jarod went on with their daily routines, rarely talking about the incident in Mobile. A strange kind of silence, denial, and deflection had set in.

The house Clevis and Veronica had occupied for so many years was filled with reminders and mementos of Veronica's life. Jarod found it difficult to look at the framed photos lining the bookcase in the family room. He avoided the portion of the house where paintings of each member of the household hung along the staircase leading to the upstairs bedrooms of the sprawling estate.

Clevis soon learned that the investigation of Veronica's death would be ongoing. It was far from over. The period immediately following Clevis and Jarod's return to Huntsville proved to be merely a temporary respite from the rigors of managing the family business while addressing the legal issues of the death of Veronica.

Unlike the industrial accident involving the lift crane, Clevis would not be provided with legal representation for the drowning. If he or Jarod was charged with Veronica's death, it would be up to Clevis to employ criminal defense counsel to represent him, or possibly Jarod. Considering the fragile status of Harrington Industry's current financial situation, the prospect of incurring substantial legal fees was unsettling, at best.

The stress of these issues triggered the instinctive 'survive and succeed at all cost' attribute of Cleve's personality. Throughout his life, Clevis has taken in stride every hardship thrown at him and ultimately turned the adverse circumstance into an outward success. Clevis knew the survival of the company he built from scratch, and, more importantly, his personal reputation as an unparalleled winner was on the line.

For the next three weeks, Lieutenant Mercer poured over all the available documentation regarding Veronica's death, including the autopsy report. One critical question remained to be answered- Was anyone, other than Harrington, moored in the cove on the night of the drowning?

Lieutenant Mercer was able to coordinate with Sergeant Palmer to investigate the possibility of a witness to the tragedy. Through Palmer's local connections, Mercer was able to obtain contact information for almost everyone who, at the time of Veronica's death, had a boat stored in one of the slips at Mobile Bay Marina.

After many cold calls to boat owners, Roy finally found a possible lead. One of the owners, Josh Gibson, told Mercer he was in the area on the night of the death. He and his son were on an overnight fishing excursion in the general vicinity of the cove.

After arranging a phone call to Gibson, Mercer said, "Tell me what you and your son were doing that evening."

Josh replied, "We'd gone out on the bay fishing for redfish and speckled trout. We started at about four p.m. When it began to get dark, we decided to move into a more protected area to try our luck. We arrived at the cove and anchored about five hundred yards from the channel outcropping. The sun was just beginning to touch the western horizon when we noticed a really high-end sea cruiser anchored not too far from where we was. We didn't pay much attention to what they were doin'. We did notice they had some music playing."

Mercer inquired, "What was so noticeable about a boat playing music in the cove area? That doesn't seem all that unusual."

"The music was really loud. You could tell they had a high-dollar sound system. I'm sure folks could hear it for a long way. After about an hour, the music stopped. It got pretty quiet."

"Did you hear anything after that?"

"Nope. Not really."

"How late did you and your son stay up that night?"

"We went to bed around eleven p.m."

"So, you didn't hear anything during the night?"

Josh paused for a minute. "Well, now as I think about it, I woke up around two a.m. I got up to get some water out of the ice chest. Just as I was about to go back to bunk down, I heard someone holler or scream. Whatever it was, it sounded to me like someone was scared or maybe in distress. It was kind of weird. It gave me cold chills. You don't expect to hear them kind of noises in the early morning hours."

Mercer responded, "A scream in the middle of the night out on a desolate area of the bay. Didn't that make you curious about what the hell was going on?"

"I suppose so. I thought about getting my spotlight and shining it in the general direction of the sea cruiser. But I didn't hear any more noise, so I figured the bright light might piss 'em off. I knew it would be kind of annoying if you know what I mean."

Mercer decided to conclude the questioning. "Thanks for helping us with this. We'll contact you if we have any further questions."

This is not going well. Too many unanswered questions.

He realized he needed to get access to Clevis Harrington's personal records. If he could get a search warrant for the house and office of Harrington, he might be able to fill in some of the gaps in the scenario of Veronica's death.

Mercer immediately filed an affidavit with the district court for the issuance of a general search warrant. After review by the judge, the application for the warrant was denied. The court findings stated there was insufficient evidence of probable cause to justify a search warrant.

Lieutenant Mercer soon learned of the court's decision. He was sitting in his office when he read the court's ruling. The last sentence of the order struck a nerve. 'The motion for issuance of a search warrant in the above matter is hereby denied.'

Roy pounded his fist on his desk. He grabbed the court order and charged down the hall to vent his frustration to his colleague, Sergeant Morrison, "Damn it, Brad. The court refused to grant a search warrant in the Harrington case. Once again, I run up against that friggin' impenetrable wall surrounding the privileged elite. 'Justice for one and justice for all.' That's total bullshit in the real world. The rich get a free pass and the poor guy gets screwed every time. If this had been some goddamned no-name street thug, the judge would have issued the search warrant without hesitation."

Mercer was well aware of the social status and reputation of the Harrington family. That alone made it difficult, if not impossible, to get access to all the information that would be discoverable by such a warrant. Despite Mercer's best efforts, no further leads materialized. The case went cold.

CHAPTER 10

1977
Atlanta, Georgia

In the early spring of 1977, The American Aerospace Manufacturers' Association was holding its annual meeting in Atlanta. Clevis was excited to be able to attend. It was his first national conference. His new company, Harrington Industries Aviation Manufacturing and Design, Ltd., was in its early years. Cleve was trying to balance business development with sound financial strategy to lay the groundwork for the company to eventually achieve the goals Cleve knew were well within his reach.

It had been years since Cleve had flown into Hartsfield-Jackson Atlanta International Airport. The airport was bustling with activity. The tightly compacted mass of passengers, with luggage in tow, flowed to and fro along the concourse, resembling the finely-tuned choreographed movement of army ants on the march through a tropical rainforest.

Clevis had decided to make this trip alone. He needed ample time to make as many business contacts as possible during his stay.

If Veronica had joined him on the trip, the opportunity to network with business prospects would have been curtailed.

After deplaning, Cleve quickly navigated his way through the crowd gathered in the baggage claim area. "The Ambassador Hotel, please," he announced to the cab driver.

After a short ride, the taxi pulled into the circular portico of the hotel. The Ambassador Hotel was an iconic and imposing structure. Built in the 1940s, the lobby area was festooned with intricate Art-deco moldings, embedded figurines, and gurgling fountains strategically placed throughout the main floor.

The conference had begun the day before Cleve's arrival. He hurriedly unpacked and returned to the hotel lobby to catch the shuttle to the exhibitor's hall.

As Clevis walked through the giant entry doors, he was astounded by the massive scale of the hall. The facility was cavernous. Exhibitors' booths lined the walls and the central portion of the hall for as far as the eye could see. The exhibitors were tightly arranged across the main floor of the hall in every direction for what seemed like several city blocks. He didn't know where to begin.

Clevis walked purposely up and down each aisle of booths, collecting business cards and introducing his company to the personnel operating the booths. After several hours of navigating through the facility, Cleve had managed to connect with several potential prospects for future business. He was particularly focused on the companies involved in subassembly of integrated aeronautical systems. His company was well-positioned to ramp up to fabricate the parts needed to build those systems.

Just before the exhibitor hall closed for the day, Cleve set out to find a restaurant nearby. He didn't know his way around Atlanta. He managed to find a small steakhouse about a block north of the hotel. Seated at a small table in the rear portion of the restaurant, Cleve leafed through the collected business cards as he ate his meal.

After dinner, Cleve wandered around for several blocks to see what was in the area. He wasn't ready to call it an evening. He decided to stop by a small cocktail bar near his hotel. It wasn't Cleve's thing to sit alone in a bar nursing a drink, but anything beat sitting alone in a hotel room in a town he didn't really know.

After a half-hour, the bar suddenly filled with customers. A large group had just walked in. Most of the tables in the small seating area in front of the massive wooden bar were occupied.

The wait staff was overwhelmed by the sudden influx of customers. In the midst of all the noise and chaos, Clevis noticed a young woman sitting alone. She seemed uncomfortable amid all the bar patrons pressing up to the bar to get the attention of the bartender.

Cleve managed to squeeze into the remaining empty barstool next to the young lady.

"Kind of crazy here this evening. I'm Clevis. Just arrived today for the big aerospace conference at the convention center."

The young lady looked unimpressed and disinterested. "I know. You still have your conference badge on your shirt pocket."

Cleve grabbed his badge and quickly stuffed it into his pants pocket. "I guess that was a dead giveaway. Not cool. Your name?"

The young lady responded, "Melissa."

Despite the rocky start, Clevis and Melissa hit it off. Cleve was physically attracted to her. Melissa was very good-looking by any measure. She was a head turner with her high cheekbones, dark brown eyes, and naturally bronze skin tone. Her overall appearance revealed her Greek lineage in a very flattering way.

As the evening progressed, some of the bar crowd drifted away. Cleve and Melissa became immersed in conversation. They eventually moved to a booth in the back corner of the room. Cleve ordered another round of drinks. They sat in the small booth for over two hours.

Around ten-thirty, Melissa accepted Cleve's invitation to return with him to his hotel. At the hotel, Cleve suggested they have another drink.

"Let's see what's in the minibar."

The time and the liquor flowed as midnight approached. "I didn't plan to stay the night, you know," she asserted.

"You're welcome to stay. It's kind of late to be traveling on the streets of Atlanta."

The hours that followed became a booze-fueled haze for the two of them.

The next morning, Cleve lurched awake and quickly began to prepare for the day. He didn't want to miss anything at the conference.

Melissa was not a morning person. She was groggy from all the liquor consumed the night before. Melissa struggled to sit up but was struck by the unmistakable sharp pain of a hangover headache.

She fell back helplessly onto the pillow, her hand firmly planted against her forehead. "Oh my God, my head hurts!"

Cleve turned in her direction as he buttoned his shirt. "Well, you drank too much last night."

Melissa glanced furtively at Clevis. "It's your fault. You never let my glass get close to half empty."

Cleve quickly grabbed his coat as he hurried toward the door. "Sorry about that. Not much I can do to help you."

Melissa slowly pulled herself together. As Cleve opened the door to leave, he said, "You can use the shower if you want. Oh yeah, would you pull the door shut when you leave? It was great to meet you."

She was conflicted about her chance encounter with Clevis. She wasn't sure why she agreed to spend the night with him. There was something about the way they clicked in the conversation. She knew she would likely never see him again. He hadn't even asked for her last name.

Melissa's life had been far from ideal by any standard. She was raised by a single mother. She had big ambitions about what she wanted to do with her life. As a small girl, she dreamed of becoming a doctor or airline pilot. But life had other plans.

When she was a teenager, she experienced an unexpected pregnancy. Her boyfriend at the time had little interest in marriage or a lifelong partnership.

Even though it was against her values, Melissa decided to

terminate the pregnancy. Abortion was the only viable choice at that point in her life. She was struggling to survive financially and emotionally. At the time, there was simply no room in her life for a child.

In a matter of weeks after her overnight stay with Cleve, Melissa suspected she may be pregnant again. A quick pregnancy test confirmed her suspicion. Melissa was overwhelmed by the prospect of having a child. But she was determined she would handle things in a more mature fashion with this pregnancy. She immediately dismissed any thought of another abortion.

She was not delusional about the situation. She realized raising a child on her meager income would be tough. But, at this point in her life, she felt she had something to prove to herself if no one else.

In January 1978, Melissa gave birth to a baby boy. The hospital assistant inquired, "Who is the father of your child?

Melissa responded hesitantly, "I'm not sure. His first name was Clevis. That's all I know."

The assistant frowned. "What name have you chosen for the baby?"

"Cody Wayne Beard. The name sounded kind of special. Maybe he'll turn out to be something special as well. I pray that be the case."

After Cody's birth, the years proved difficult for both Melissa and Cody. Melissa drifted from one dead-end job to another. Her high school education was not enough to land a good job with a decent income. Life on minimum wage was challenging at best.

As Cody grew up, he attended different schools depending on where he and his mother lived. Cody never felt grounded in any substantial way. His friendships were fleeting. On occasion, Cody would be forced to leave school in the middle of the academic year. Moving to a new city in pursuit of another job opportunity became the norm.

The biggest impediment to Cody's development was the absence of a father figure. Even at a young age, he was keenly aware he didn't have someone there for him in a way his mother could never fulfill.

Cody felt deficient because of his chaotic and unstructured life. In his early adolescence, he began to rebel. By his teenage years, he was running with the wrong crowd. To him, the "screw you" mentality of the rebels and gang members was more than simply enticing. It filled a void as nothing else could.

Cody was naturally short in stature, particularly for his generation. He had obviously taken after his mother. Her height was roughly the same as his. At five feet, two inches, he developed a tough guy demeanor. That was an essential tool for survival in the world of street crime and dominance by force and fear.

By the time Cody was eighteen, he was totally out of control. At that point, Melissa had little influence on him. Cody knew the deck was stacked against him in a big way. He figured the only chance he had was to game the system of life. He had no problem taking opportunistic advantage of any circumstance he encountered or anyone he met along the way.

In his senior year of high school, Cody became involved in the illegal drug trade. His closest friend, Johnny "Hawk" Elliott, introduced Cody to the lucrative world of drug sales. Using some of his off-the-books drug income, Cody purchased a 1984 Chevy Caprice sedan.

Over the years, Hawk groomed Cody. Hawk protected him from the threats of rival gangs and secured an income for Cody in the illicit drug world. In 1998, Hawk enticed Cody to become a drug runner for one of the Atlanta cartels.

After a couple of years, Cody's primary source of income was the money earned as a drug runner. His routine was to run heroin shipments out of Mexico into the Atlanta area. He was paid by the kilo, in cash, at the point of delivery in Atlanta. It was a dangerous lifestyle. The risk of apprehension by the law was constant.

The biggest threat was rival drug gangs. If something went off the rails, summary execution by the cartel was an absolute certainty.

Despite all the negative influences and the constant chaos of the illicit drug world, the one thing that most troubled Cody was the question of his parentage. Who was his dad? The question was so vexing. That mystery had followed him throughout his life.

Cody was street-smart to a fault. He'd learned how to navigate through all elements of society. It was a life skill he acquired at an early age. He could be crude and ruthless as needed. Or well-spoken, if it served his purpose.

At one point, he'd heard about genetic testing which had recently become available.

This might be the answer to the question- Who the hell is my father?

Cody pulled the money together through illicit sources and ordered a test kit. Shortly thereafter, he spit in a tube and sent it off to the lab for testing.

Some weeks later, the results came back. The report showed a DNA match. There was a 99% chance his biological father was a man named Clevis Harrington.

At first, Cody had no idea who Clevis Harrington was. After some preliminary research, he was shocked to learn his dad was a self-made billionaire and high-profile socialite living in Huntsville.

Cody's thoughts ran wild. *This is too damn good to be true. I've spent my entire life dodging the law and gaming the system just to survive. This may be the mother lode. Hallelujah!*

After Cody learned of his parentage, he quickly concocted a plan to cash in on his newfound good fortune. Later that month, Cody traveled to Huntsville in his beat-up Chevy Caprice. He had some reconnaissance to do in the Huntsville region. He was determined to devise the best strategy to shake down his billionaire father.

It was late on a Thursday evening. Cody had reached the outskirts of Huntsville. He found suitable lodging. Cheap shelter at a seedy pay-by-the-week dump of a motel on the wrong side of town. He quickly began to scout the area. It was not long before he located Cleve's residence and the address for the main office of Harrington Industries.

Based in his old Caprice parked down the street from the

entry drive to the Harrington residence, Cody observed Clevis in his daily routine of traveling to and from work. It was a calculated risk. His dilapidated vehicle could draw unwanted attention in an upscale neighborhood.

Cody studied the location of the company's main office. He was able to obtain the name of Clevis' personal assistant, Rita Goodman.

Through his observations, it became apparent that Clevis Harrington and the Harrington family had achieved a level of prominence unsurpassed by any other family dynasty in the Huntsville area.

A month later, Cody returned to Huntsville to initiate his plan. He contacted Ms. Goodman under the pretense he was a representative of a potential customer. Ms. Goodman fell for the scheme. She set up an appointment for Cody to meet with Mr. Harrington at the company's main office.

Upon arrival on the day of the appointment, Cody introduced himself to Ms. Goodman. "Good morning. My name is Cody Beard. I have an appointment with Mr. Harrington for ten this morning."

"Yes, sir. He's expecting you. Please, go right in."

Cody entered through the large, ornate wooden double doors into the expansive offices of Harrington. The over-the-top lavishness of the design and décor of the executive offices confirmed Cody's instinctive hunch. This could be the big payday.

He wasted no time getting to the point. "Mr. Harrington. My name is Cody Beard. I know you've never heard of me. I was born in 1978 in Atlanta, Georgia. My mother is Melissa Beard. Perhaps you remember my mother."

Clevis interrupted, "What's the point of this personal biography recital?"

Cody replied, "I'll get to that. My mother told me I was the product of a one-night stand in the spring of 1977. But she never told me who my father was. That bugged the hell out of me for all these years. When I got older, I wasn't going to settle for that answer. I obtained a genetic test, hoping to get the name of my father. I got the answer I was after Mr. Harrington. The test revealed the truth. You're my father. I am the result of your fling in Atlanta all those years ago."

Visibly angered and shaken, Clevis asserted, "What's this got to do with me? I don't know you. I have no idea what the hell you're talking about."

Cody calmly continued, "Let me explain. I've done my research. I'm your biological child. I can prove it. I know you and your other son are well-known here in Huntsville. From what I can tell, your family travels in some pretty damn high circles."

Clevis sat behind his desk in stunned silence as Cody spoke.

Cody elaborated, "If people ever figure out you have a 'love child', your pristine reputation would be trashed. If you want to avoid all the trouble of dealing with that messy situation, you can pay me a million dollars in cash, and I'll go away."

Clevis reared back in his chair. He slammed his clenched fist against the desktop. "That's insane. You are absolutely delusional. I'm not paying you one goddamn dime."

Clevis stood up and moved menacingly closer to Cody. His six-foot-two-inch frame loomed over Cody as he shouted, "Do you think I'm going to sit back and let you issue threats and make demands on me? Do you think I'm a fucking idiot? You little piece of shit! I'll cut your balls off and throw them in the Flint River. I'll annihilate you if you try to take me on. If you come around here again, I'll make sure you're out of the picture for good."

Cody abruptly rose from his chair, surged toward Clevis, and slammed his fist against the top of the desk, knocking a vase to the floor. "Look, old man, I'm not afraid of you or your family. I'll make sure you regret this. I'll make you pay. Just remember, I've got you by the balls. I'll eventually win. I'm damn sure of that."

Clevis immediately paged his assistant. "Ms. Goodman, get Security to my office immediately!"

A security guard quickly showed up. Despite Cody's aggressive efforts to resist, a two-point restraint immobilized Cody from behind. Cody was rushed out of Cleve's office and escorted off the company grounds.

Cody was undeterred by the experience. He returned to Atlanta to consider his options. He was convinced he had the upper hand. He knew there was money to be made. His ace in the hole was his claim as an omitted child of the Harrington estate after the death of Clevis.

The way he saw it, even if his claim to a portion of the Harrington estate didn't work, the threat was all he needed to extort money from the family.

Cody had proven to be a cunning operator in the past. He had done his research. He knew Clevis would never acknowledge the existence of a child from an impulsive drunken tryst. It would be an unacceptable blemish on Harrington's reputation.

Cody had always been confident he'd find a way to get his hands on a steady stream of money. Confidence came naturally for him. It was a trait he learned early in life. In his view, the revelation about his billionaire father was his ticket to a healthy source of revenue without the risks of the drug-running world.

In the meantime, Cody needed a new infusion of cash. The phrase "easy come, easy go" was an accurate description of his financial life. Cody had an expensive cocaine habit. He also was known to his friends as 'The Big Tipper'. Money flowed through his hands like water down a raging river.

Johnny "Hawk" Elliott was Cody's high school friend. In the summer of 1998, Hawk introduced Cody to drug dealing. Over time, Hawk became a major influence in Cody's life. Hawk had groomed Cody to be a drug-running mule for the drug cartel operating in the Atlanta area.

To Cody, Hawk was the role model he sought to emulate. Hawk seemed to have all the answers. Supremely confident in his manner and a natural "chick magnet."

Hawk's lifestyle was 'badass' Very appealing to Cody's adolescent mind. Hawk was known locally as the main pump in the regional drug trade. He was the kingpin for scheduling Mexican heroin runs.

"Hey bro, I've got another run for you," Hawk announced to Cody. "This one's big. Five kilos. You'll have to stuff that shit all over that Chevy of yours. You better do some quick thinking about how you plan to hide all that smack from border patrol."

Cody was used to the risk of running heroin out of Mexico. His biggest concern was the drug-sniffing dogs. He'd been lucky so far. The dogs hadn't alerted to his vehicle as he passed through the international checkpoint. A couple of close calls in the past, but fortunately, the dogs passed him by. But he worried his luck would run out someday.

Cody had chosen his Chevy Caprice because it looked extraordinarily ordinary. Kind of blended in with the domestic crowd making their way back and forth across the bridge at Laredo. Not too fancy. Not too junked out. He made a point to look as unremarkable in the eyes of the border patrol as he possibly could.

Experience had taught him that the best time to make the crossing at the international checkpoint was during peak traffic hours on the busiest day of the week. When it was busy at the port of entry, things had a way of slipping through. Cody was more than ready for another cash payday. The way he viewed it, if you're not willing to take a big-time gamble, you're not going to get the big payoff.

It was four a.m. on a chilly October morning. The pitch-black darkness of the winter night had not yet yielded to the first light of dawn. Cody loaded his car with enough food and water to make the entire trip without stopping, except for gas and to use the bathroom along the way. The fewer the stops, the safer he'll be.

He quickly checked his vehicle to see if all the lights and turn signals were in working order. The highway patrol along the entire length of Interstate 10 was lying in wait to make a routine traffic stop for cars like Cody's as a pretext for a full drug and contraband search.

Cody was very aware from past trips that it would take him more than sixteen hours of driving time each way to make the eleven-hundred-mile journey. He'd like to make it in less than sixteen hours, but the first rule of drug smuggling was 'Don't exceed the speed limit'.

Just before departure, Cody made a final check of each

concealed compartment stealthily engineered into the interior framing of the vehicle. The hidden spaces were designed to be accessible through the side paneling from the interior of the back seat area. His strategy was to spread the shipment out into all of the compartments to minimize the possibility a drug-sniffing dog would alert to a scent.

The border patrol was always looking for the biggest fish they could catch. Hawk and Cody knew it was best to keep the shipment just small enough to avoid undue attention.

Cody was not a religious guy. But he always kept a set of rosary beads hanging from his rearview mirror. He thought it added the desired effect of making him look like the masses of people passing through the checkpoint at the southern border.

It was five a.m. Time to hit the road for the long and arduous drive to Laredo. About an hour before sunrise, Cody stopped for gas just outside of Atlanta. He squeezed every possible ounce into the tank. If things went as planned, there would be no stopping again until he was on the outskirts of Baton Roug

CHAPTER 11

As Cody drove west on I-10, the morning sun had just begun to cast first light into the eastern sky. The orange rays pierced the darkness and illuminated the coral-hewed clouds in a brilliant display of natural beauty. He'd made this trip so many times. He'd become immune to the unique display of first morning light and the serenity of driving along a desolate stretch of highway in the early hours of a beautiful fall day in the deep south.

About ten miles east of Baton Rouge, Cody noticed a state trooper's vehicle had gracefully maneuvered into place directly behind him. The trooper kept a distance of about six car lengths for several miles as they approached the outskirts of the city.

Cody became increasingly nervous when he realized the trooper changed lanes in unison with him each time Cody passed a car. Five miles east of Baton Rouge, the trooper activated his emergency lights. Cody quickly pulled onto the right shoulder. His breathing suddenly took on a rapid cadence. His heart pounded incessantly. He struggled to stay calm.

This could be a big f'ing problem. What the hell did I do wrong? I didn't do anything. I can't let him find the shipment compartments or the cash. Stay calm!"

Cody took a deep breath, trying to relax. He incessantly repeated, *"Just stay cool. Just stay cool."*

The trooper sat in his vehicle for what seemed like an eternity. Cody knew the trooper was checking his license tag for wants or warrants.

Finally, the trooper emerged from his patrol unit and approached Cody's car. "Can I see your license, proof of insurance, and vehicle registration, please?"

"Yes, sir. What did I do? I wasn't speeding."

"You failed to use your turn signal when you changed lanes about a mile back."

"I did? I thought I signaled. Maybe I forgot. I'm on my way to my grandmother's funeral. I guess I got a little distracted."

The trooper carefully studied Cody's license and registration. He methodically aimed his flashlight beam into the interior of the car, scanning back and forth along the front and rear seats. The trooper paused for a moment, looked intently at Cody's driver's license, and then glanced back at Cody's face. "Well, I'll let you go this time. Just remember to use your turn signals in the future."

As the trooper pulled back onto the highway, Cody's heart was racing.

That could have been a friggin' disaster. I'm damn lucky the trooper wasn't on a drug enforcement detail. A good drug dog would have no problem finding the big stash of cash under the back seat. Those rosary beads are working for me.

Following a quick stop for gas and a bathroom break, Cody headed southwest toward Laredo. He'd been driving for a grueling nine hours. He was exhausted and ready for a rest stop. Cody knew that was a dangerous thing to do under the circumstances. Instead of a much-needed rest break, he grabbed a cold sandwich and warm soda out of his knapsack and pushed on toward his final destination.

After several more hours of driving, the international border crossing came into view. Cody knew the border patrol would wave him through. The southbound vehicles into Mexico weren't the focus of the drug interdiction unit. It was the northbound traffic that received all the scrutiny. Without incident, he passed across the bridge into Mexico.

Turning onto the main thoroughfare, Cody navigated his way through the narrow streets of Nuevo Laredo. The rundown buildings and abandoned automobiles lining the street were an ever-present feature of this struggling border town.

The designated pickup point for the transaction was a dilapidated gray stucco building on the northeast corner of AV Riva Padrino and Madero Street. A large white wooden sign with faded black letters hung over the garage door entry, "Reparacion de autos de Pedro" (Pedro's Auto Repair). The proprietor, Pedro Escarro, was waiting for Cody's arrival.

As Cody pulled into one of the repair bays of the garage, the metallic clanking of the chain drive and whir of the electric motor closing the mammoth wooden door echoed through the shop.

Pedro was a rotund man. Approximately five feet one inch tall. His razor-thin black mustache extended out beyond the corners of his mouth, culminating in an upward twist resembling the horns of a Brahma bull. Pedro's most distinguishing characteristic was his mammoth belly projecting proudly from under his sweat-stained tee shirt, reminiscent of a Black Diamond watermelon wrapped in cotton cloth.

Pedro immediately spoke to Cody in broken English, "I have bad news for you, Amigo. Our costs have gone up. The price we quoted for the shipment is now three hundred thousand US dollars."

Cody was stunned. "What is this? We agreed on the price. It's two hundred fifty thousand, not a penny more."

Pedro shook his head. "So sorry. That's the way it is, Compadre. Nothing I can do about it."

Cody realized he had to do something. He couldn't return to Atlanta with no shipment. He knew it was impossible to get the additional money on such short notice. The source of funding for a criminal drug enterprise was complicated.

I don't have a choice. I've got to try to negotiate this.

He blurted out, "I can't get the extra money. There's no time. We'll have to buy less product."

Pedro stared at Cody. He was noticeably incensed at the suggestion he wasn't going to get his asking price for the smack. He raised his hand in a gesture for Cody to hold on. Pedro walked through the open door into his office to make a phone call.

Cody couldn't understand what was being said. The conversation was in Spanish. However, Cody could see Pedro gesturing wildly as he spoke.

Twenty minutes later, Pedro returned. "Okay, Amigo. We'll sell you fifteen percent less product. The price will be two hundred fifty thousand dollars."

Cody reluctantly agreed. He was aware he had no choice. He had to take the risk. He had to make the deal to get the load on board and out of Mexico.

Cody had to make a quick turnaround. He couldn't relax until he was back across the border.

The longer he remained in Mexico, the riskier it was. He'd always feared a rival cartel would discover his routine. If that ever came down, he was as good as dead. The rival Antauvio drug cartel would kill him in an instant to eliminate the competition.

As Cody began to stack the neatly tied bundles of one-hundred-dollar bills onto the desk in Pedro's ramshackle office, Pedro methodically checked each bundle with a counterfeit detector pen.

Pedro exclaimed, "I can't take any chances, Compadre. I can't afford to take any fugazi bills."

Cody paced nervously back and forth. "Hurry up, man. I need to get on the road."

Pedro gestured with his open hand, waving up and down, "Calm down, my friend. I have to confirm the transaction. I know the product I sell you is good, but I can't take your word for the cash."

Cody responded impatiently, "Ten more minutes is all I have. I got to get out of here now!"

After completing the purchase, Cody loaded the heroin into the hidden compartments of the car, being careful to maintain the seals on the bags containing each brick of smack. Any broken seal on a package would be a red alert to a sniffer dog. Cody's hands trembled noticeably as he slowly drove out of the front entrance of the garage onto the narrow street.

He had very little time to calm down before he would arrive back at the Laredo port of entry. He drove west on Madero Street for five blocks to the intersection of Genova Boulevard. He turned north onto Genova, driving slowly to avoid drawing the unwanted attention of the Mexican Federales.

Finally, Cody could see the port of entry straight ahead. He quickly pulled into the lane with the shortest line of cars. Two more vehicles entered the same lane, filling the space behind him.

It was two p.m. when Cody entered the northbound Lane Five for re-entry into the United States. At that time of day, all of the lanes were stacked with cars and trucks making their way into the United States.

As he sat in the long line of vehicles, Cody nervously glanced left and then right, scanning the area to see if the sniffer dogs were on duty. Suddenly, straight in front of him, a border patrol officer with a large silvery-gray German Shepard in tow, bobbed and weaved back and forth between the cars and trucks like the dance of a heavyweight prizefighter in the first round of a championship bout. Cody had been in this situation many times in the past. All he could do was wait and hope for the best.

As the dog steadily maneuvered toward Cody's car, the patrol officer abruptly pulled back on the leash to cue the dog to check the utility van directly in front of Cody. The routine search effort quickly escalated into the frenetic movement of dog and officer when the canine alerted to the right rear area of the van.

The officer motioned for the van to pull into one of the search bays off to the side of the through lanes on the bridge. Cody quickly pulled forward into the spot where the van had been initially searched.

He knew it was always a crap shoot in this all-or-nothing

gamble to escape detection. If the officer and dog had returned to his lane in time, he would likely have been detained for a complete search. The traffic finally began to inch forward toward the U.S. side of the border.

He felt a great sense of relief as an officer up ahead signaled the traffic in his lane to move on through. Cody mumbled, "Oh my God, that was friggin' close."

He realized if he'd been just one vehicle farther up in the lane, he'd have been detected and searched. He mumbled under his breath, "I'm getting too old for this shit. But the money's too damn good to give it up any time soon."

The trip back to Atlanta was routine by Cody's standards. He was ready to be finished with this run.

He dreaded the prospect of dealing with Hawk when he found out the shipment was short. Hawk was a survivor in a world where death was common. If Hawk didn't buy Cody's story about the short shipment, Cody was as good as dead.

As they began to unload the product into Hawk's ramshackle rented warehouse, Hawk exploded, "What the fuck do you mean, the shipment is short?" Hawk moved menacingly close to Cody's face. "I'm no goddamn fool. If you're stealing from me, bro, I'll personally slit your throat and gladly watch you die."

Cody knew Hawk would react that way. Drug running was a mega-money blood sport where trust is a foreign concept.

Cody backed away from Hawk and stuck his hands in the front pockets of his jeans. He leaned against a desktop.

"How damn stupid do you think I am? Would I try to steal from you right under your fucking nose? Do you think I had time to stop somewhere to unload a portion of the stuff? Where the hell would I hide the shit? I couldn't just pull some out and leave it along the goddamn road." Cody stood up, walked over, and stared directly into Hawk's eyes. "I didn't steal the damn heroin. The cartel suddenly demanded more cash. I didn't have the frigging funds to pay them."

Hawk forcefully jammed his fist into Cody's face. "I don't

believe you at all, you little mother! I don't trust you. If this happens again, you're dead."

Cody's hands trembled as he walked away. He knew Hawk meant what he said. After the encounter with Hawk, Cody just wanted to escape all the drama and stress of the drug world. It was lucrative in the best of times, but deadly at its worst.

To kick back and celebrate the successful run to Mexico, Cody invited his friends to a party at his apartment in the West End district of Atlanta. Cody's apartment suddenly seemed exceptionally small, with eight people crowded into such a tiny space. The alcohol and weed flowed freely throughout the evening.

Emboldened by his recent success, Cody felt the need to boast about his recent discovery. Late in the evening, Cody announced to his friends, "Hey guys, quiet down. You won't believe this shit. You know I've been trying to find out who the hell my old man is. My mother wouldn't say. She told me she didn't know his last name. That must have been a hell of a relationship. Anyway, I got one of those DNA test kits to see who's in my family tree. You won't guess who my dad is. None other than Clevis Harrington in Huntsville."

Joey Westman, Cody's friend from third grade, asked, "Who the hell is Clevis Harrington?"

Cody replied, "Well, I'll tell you. When I found out this guy is my dad, I checked him out. He's a rich dude in Huntsville. Built a big business there."

Tony Baker reacted, "I've heard of him. My uncle worked for Harrington Industries when he lived in Huntsville. Read a news story about Harrington a while back. He's a big shot. In the newspapers all the time. The real jaw-dropper is the story most people don't know."

"What story are you talking about?" Cody asked.

Tony replied, "The story that his son is a funny boy."

Joey asked inquisitively, "What do you mean?"

Tony replied, "He's gay. His son is gay."

Joey asked, "How'd you know that?"

Tony scowled. "I've got my sources. I saw a story online in the

Atlanta Underground Review about the cops targeting some of the gay bars in the badass part of town. The story said the police report mentioned Jarod Harrington as one of the poor bastards temporarily detained in a raid on a homo bar called The Man Cave. The article said Jarod was arrested and booked for public intoxication. What caught my attention was the part that said Jarod was the son of a prominent businessman in Huntsville."

Joey scratched his head. "So, what's the big deal?"

Tony walked toward Joey. "Well, as I said, my uncle used to work at Harrington Industries. I figured the bigshot mentioned in the article must be Clevis Harrington. My uncle told me everybody at the company knew Clevis was a straight-arrow ex-Marine. A real hardass. One of those right-wing ultra-conservative guys with a "my way or the highway" attitude. Those guys don't typically take kindly to no homo. Especially if he's one of the acorns off the old oak tree. If Harrington found out his son's gay, I'd bet he'd kick his ass to the curb."

Cody looked up from his phone. "Wait a minute. Clevis Harrington's son is gay?"

Tony smiled wryly. "Yeah. That's what I've read."

Cody leaned back in his chair, his hands behind his head. "That's too damn good to be true."

Tony shrugged. "You can't make this shit up, you know. Friggin' wild, wouldn't you say?"

Cody sat quietly for a moment. "How do you know all this shit? He's up in Huntsville. Have you been hanging out with the light-in-the-loafers crowd?"

Tony shook his head. "No. Didn't you hear what I just said to Joey? Get the shit out of your ears and listen up, man."

Cody looked askance at Tony. "What makes you so sure Harrington don't already know about Jarod?"

Tony glared at Cody. "Do you think old Clevis Harrington reads an online underground rag like the neo-Nazi Atlanta Underground Review? Come on, man, really?"

Joey danced across the floor and trumpeted, "Big stud Cody's got a gay bro. Who'd guessed? Maybe this runs in the family."

Cody looked back at Joey with a deadpan stare. "Well, I don't know about brother Jarod, but I can tell you for damn sure. This fruit of Clevis's loins don't lean toward the faggot side. Just ask the bitches I've done over the years." Cody's voice suddenly resonated with a serious tone. "I'm still not convinced about Jarod. It all sounds kind of like a bigass guess to me. I'll have to check this out to see what's the straight shit. Being gay's no big deal nowadays, but I'd bet it's a deal killer to somebody like Clevis Harrington."

The party finally wound down around midnight. It would have continued long into the night, but Cody ran out of booze. The group drifted out onto the parking lot next to Cody's apartment building.

As everyone headed toward their cars, the squeal of tires pierced the night air as the sound of high-caliber gunshots echoed off the three-story apartment buildings scattered throughout the complex.

The barrel of a forty-five-caliber revolver could be seen projecting through the open passenger window as the car sped away. In an instant, the mood went from celebration to chaos. Cody had been hit.

Three entrance wounds were clearly visible through Cody's shirt. He'd taken the rounds in the chest and abdomen. He lay bleeding out on the asphalt pavement. His head rested against the curb.

"Someone call 911. Cody's been hit. Damn it, hurry the fuck up! He's bleeding real bad."

The ambulance arrived within minutes. To Cody's friends, it seemed more like an hour. Cody was rushed to Memorial Regional Hospital about four miles north of the scene. The paramedic crew had witnessed this situation all too often. In metro Atlanta, gunshot injuries were standard activity on any night of the week.

Cody had massive blood loss. The emergency room staff immediately administered blood to maintain adequate blood pressure to help prevent hypovolemic shock.

After an hour and a half in surgery, Cody was transferred to the intensive care unit to monitor his condition. Dr. Chris Turner, chief emergency room physician on duty at Memorial that night, remarked, "Another fifteen minutes out there and Cody would have been dead. That kind of blood loss is irreversible if too much time goes by without a transfusion. He's a lucky guy."

Over time, Cody's condition gradually improved. He was eventually transferred out of the ICU.

Dr. Turner commented that one of the bullets came within a half-inch of his heart, fracturing his rib cage at the point of penetration. Turner also said Cody had a punctured lung and a ruptured spleen. He had a long road ahead to reach full recovery.

As Cody lay in the hospital bed, he racked his brain, trying to figure out who was after him. His first thought was Hawk.

The threats Hawk made to me after the latest run to Mexico kind of fit how this shooting came down.

Cody knew Hawk relied on him to make the drug runs. The drug revenue was Hawk's sole source of income. Hawk didn't like to admit it, but Hawk needed Cody more than Cody needed Hawk. After sixteen days in the hospital, Cody was released. It would be several months before he was anywhere near one hundred percent.

Following weeks of gradual improvement, Cody felt well enough to get on with his plans. He'd given this a lot of thought. He was getting tired of all the drama and danger of the drug trade. He was hoping to find a lucrative enterprise without the risk of being shot.

Tony Baker's comments at the party still lingered in Cody's head.

If Harrington found out his son's gay, I'd bet he'd kick his ass to the curb.

Deep down, Cody knew that a gay lifestyle was no big deal. But he never passed up a chance to deploy his opportunistic skills for the sake of money. From his tumultuous meeting with Clevis, he was well aware that Mr. Harrington was "old school." Ultraconservative in every way.

Cody decided to try to arrange a meeting with Jarod in Huntsville. From all indications, Jarod was a rising star at Harrington

Industries. Cody knew Jarod had a big future ahead of him. There was a lot to lose if something went off the rails.

Nothing new surfaced in Cody's search for solid proof of Jarod's homosexual lifestyle. But Cody was not discouraged. He was determined to press on with the plan. Logic told Cody if Jarod was as straight as his dad, Jarod would react with unmitigated indignation at the accusation he's gay.

In his exhaustive search, Cody came across a very useful piece of information. A review of archived issues of the Huntsville Tribune revealed an article reporting that Clevis Harrington and Harrington Industries had shown a pattern of discrimination toward employees over a period of years.

The story pointed out that employment discrimination charges had been filed against Harrington by male employees in two separate incidents. The report stated that one of the employees was a senior manager, and the other was a department supervisor.

The details revealed that Clevis Harrington had created a toxic work environment by making homophobic slurs and remarks about the employees. Harrington later terminated both of them without a stated reason for the firing.

According to the report, Harrington had entered into a settlement agreement in each case admitting discrimination evidenced by wrongful termination of employees on the basis of sexual preference.

Cody had all the information he needed. He turned to the question of how he could get a meeting with Jarod. He needed a reason that wouldn't raise any suspicion. After considerable strategizing, Cody had a plan.

One of Cody's strengths was an uncanny ability to disguise his natural street thug persona whenever it served his purpose. In this situation, he needed to come off as business-like and well-educated.

He called Jarod's office. He told Jarod he was an independent consultant involved in strategic planning and business development for aerospace-related companies. Cody mentioned he may have critical proprietary information that could impact Jarod's business.

Jarod took the bait. He was willing to drive to Atlanta to learn what Cody had to offer. The two agreed to meet for lunch at eleven-thirty at the Dixieland Grill on Beale Street in the south end of Atlanta.

On the day of the meeting, Cody arrived early at the restaurant. He asked to be seated at a table away from the center of the crowded main dining room.

It was twenty-five minutes to noon when Jarod walked in the front door of the restaurant. Cody had never met Jarod. But he instinctively knew the tall, dark-haired young man waiting at the hostess kiosk was undoubtedly him.

Cody approached Jarod and introduced himself. "You must be Jarod. I'm Cody Beard." The two walked to the rear area of the restaurant and sat down at their table. Cody thanked Jarod for taking the time to meet with him.

After lunch was served, Cody began to reveal the purpose of their meeting.

"I wanted to meet you away from your office. You'll understand why when I explain the reason I'm here."

Cody glanced around the room. "I guess there's not much reason to beat around the bush. I want to give you some background. A single mom raised me. We moved around a lot. It was hard for her to keep a job."

Jarod interjected, "I don't understand. I thought we were going to discuss business development opportunities."

"Yes, I know that's what I told you, but there's another purpose for our meeting. I told you about my childhood so you'd understand what it was like to grow up desperately poor without a dad. I never knew my old man growing up. He was never there. I asked my mother many times to tell me who my father was. All she ever told me was his first name. When I was old enough to understand, she said I was the result of a very brief encounter. She never got his last name. I know this doesn't mean shit to you since you grew up with two parents. But, let me tell you, man, it gnaws on you as the years go by. When I was older, I ordered one of those genetic test kits. I was desperate to find out who my dad was. The results were damned surprising."

"I'm not following. What are you trying to say?"

"Hang on. I'm about to tell you." Cody paused briefly. "The report said there was a ninety-nine percent chance my father is Clevis Harrington."

Jarod was totally shocked. His eyes grew large as he stared at Cody. "Let me get this straight. You're trying to tell me my father is also your father? That sounds like a bunch of crap to me."

Cody quickly replied, "I've got the DNA test to prove it."

"I'm not buying it. This is some kind of scam." Jarod retorted.

Cody went on to say he'd already confronted Clevis with the same information. Clevis became enraged and threw Cody out of his office. Cody elaborated, "He went frigging ballistic when I told your dad I was his son. I didn't buy his reaction. He knew it was true. As you know, our dad kind of goes bat-shit crazy when things don't go his way. He may not have realized it before that moment. But I could tell it was sinking in. It hit him like a sucker punch to the gut. He had a child in Atlanta. I could tell by his reaction the pieces of the puzzle came together for him that day." A slight smirk emerged on Cody's face. "You and I are bros, and Clevis is our dad. Are you going to welcome me into the family?"

Jarod sat there for several minutes, staring at Cody, shaking his head. Then he exploded, "I think you're a goddamned con artist! You get me to drive all the way to Atlanta to meet with you on a trumped-up premise about business development, and then you drop this shit on me? Let me make this very clear. If you tell anyone else about this, you'll need to watch your back."

Cody asserted matter-of-factly, "You realize I can cause you a lot of trouble. Especially after your dad dies. Or should I say "after our dad dies?" The estate could get very messy, very quick." Cody paused to let that sink in. "But that's not really why I'm here. The bit of information about our shared old man is definitely interesting and may eventually be very profitable for me. But let me get to the real point of our meeting. I've read your father's bio. It's not difficult to find. I'm sure you know he spreads it on thick about his success every chance he gets. I've read it all. Star quarterback in high school. Ex-marine in the infantry. Bronze Star for valor. Gun enthusiast. Self-made billionaire. Ultra-conservative politically. A mover and shaker in Huntsville. Should I go on? My guess is he's a strait-laced, traditional man's man kind of guy. A reincarnation of John Wayne and General Patton, all rolled into one, wouldn't you agree?"

Jarod shifted in his chair. "What's your point?"

Cody continued, "So, what do you think his reaction would be if he found out his son is gay? I'd bet you've kept that little factual tidbit to yourself all these years. Am I right? He might accept this and take it in stride. But I'd bet he'd throw your ass out of the family and cut you off from the estate faster than you could say, Daddy Warbucks."

Cody sat silently for a moment, assessing Jarod's reaction.

"But I'm going to assume he has no clue."

"You'll regret this." Jarod proclaimed.

Cody went on, ignoring Jarod's overt threat. "You know it doesn't take an Einstein to figure out that ole Clevis doesn't like blemishes on the public perception of the Harrington dynasty. He spent too many years building the empire. To avoid any disclosures to Mister Clevis, I want one hundred thousand dollars in cash."

Jarod abruptly stood up from the table. He stared down at Cody and bellowed, "You're wasting your time. I don't intend to pay you one damn cent." Jarod took a sharp breath. "But I will tell you this: I'll do whatever it takes to protect my reputation with my family. I think you're trying to play a very bad poker hand. Mark my words; I'm calling your bluff. My dad didn't pay you a damn thing, nor will I."

Jarod turned and swiftly walked out of the restaurant. The diners sitting adjacent to Jarod's table were visibly startled by the commotion. The muffled sound of voices resonated through the restaurant as Jarod stormed out the door.

Cody was totally surprised by Jarod's reaction. He thought

maybe he'd misread him. He expected Jarod to have been more defensive. More concerned about the possibility Clevis might find out what Jarod had spent decades hiding.

I'm not about to give up. That's not my style.

Cody had a long track record of successfully executing his devious schemes. He was motivated by a natural resentment for Jarod and his pedigreed lifestyle.

There was a lot for Cody to hate. Jarod was almost ten inches taller than Cody. Jarod was a handsome young man. Cody, through no fault of his own, had the unmistakable appearance of low breeding and lack of opportunity.

From the time of their first meeting, Cody saw Jarod as a member of the privileged elite. To Cody, that was a damn good description of Jarod's life.

Cody persisted with his scheme. He mailed a letter to Jarod. He was sure Jarod had a breaking point and would ultimately yield to Cody's demands. The letter outlined their discussion at the restaurant. It ended with an ultimatum, "You've got until next Thursday to call to arrange to pay the money. If you ignore this, I'll contact your old man to tell him everything I know about your secret life."

In three days, the letter arrived in Jarod's mail. The letter said it all. It was obvious. Cody was not giving up.

In response to Cody's demand, Jarod called Cody.

"I'll figure out some way to get the money, but I'll need some time."

Cody had Jarod's back to the wall. "You'd better damn sure figure it out. I don't intend to wait around. If you want to keep your shit together with our dad, you have to pay the money now!"

Two weeks following the phone call, Jarod was finally able to obtain the cash. It took much longer than he had thought. Suppressing his instinctive desire just to kill the bastard, Jarod placed a call to Cody.

"I've got the money. I guess we need to meet somewhere to get this done."

Cody indignantly replied, "It's about time. You've been

pushing your damn luck taking so long. I don't like being screwed around."

"Nobody's screwing you around! It just took some time to get the money."

Cody began to explain, "There's a little coffee shop at the Rooster Inn in Anniston, Alabama. Do you know where that is?"

"Never heard of it."

"It's a little hole-in-the-wall place about halfway between Huntsville and Atlanta. The motel is located on State Route 202, just off of I-20 West. We can meet there. Plan on ten a.m. next Saturday. Don't stand me up. It wouldn't be good for you."

At the end of the call, Jarod was livid over this classic shakedown. Should he comply with Cody's demand or to tell him to stick it? If he told Cody the deal's off, he'd never know when Cody might contact Clevis to make the big reveal.

The idea of having this bomb waiting to explode at any time was a daunting proposition. He may be able to call Cody's bluff. But if Cody's determined to make good on the threat, Jarod ran the considerable risk of eviction from the Harrington family dynasty.

As the days grew closer to the appointed time for the meeting, Jarod pulled himself together. He just wanted to get this behind him.

Once this is out of the way, I've got a lot better chance this whole thing will go away for good.

The following Saturday, Jarod checked the small canvas bag in his glovebox to be sure he had all the cash demanded by Cody. As he drove to Anniston, a myriad of questions circled in his head.

How'd I get into this? How do I make sure Cody never shows up again demanding something more?

As Jarod pulled his SUV into the parking lot of the Rooster Inn, he spotted Cody walking through the front door into the lobby of the hotel. This time, Jarod knew Cody on sight and vice versa.

The meeting was brief. No small talk. No lunch together. Jarod simply handed the bag to Cody. Cody turned to walk away.

"Aren't you going to count it?" Jarod asked.

"No need. If it's short, I know where to find you."

Cody walked out the lobby door and disappeared across the parking lot.

Jarod stood there, assessing what had happened. More importantly, what may yet happen in the future?

Based on the unsettling experience of his recent brief exposure to Cody, he knew this may not be the end.

CHAPTER 12

2005
Huntsville, Alabama

F ollowing the untimely death of his mother, Jarod returned to Huntsville and quickly became immersed in his daily activities as Vice President of Operations at Harrington Industries. Clevis had gradually increased the workload for Jarod. He was now overseeing all of the various departments, including production, shipping, manufacturing logistics, and human resources.

It was Jarod's responsibility to hold weekly meetings with each department head to evaluate the progress of all of the pending orders currently in the system. Clevis was testing Jarod's mettle to see if he had what it takes to serve as the President and Chief Executive Officer of the company.

Clevis learned the business by building the business. He knew organically all the intricacies of a manufacturing company from order to final delivery and payment. The company had grown significantly since his early days in the business. The rigors of daily management of the entire operation had increased exponentially.

Time passed quickly. It had now been more than a month since Veronica's death. Jarod tried to throw himself into his work. Anything to suppress his horrific memories about the family outing to Mobile Bay.

During a routine meeting with his father, Jarod came to the realization he had to have answers. The disturbing questions surrounding his mother's demise were slowly consuming him

In the midst of a meeting in Cleve's office, Jarod exclaimed, "Dad, I know you don't want to talk about Mom. I can't handle the silence. I've got to know what happened the night she disappeared."

Clevis leaned back in his chair. His eyes narrowed as he stared at Jarod. His jaw tightened. "I thought we've already discussed this."

"I need to know what really happened. All I know is what you've told me. I wasn't there when she went into the water."

"Well, I wasn't either. We were both asleep."

"Oh really? Is that the way it happened?"

"Get off it, Jarod. You know all I know. Your mother had too much to drink. She was already unsteady on her feet after her leg injury from the car wreck. It's easy to see how she could've just lost her balance and fell into the water."

"Something's bothering me about that. I think Mom would have screamed or done whatever it took to try to save herself. You're telling me she just quietly fell into the water?"

"I don't know for sure. I was asleep. She may have screamed or cried out. You know as well as I do, neither one of us heard anything."

Jarod nervously rocked back and forth in his chair. "I've got to ask. I have to know. Did you kill Mom?"

Clevis took a sharp breath, his chest heaving in and out. "Hell no! I didn't kill Veronica. Why would I do that? I loved your mother. We were finally getting our relationship back on track. You know that."

"But you never showed any emotion after she died. You acted like it didn't really bother you. I never saw you cry. Not once."

Clevis hesitated. "I know we don't talk much about family matters. I realize I've never been the best father figure a boy could ever want. But you have to understand, I've always had difficulty expressing emotion. I came by that naturally. My dad was very remote. I guess that hardened me as I was growing up. I've never been a truly sensitive person. I know you'll find it hard to believe, but I have feelings. I have emotional reactions. It's just all bottled up inside. I hate it, but that's the way it is."

After that conversation, Jarod walked slowly toward his office. His heart pounded. His hands grew clammy with sweat. He was confused and conflicted. For the first time, his father had exposed a vulnerable side Jarod believed never existed.

It was no surprise to Jarod that his father unequivocally denied any involvement in Veronica's death. If his dad was the killer, Jarod would never learn the truth from Clevis. At least he did ask the ultimate question. That was all he could do. It was time to move on.

After the encounter with his father, Jarod's workload continued to leave little time to contemplate anything but work. He had always been very private about his personal social life. He had little opportunity in the early years of his adult life to spend time looking for a potential life partner.

It was particularly meaningful when he finally found Matt Weaver. It had been two years since they first met. They quickly realized they had a lot in common. Both were about the same age. Jarod felt relaxed and comfortable around Matt. Both of them were painfully aware of the risk their relationship posed to Jarod's career.

Jarod told Matt that his dad was rigid and intolerant beyond belief. Jarod hated the word 'homophobe', but it fit his father to a tee.

As their relationship grew, Jarod knew he had to let Matt know the challenges Jarod faced working around his father.

On a cold Saturday morning in late September, the two met for breakfast at the Waffle Stop café on old Highway 99 on the outskirts of Huntsville.

Jarod and Matt were somewhat apprehensive about being seen together. However, from the perspective of Clevis, Jarod, and Matt were just 'best buds'.

Jarod slowly sipped his coffee as he spoke. "I've been thinking about the situation with my dad. He's a real threat to me. And to us, for that matter. If he ever figures out I'm gay, he'll go ballistic. He's asked me repeatedly over the years if I had a girlfriend. He tried to "fix me up" more than once with some girl he knew from the office. I always had some lame excuse for declining the offer. When I was in high school, I asked some girl out just long enough to be able to introduce her to Dad so he'd think I was dating. I never had a regular girlfriend. Dad must have assumed I was a confirmed bachelor."

Matt responded empathetically, "That would drive me crazy. I guess I'm lucky. My parents don't seem to care what I do in my personal life. They just want me to be happy. They told me they accept me as I am."

Jarod took a deep breath. "I can't even imagine having a parent with such understanding. I think my mother knew or at least assumed I'm gay. She never said anything to me about it. She was that way. I'm certain she wanted to protect me from Dad. She realized he would go off the deep end if he found out."

Matt reached across the table to stroke the top of Jarod's hand. "Thank God society is slowly evolving. The Neanderthals, like your dad, are now the exception rather than the rule."

Jarod pursed his lips. "It's a screwed-up world where people judge you based on your sexual preference."

Matt quickly added, "But unfortunately, that's our world. Sometimes I think there's no changing it, at least not in our lifetime."

"You know, something has always bothered me. For all my life, I longed for the approval of my father. He knew I could never be like him. I don't want to be like him. But I desperately yearned for some type of acknowledgment that he accepted me as I am. That never came. When I was young, he was oblivious to my feelings.

I've always thought he didn't give a damn about my emotional needs."

"That would have been a tough way to grow up."

"It was tough. But I knew better than to expect his love and understanding."

Matt leaned toward Jarod, eyebrows drawn inward, his face etched with empathy and concern. "You never talk about the death of your mother. Why is that? Are you doing okay?"

Jarod's eyes quickly welled with tears. He bit his lower lip. "I don't know. I've tried to keep it all inside. I had to be tough for Dad." The tears streamed down Jarod's face. "I'm telling you, Matt, I'm so confused. I miss her so much. Life was surreal after she died. After she was gone, everything I saw or did played out in slow motion. I was untethered for a long time. She was my rock. I'll miss her forever."

Matt looked at Jarod, then spoke hesitantly. "I don't know how to say this. You know your dad better than anyone."

"What are you saying?"

"Well, I've given this a lot of consideration. I know your dad says your mom's death was an accident. But --"

"You think Dad killed her? Is that what you think?"

"I didn't want to say, but I suppose ---"

"You don't have to say anything. It's haunted me ever since that night on Mobile Bay. I've always thought I knew Dad. It doesn't make sense that Mom fell off the boat and drowned. My heart tells me to accept all this as a terrible accident. My head tells me it may have been something worse. Much worse."

Jarod and Matt sat quietly for several minutes, Jarod's eyes gazing downward.

Finally, Jarod looked up and took a deep breath. "I've never told you this before. I discovered I have a half-brother. He lives in Atlanta. He contacted me not too long ago. We went to lunch together. He'd conned me into meeting him under some bogus story he'd made up about business development. I had no clue this guy existed."

"Who is he?"

"His name is Cody Beard. As it turns out, he'd obtained a genetic test. Are you ready for this? It showed his biological father is my father. That was a hell of a surprise."

"That's a little over the top. Do you believe him?"

"I didn't at first, but he was very convincing. Said he had proof."

Matt looked stunned at the news. He slapped his forehead with his open palm. "Wow! That would be a shocker."

Jarod nodded. "But wait, there's more. A hell of a lot more. The worst part of this was Cody was not just paying me a social visit. He'd found some information. He said he was convinced I'm not the super-masculine hetero my dad expected me to be. Or, at least, that's what he said. He told me he'd already tried to black-mail my dad with a threat to upend the Harrington dynasty by inserting himself into the family estate. According to Cody, my dad threw him out of his office and told him never to come back." Jarod hesitated. "I'm not sure why he shared the information with me. Probably just a tactic to let me know he could play hardball and doesn't give up. I guess the skirmish with my dad scared him off for a while. Based on what he told me, he'd apparently done his homework."

"What do you mean?"

"Well, he found a bio about Dad online. It wasn't hard for Cody to figure this out. Dad's online profile clearly shows he's an ultra-conservative macho guy. A classic example of a quin-tessential right-winger." Jarod mindlessly twirled an empty sugar packet as he spoke. "I hate to admit it. Cody managed to con me out of a hundred thousand dollars. I guess you'd call it blackmail. I don't have that kind of money sitting around. It took me weeks to come up with it. I had to dip into my savings and my retirement account."

"Why'd you pay the money?"

"He threatened to go to Dad if I didn't pay. He planned to reveal I'm gay. I could tell Cody is a real sleazeball. It was obvious to me. He was more than capable of carrying out such a threat. Since the moment this all happened, I've regretted ever going along with the whole scheme. It was obvious Cody was a manipulative operator. I later realized I had no guarantee he wouldn't be back for another blackmail attempt. I felt like a damn fool."

Matt's expression turned somber. "I can't imagine how I would have handled it if that happened to me."

The two sat quietly for several minutes, and then Jarod spoke. "I just wanted to tell you about the incident. It shows how dangerous it is for us to spend a lot of time together. At least as long as Dad's alive. I don't like it, but we have to continue to keep a low profile. I hate it. I wished I had a normal dad who accepted people for who they were. You know Matt, sometimes life really sucks."

Matt leaned across the table, gazing directly into Jarod's eyes. "I'll tell you one thing. You don't want to be like your dad. From what you've told me, he started out as a normal guy growing up in a small town. Sounded like an idyllic existence."

"Yeah, you're right. That's the way Dad always described his early life."

"That's my point. Something happened along the way. Your dad went from being a normal guy to some kind of driven manic automaton hellbent on success at any price."

"I damn sure don't want to be like him. I want to be successful in my own right. I want to stand on my own. It's become obvious to me. Dad is standing in the way. At least, he's making it more difficult with his horse's ass approach to anything not exactly aligned with his ultra-conservative values."

Matt nodded in agreement.

Jarod continued, "I think he's become a sociopath. It scares me. He's definitely gone off the rails."

A reassuring smile emerged on Matt's face. "Remember what I just said. You don't want to go down the same path as your dad. It's not worth it."

The recent blackmail incident with Cody continued to haunt Jarod. The money was gone. At this point, there was nothing to stop Cody from coming back with a new threat, demanding more.

Since Cody's shakedown, Jarod was haunted by remorse and regret.

As time passed, Jarod became more and more obsessed with the reality of the situation. His thoughts frequently visited a very dark place.

He began to think he'd have been better off to have used the money to eliminate Cody for good. After all, Jarod's career might be at stake. Jarod was certain no one would miss Cody. Society would be better off.

Jarod continued with his life in Huntsville. He tried to remain focused on his job but found himself repeatedly assessing the impact of his decision regarding Cody's successful blackmail scheme.

At the same time, Cody and Hawk were planning the next drug run to Mexico. Cody had been, at one point, flush with cash from his surreptitious endeavor with Jarod. But he quickly burned through the money, living the life of the big man on the streets of Atlanta.

Cody needed a new infusion of cash. His earlier misgivings about continuing to do drug runs were simply a distant memory, given the prospect of another installment of funds upon his return from Mexico.

Cody was aware of the existential risk each time he traveled down I-10 to Nuevo Laredo. He had survived each run unscathed to live another day. He'd been making those runs for such a long time. He was either really good at it. Or maybe just damn lucky.

Unfortunately, he had achieved unwelcome notoriety as a highly successful drug runner in the southern region of the United States. His reputation grew by the day. He was aware that notoriety was not good in the world of drug running. But, in Cody's eyes, it simply went with the territory.

Three days prior to his planned departure to Mexico, a call came into the Atlanta 911 dispatch center.

"911, state your emergency."

In a very excited voice, the caller told the dispatcher, "I was driving down County Road 412 just south of the metro. I came upon a car sitting in the middle of the road with the engine running. I stopped to see if I could help. There's a young man slumped down in the driver's seat. Looks like he'd been shot. Lots of blood in the car and on the guy's chest."

"What's the precise location?" the dispatcher asked.

"It's on County Road 412, I'd say about half a mile east of Medina Drive."

"We'll get someone out there."

In less than ten minutes, a police cruiser pulled up. Officer Jake Wheeler emerged from his unit and began to investigate. As he approached the victim's car, he noticed several small plastic pouches on the ground. Wheeler peered into the driver's seat area. Based on the condition of the body and the massive blood loss, it was obvious the subject in the automobile was deceased.

Wheeler returned to his patrol unit and requested a backup officer and a crime scene unit to be dispatched to the area. Within minutes, Officer David Jacobson arrived to assist. Jacobson had seen just about everything in his long career.

As he walked toward the victim's car, he hollered at Officer Wheeler. "Hey, Jake. What's going on out here?"

Wheeler responded, "Apparent homicide. Looks like a fairly young man. Definitely, a mafia-style hit. I don't see a gun anywhere. My guess is the shooter left with the weapon."

Jacobson began to search the roadway near the bar ditch adjacent to the road. "Did you check to see if the shooter tossed the gun into this ditch?"

Wheeler replied, "Affirmative. I didn't find anything. But it's highly likely there's one or more shell casings around here somewhere. Looks to me like this whole thing happened really fast. The perpetrator didn't stick around to look for shell casings."

Officer Jacobson approached the vehicle to get a better view of the deceased. Despite his years on the force, Jacobson was startled by the brutality of the killing. The body, encrusted in coagulated blood, was lying in a contorted position as if thrown onto the car seat like a discarded sack of trash pitched to the curb.

The limp body was arched toward the center console, the right arm unnaturally jammed between the lower torso and the seat back. Massive quantities of blood blanketed the body, resembling bright red congealed lava from the bowels of a pulsing volcano. It was a truly gruesome sight.

Shortly thereafter, the Atlanta police CSI unit arrived. After searching the immediate area for possible items discarded by the shooter, the investigators began to survey the ground around the vehicle. Small plastic pouches found lying near the vehicle were photographed. Pursuant to police protocol, the pouches were collected using sterile techniques to avoid cross-contamination.

Photos were taken of the victim's body and the interior of the car. A search was made for spent shell casings. Only one was found.

The homicide appeared to have been carried out by someone with experience and sophistication. The scene revealed this was not the killer's first hit job. Once the initial investigation was completed, the Atlanta medical examiner's office was called to transport the corpse.

The medical examiner easily identified the body based on the contents of the wallet found in the deceased's pants pocket. He was Cody Wayne Beard. The driver's license showed an Atlanta home address. Under standard protocol, a search for the identity and contact information of the next of kin was made and an autopsy was conducted on the body.

The information regarding the medical examiner's autopsy report and identification of the victim was transmitted to the homicide division of the Atlanta police department. Detective Jay Tillson was assigned to the case.

Tillson had been with the Atlanta homicide division for sixteen years. Prior to that, he was a patrol officer working in the south quadrant of Atlanta.

Detective Tillson, a tall, lanky man with thick, silvery hair, picked up the file and read the medical examiner's autopsy report and the crime scene report prepared by the CSI unit lead investigator.

Tillson had seen this many times before. Someone was out to

eliminate the victim. This was no suicide. No gun was found at the scene. Other than the single shell casing, no telltale evidence was apparently left behind. Whoever did this knew exactly what they were doing.

One of the curious components of the crime scene was the small plastic pouches found lying on the ground near the victim's car. Tillson called the crime lab to get a reading on the contents of the pouches.

"This is Detective Jay Tillson at Metro Atlanta PD. I just signed on to a new case. It was a homicide that happened last Wednesday out on County Road 412. The case reference number is 2408. What can you tell me about your findings?"

The person answering the phone responded, "I'll have to transfer you to someone in the lab records division. Please hold."

After a long pause, someone finally picked up the call. "Lab records, this is Margaret Williams. How can I help?"

"This is Detective Jay Tillson with Atlanta metro police. I need to get some information on case no. 2408. I'm looking for toxicology results on the homicide victim. I also need any information you have on the small plastic pouches found at the scene."

Williams pulled the records for the case and responded, "Well, it looks like the lab results just came in. The toxicology was negative for the victim's blood. On the pouches, it says the material was a powdery substance."

"What kind of powder?"

"Tested positive for cocaine. That's about all we have at this point."

"Thanks. That'll help. Can you forward the information to me at Metro?"

"Will do."

As a part of the initial investigation, Detective Tillson searched the contents of the victim's vehicle. Among the papers strewn around the interior of the car was a small envelope with a company name imprinted on the outside- "Assurance Genetic Testing, LLC."

Inside the envelope, Tillson found a test report showing the subject of the test was Cody Beard. Under the category of likely ancestral links were the names of several persons, including Melissa Beard and Clevis Harrington.

At first glance, Tillson had no reaction to this information. After some basic research, he found a recent street address listing for Melissa Beard in Atlanta. Rather than attempting to reach her by phone, Tillson decided to drive to the address to see if he could connect for an onsite interview.

The information Tillson obtained showed an address in the 4200 block on Parkland Street in the Clarkston area of Atlanta. Tillson entered the address into his phone. The location was a twenty-minute drive from headquarters.

As he approached his destination, the obvious signs of destitution and dilapidation were all around him.

This is definitely not an area where a person would choose to live if they had any other options.

The designated address was a World War II-era craftsman-style bungalow. From all appearances, it undoubtedly had been the proud home of occupants from long ago.

The aging structure still reflected some of its original classic charm. The large front porch was accented by trapezium-shaped columns connected to a concrete shelf ledge surrounding the front and sides of the entry.

The house had seen better days. The wood decking on the front porch was interspersed with large voids where wooden floor planking had long since surrendered to the passage of time. The curled edges of peeling lead-based paint accentuated the rotting clapboard siding surrounding the weather-worn wooden front door.

Tillson knocked on the battered outer aluminum storm door and waited for a response. At first, it appeared no one was home. As he turned to leave, the door opened slightly and a middle-aged woman appeared within the narrow space of the partially-opened front door.

"Yes. What do you want?" she inquired in an aggravated tone.

"I'm Detective Tillson with the homicide division of the

Atlanta police department. I'd like to ask you a few questions, if you don't mind."

She snapped back impatiently, "What's this about? I don't have any information about any homicide."

Tillson replied reassuringly, "I know, ma'am. I'm just trying to identify some people. I thought you might be able to help."

Melissa opened the door wider and stepped out onto the porch.

Tillson continued, "I'm investigating a homicide that occurred on the outskirts of Atlanta. Out on County Road 412. You might want to sit down."

Melissa cautiously moved to the swing at the edge of the porch, looking confused and concerned.

"One of the reasons I'm here is to locate the next of kin of a homicide victim."

Tillson could see that Melissa looked somewhat confused.

"What homicide victim?"

Tillson didn't immediately respond. "Your name is Melissa Beard, is that correct?"

"Yes," she replied nervously.

"Well, the victim in this case is Cody Beard. We obtained information from his personal effects, which showed you may be related to him. Are you his mother?"

Melissa, visibly shaken, sank down on the porch swing. "Yes. Cody is my son. Oh my God! Has something happened to him? Tell me he's okay."

"He's deceased, ma'am. He was shot last Tuesday night. We don't yet know the identity of the shooter. That's the reason for my investigation. I'm sorry for your loss. I hope you can provide information that will help us find whoever did this."

Melissa buried her face into the palm of her hands.

"Why don't you tell me a little bit about your son? Do you have any idea why someone might want to kill him?"

Melissa looked up. She shrugged and sank lower in the porch swing. "Oh my God! I can't believe this. I don't know of anyone who would want to kill Cody. But I've kind of lost contact with him in the last few years. Cody was a good boy when he lived at home with me. I can't believe he's dead."

"Tell me about Cody. What did he do for a living? Who were his friends? That kind of thing."

Melissa took a deep breath as she began to speak. "We struggled together just to get by. He was exposed to so much hardship. He learned way too early how tough life can be. I know he took a turn toward the wrong side of life. Before he moved out on his own, he was hanging out with a very tough crowd. I wanted him to go to college. To be somebody. Despite all my effort, he barely made it through high school."

"He moved out after high school?"

At that point, Melissa had difficulty speaking. Her breathing had become noticeably labored. "Yes. Cody thought he could succeed his own way. He was very headstrong. I tried to tell him he needed to get an education if he wanted to succeed, but he didn't listen. When he went out on his own, I was afraid he would end up in prison or dead. I guess my worst fears turned out to be right."

"We found a genetic testing report in your son's possession. The report showed the father to be Clevis Harrington. Is that correct?"

Melissa hesitated as tears streamed down her cheeks. "Yes. I never really knew his last name until now. I'm embarrassed and ashamed. I was so impulsive and foolish in my younger years. Clevis and I met one evening in a bar here in Atlanta. He seemed so charming. Interesting to talk to. I guess I got sucked in by his charm. One thing led to another. Well, you can guess the rest of the story. When I found out I was pregnant with Cody, I decided to have him. I didn't want another abortion. I knew it would be tough, trying to raise a child on my income. I never told Clevis about Cody. I wouldn't have known how to get ahold of him if I wanted to. I was determined to make the best of a bad situation. When I was raising Cody, I never dreamed it would end up like this."

"Tell me what you know about his friends and anybody he associated with."

"Well, he did have friends when he was growing up. As I said, I lost track of him after he moved out. I guess I really don't know who he hung out with in the later years. I'd heard Cody had gotten hooked on cocaine. That's probably the result of the influence of his bad-boy friends. I wish I could have turned him in a different direction before it was too late."

Tillson wrapped up the questioning. "I think that's all I have for now. I'll be back in touch if we have any new developments on the case. Please let me know if you get any new information. We want to find who killed your son."

As he carefully negotiated the rotting wooden porch steps leading down to the sidewalk, Tillson turned momentarily, glancing back at Melissa. She sat motionless on the swing, her head bowed in deep contemplation. She was the essence of a defeated woman.

Detective Tillson returned to central headquarters. He decided to contact the Huntsville police to seek their assistance. He needed someone to question Clevis Harrington. Tillson suspected Clevis didn't know anything about the homicide. From what Melissa told him, Harrington probably didn't know Cody existed.

Tillson called the homicide division of the Huntsville PD. He was referred to Lieutenant Roy Mercer. Tillson introduced himself and described the facts and circumstances regarding the homicide.

As soon as Tillson mentioned Clevis Harrington, Mercer abruptly interrupted, "Oh yeah, Clevis Harrington. I helped a detective down in Mobile with an investigation of the drowning death of his wife, Veronica. Based on my experience, I'd have to say he's not a particularly pleasant man to deal with. That case went cold some time back."

"Why's that?" Tillson queried.

Mercer continued, "The circumstances of the death were very suspicious. Lots of unanswered questions. I ran into a wall when I asked the court for a search warrant on Clevis. He's so damn well connected and respected in Huntsville, he's practically untouchable."

"It sounds like you have your hands tied. I would appreciate any help you can provide on the Cody Beard homicide."

Mercer proudly declared, "I don't give up easily. I'll arrange an interview with Mr. Harrington as soon as possible."

Mercer was not looking forward to talking with Harrington. He suspected Harrington may prove to be a key part of the investigation of the death of Cody. In addition, Lieutenant Mercer was still looking for more information on Veronica's death. He needed to figure out a way to get Harrington to be more forthcoming.

After several attempts, Mercer was able to arrange for an interview with Harrington. To Mercer's surprise, Clevis agreed to come down to police headquarters for the interview.

On the day of the questioning, Clevis arrived ten minutes late. Lieutenant Mercer escorted him into one of the interrogation rooms. Mercer had the home-court advantage at headquarters. All of the interrogation rooms were equipped with sound and video recording systems.

Mercer told Clevis, "Please have a seat at the table, Mr. Harrington. May I call you Clevis?"

Harrington responded, "You can call me Cleve if you want."

"Thanks. That'll make this a little easier. I don't know exactly where to begin. I'm not sure how much of the underlying facts you already know regarding our current investigation. I was called into this case by a detective in Atlanta. He contacted me regarding a homicide that occurred recently on the outskirts of the city."

"So, this is not about the death of my wife? What's a homicide in Atlanta got to do with me?"

"There appears to be a connection. The homicide victim was Cody Beard. Do you know him?"

Cleve's expression immediately changed. Harrington's jaw clenched. His brow lowered in a scowl. Anger and frustration were visible in his eyes. Clevis emphatically asserted, "I don't know a Cody Beard. Never heard of him."

Mercer was prepared for possible stonewalling. "I can show you documentation that proves Cody Beard is your biological son."

Harrington retorted, with noticeable indignation, "I don't give a shit about your documentation. I'm telling you, I don't know Cody Beard. I have one son, Jarod Harrington."

Mercer pulled his chair closer to Clevis. "Look, Cleve, let's cut the crap. If you don't cooperate, we'll consider you to be a suspect in this homicide. We know, and you know, Cody is your son, and Melissa Beard is Cody's mother. We've already talked with Cody's mother, Melissa. She was very cooperative. She told us all about the weekend you spent in Atlanta for a conference. She told us you met her for the first time in a bar. The two of you spent the night together in your hotel room. Is this all coming back to you now, Mr. Harrington?"

Suddenly, Cleve's expression changed from self-righteous indignation and anger to a modicum of acceptance and realization. Lieutenant Mercer could tell that Harrington realized his stonewalling tactic wasn't going to work.

Cleve's jaw stiffened. He repeatedly bit his lower lip. "All right. I've been told Cody is my child. I'm not saying I'm totally convinced. I guess I'm not going to change your mind about that."

Mercer resumed his inquiry. "Okay. Let's get down to the facts. As I told Melissa, the Atlanta police department called us into the case. Atlanta had investigated a homicide that occurred on County Road 412 just outside the city limits of Atlanta. The victim was identified as Cody Wayne Beard. He'd been shot in the chest, execution-style. There was a lot of blood on the victim and on the driver's seat."

"I still don't know what this has to do with me."

"Do you have any idea why someone would want to kill Cody?"

Clevis pulled his head back and furrowed his brow. "How would I know? As I told you already. I don't know Cody Beard. I damn sure don't know his lifestyle. To me, it's just another street punk killing. It happens every day in a big city like Atlanta."

"Where were you on the evening of August 7, 2009?"

"I have no idea. It depends on what day of the week it was."

"A Friday."

Cleve's jaw clenched. He spoke in a slow, deliberate manner. "I was at the office until about six p.m. That's my typical time to leave at the end of the day. I went directly home. I stayed there until the next morning."

Mercer leaned to the side. He propped his elbow against the arm of the chair. "Was anyone with you that evening?"

Harrington shook his head. "No. Since the death of my wife, I'm typically alone when I'm at home." Clevis took a deep breath. He stared directly at Mercer. "I know what you're trying to do. I had nothing to do with any homicide. There were people at the office who could confirm. I was at work during the day until about six p.m. After that, I wouldn't have had enough time to drive from Huntsville to Atlanta to commit the murder. It's absolutely asinine anyone would think I could have done such a thing. Why would I want to kill someone I don't even know?"

"That's what we intend to find out, Mr. Harrington."

Clevis abruptly rose to his feet and headed toward the door. "This interview is over."

Lieutenant Mercer made no attempt to stop him. At best, Clevis was simply a person of interest. Yet, over the years, Roy had learned a valuable principle. When someone is defensive and contemptuous during an initial interview for a criminal investigation, there's usually something more to the story than they're willing to reveal.

Mercer had hoped to use this opportunity to question Harrington about the death of his wife down in Mobile. But it was obvious the time wasn't right for that.

Based on what Sergeant Palmer told Roy, Palmer had already asked the most obvious questions. Mercer knew he needed more evidence about the drowning of Veronica before he could pursue any meaningful follow-up.

Foremost on Mercer's mind was the obvious issue.

I need to find a way to get a search warrant for Cleve's house and office.

Unfortunately, the death of Cody won't provide sufficient probable cause for a warrant.

Shortly after Clevis was questioned, Mercer arranged for an interview with Jarod Harrington. To expedite the matter, Roy opted to talk with Jarod by telephone rather than ask him to come down to the police station.

The next day, Mercer called Jarod. Lieutenant Mercer explained the reason for the call. Unlike Clevis, Jarod didn't pretend he didn't know Cody. Jarod sounded shocked to learn Cody had been murdered.

Mercer asked, "How long have you known Cody? I know the two of you didn't grow up together."

"I didn't know anything about Cody until recently. I didn't know he existed. I met him when he told me we may be brothers. Boy, that news was a real shock."

"What do you mean?"

"Cody and I had lunch in Atlanta. I drove to Atlanta to meet him."

"Why were you willing to drive all the way to Atlanta? Did you already know he was your half-brother?"

"No. Not at that point. He had told me he was a business consultant affiliated with the aerospace industry. Of course, that turned out to be a lie. Based on what he told me on the phone, I thought he might be someone who could help with business development. I later learned his purpose for the meeting was to tell me he'd discovered we were biological brothers! I about fell out of my chair. I didn't believe him. I told him he was full of crap, but he said he had a genetic test to prove it."

"Did you discuss anything else?"

"Well, not that I can recall. The information about our family connection was enough for one day."

"Do you have any idea why he wanted you to know he was your brother?"

"I guess he thought it would be good for us to know each other. I'm not really sure."

Mercer pressed further. "Do you have any idea who might have been out to kill Cody?"

Jarod paused. "Not at all. I haven't been around him other than our lunch together. I don't know any of his friends. Or anyone else he was associated with, for that matter."

Mercer elaborated. "We've determined Cody was living a fast-paced lifestyle on the wrong side of the law in the Atlanta area. We've learned he had connections with known Atlanta-based drug operatives."

"That doesn't surprise me. I could tell he was a bad news guy."

Lieutenant Mercer hesitated. "I do have one more question. I was recently called into the investigation of the death of your mother down in Mobile. One of the lingering issues in my mind was how your mother accidentally fell off the boat into the water. Do you have an opinion on that?"

Jarod remained silent for several seconds. "As I told Sergeant Palmer, I was asleep when she fell overboard. I didn't hear anything. There were no loud sounds that I know of."

"So, you didn't hear anything?"

"That's right. I'm a very sound sleeper."

"Your father told us she may have slipped off of the back of the boat because of some type of prior leg injury."

"My mother had been involved in a bad car wreck in Memphis. She had severe damage to her left leg. She walked with a limp. The other driver was totally at fault. Mother ended up suing the driver for negligence."

"How'd that turn out?"

"They settled the case. I don't know for how much money. I think it was several million dollars."

"You don't know how much she got in the settlement?"

"She couldn't discuss the details. She signed a non-disclosure agreement."

"So, you think she lost her balance and fell overboard because she was unstable on her feet?"

"I suspect that's how it happened."

Lieutenant Mercer wrapped up the interview. He thanked Jarod for taking the time to talk with him.

Following the phone interview, Roy had a gut feeling Jarod wasn't being totally truthful with him, especially about Cody's death. Mercer wasn't sure what Jarod had to hide.

As the investigation of Cody's death proceeded, Lieutenant Mercer was dissatisfied with the lack of progress. Roy knew there was always a particular point in any criminal investigation when there were more questions than answers. He was determined to turn that around as soon as possible.

From the beginning, Detective Tillson had asked Mercer to take the lead in the investigation for the Huntsville portion of the probe. Roy's style was to do whatever it took to solve the case. To go wherever the facts lead him. Roy was never one to color inside the lines.

Mercer thought, *"I need to get down to Atlanta to personally search the crime scene. To check Cody's vehicle. It may be a waste of time. But there's not much else I can uncover at this point in Huntsville. The forensic evidence is in Atlanta."*

The following week, Roy contacted Detective Tillson. He wanted to let him know he planned to come to Atlanta. He told Tillson he wanted to be a 'second set of eyes' in this probe. Just in case something was overlooked by Atlanta CSI.

Lieutenant Mercer knew that Atlanta was the proper jurisdiction for prosecution of the homicide of Cody Beard. But the very real possibility that either Clevis or Jarod might have been involved in Cody's death put the Huntsville aspect of the investigation squarely in Mercer's lap.

Mercer was well aware the clock was ticking. When exposed to the elements, any possible physical evidence remaining out on County Road 412 would soon degrade or disappear.

Upon arrival in Atlanta, Roy drove directly to the site of the homicide. He went alone. He could get more done that way.

Based on the crime scene photos Tillson provided, Mercer was able to confirm the precise location of Cody's car on the evening of the incident. The CSI photos showed small pools of blood in the vicinity of the driver's side door of Cody's car. On arrival at the crime scene, Mercer noted the blood was no longer visible on the ground.

The CSI report indicated one shell casing from a .38 caliber cartridge was found at the scene. The murder weapon was never located.

As he looked around, Roy noticed thick grass and vegetation growing in the bar ditch at the site. With that much dense ground cover, he concluded it would be worth a second look. Just to be sure nothing was missed in the initial search.

Roy was old-school. He'd learned a trick many years ago. In his vehicle, he carried a small metal detector to pick up signals of metal objects located on or near the surface of the ground.

"The report said a visual search had been done of the roadway and the interior of the vehicle. Only one shell casing was found."

Roy knew if any other shell casings were there, his metal detector would likely find them. He walked back and forth along the road and in the bar ditch, swinging the detector from side to side. Most of the items triggering a signal on the detector were just junk--- nails and old steel bottle caps.

After numerous passes through the grassy area of the bar ditch, the detector suddenly emitted a shrill, steady pitch. Mercer slowly ran his palm back and forth over the grass overgrowth. He methodically separated the clumps of grass with his fingers, searching the ground beneath for anything that looked out of place.

Initially, nothing was visible. Then, lodged just below the surface of the grass and weeds, a shell casing lay on the ground, partially covered with dirt and mud. Roy couldn't contain his excitement.

"Hot damn! Thank you, Lord. This is what I've been looking for."

Roy inspected the casing. It was a .38 caliber.

Lieutenant Mercer photographed the precise location where the casing was found. He donned a pair of vinyl gloves and placed it into a plastic evidence bag.

His search of the area continued into late afternoon. If any further evidence was present, the crime scene wasn't revealing its secrets.

As the sun slowly sank into the western sky, no further evidence turned up. The discovery of the shell casing was a significant find.

Mercer now had a basis for his working theory as to how this murder all came down. But he needed something more.

CHAPTER 13

After searching the scene of Cody's brutal murder, Lieutenant Mercer stopped by the central headquarters of the Atlanta police department to talk with Detective Tillson. Mercer told Tillson, "You were right about luck on this one. I found a second shell casing in the bar ditch. Just to the east of where Cody's car was located at the time of the shooting. It's the same caliber as the first casing Atlanta CSI found. I turned it in to the crime lab property department."

Tillson looked surprised. "Excellent sleuthing, Roy."

Mercer went on, "I got to thinking. With your permission, I'd like to do my own inspection of the victim's vehicle. And, if it's okay with you, I'll want to order some additional tests on the body."

"What've you got in mind?"

"I've got a theory, but I need some more information, you know, to either confirm my idea or to shoot it down."

Tillson shrugged indifferently. "Sounds fine with me. Knock yourself out."

Mercer drove to the police property impound yard on the south side of metro Atlanta. The yard manager, Harvey Mason, escorted him to Cody's vehicle stored inside a large warehouse facility. The cavernous warehouse was filled with cars and other items being held as evidence for pending cases.

Standing next to Cody's vehicle, Roy searched his pockets for the list of things he wanted to check.

Mercer approached the car. He donned protective vinyl gloves to avoid possible cross-contamination or destruction of evidence by his own fingerprints. He aimed his flashlight into the interior.

He knew what he was looking for. After a thorough inspection of the car, Roy began to take photos. At each step, he entered notes for future reference. Lieutenant Mercer carefully photographed the upper headliner, seat cushions, and seatbacks in the passenger compartment. He looked under the floor mats, the center console, the glove box, and the front seats.

As he completed his search, he noticed something unusual. For an instant, the bright beam of his flashlight glinted off something conspicuously out of place. It appeared to be a single strand of hair lying just under the front edge of the driver's seat.

Roy immediately returned to the yard manager's office.

"Harvey, can I get another evidence bag? I found something in Cody Beard's car. It may not be anything useful, but I intend to find out."

Roy returned to the car and slipped on a fresh pair of gloves. Leaning in, he carefully plucked the single hair from its resting place and inserted it into the collection bag.

Following standard procedure, he labeled the bag with the appropriate identification information. Roy stopped by the manager's office on his way out to let him know he was finished.

Later that day, Mercer dropped by the Atlanta medical examiner's office to request additional testing of Cody's remains. He met with Charles Martin, the senior administrator.

"Charles, I'm Lieutenant Mercer out of Huntsville. I'm working in conjunction with Detective Tillson here in Atlanta. We're tag teaming a homicide that happened down here. The victim's name is Cody Wayne Beard. It may also involve some folks in Huntsville. I spoke earlier to Detective Tillson. He approved my request for some additional testing."

Martin replied, "Okay by me. What do you need?"

"I'd like to get a gunshot residue test on both hands. Also, on the face and neck of the victim."

"You got it. Anything else?"

"Yes. I found a hair specimen in the victim's car. It's a single strand. As far as I can tell, it looks like the hair follicle is intact. At least, that's what I hope. I need a DNA test on that strand of hair."

Martin admonished Mercer, "It may be a while before we'll have the DNA results. The lab has a huge backlog right now. Way too much crime going on around here. We'll let you know as soon as we have the report back."

Mercer reached for his wallet. "Well, I know you'll do the best you can. Here's my card with my contact information. Just let me know what you find out."

"Will do."

"Thanks."

Roy had obtained all the information he could at this point. All he could do now was wait for the test results to come in.

On his way out of Atlanta, Roy stopped by Detective Tillson's office. "I guess I'm done here. At least for now. I checked the vehicle and stopped by the medical examiner's office." Lieutenant Mercer paused. "One interesting thing. I found a single strand of hair in the victim's car under the front driver's seat. It was hard to see at first. When I shined my flashlight on it, it looked out of place. The hair was long. I noticed when I viewed Cody's body at the morgue, his hair was short. Who knows? Maybe it's something important, maybe not. Only time will tell."

"Worth a try, at least."

In the recent phone interview with Jarod regarding Cody's death, Lieutenant Mercer came away dissatisfied for reasons he couldn't fully identify. There was something about the way Jarod answered the questions. Mercer instinctively sensed Jarod had not been forthcoming. It wasn't what Jarod said in the interview; it was what he didn't say that was bugging Roy.

Mercer concluded he had no choice but to treat Jarod as a suspect in the investigation. At least until something turned up to exonerate him. Mercer's take was Jarod seemed like a mild-mannered guy. But under duress and Cody's threat to upend the Harrington dynasty, it wasn't out of the realm of possibility that Jarod could have been the killer.

To Roy, the more likely scenario was Cody's death was a contract killing. The murder scene looked like a professional assassination. A classic hit job. Anyone with an interest in having Cody eliminated could have hired a killer to complete the task.

Mercer contemplated the fact that, for years, Jarod appeared to be an only child. Until Cody showed up.

He mulled the situation in his mind.

When you consider the Harrington Industries empire Jarod stood to inherit, just having a second potential heir, especially a guy like Cody, created a pretty good motive for murder.

After searching Cody's car, Lieutenant Mercer decided to extend his stay in Atlanta. Mercer wanted to do a search of Cody's apartment. He knew it was a long shot. But there may be something in Cody's personal possessions that could shed light on the case.

Working with Detective Tillson, it wasn't difficult to obtain a warrant. The existence of a homicide victim was a compelling reason for a court to allow a search of the victim's residence.

Up to this point, Tillson had not had time to conduct a search of Cody's apartment. The initial focus had been on the crime scene and the contents of Cody's vehicle. It was far from ideal, but the press of Tillson's caseload limited the time he could spend on each homicide.

Armed with the warrant, Mercer checked the address as he headed toward his destination- 2318 S. Independence Drive. Upon arriving at the address, Roy noticed the general area was surprisingly well-maintained. The apartment complex was typical for the Atlanta area. Multiple buildings surrounded by numerous parking areas with two swimming pools interspersed among the units.

Roy stopped by the manager's office to obtain a passkey for Cody's apartment. He introduced himself, extending his police badge toward the manager's face. "Good morning, ma'am. I'm Lieutenant Roy Mercer. I have a search warrant to inspect apartment 4B."

The manager appeared startled by the request. "What's going on? Police don't generally come around here with search warrants."

"We're investigating a homicide involving the tenant for that unit."

The manager registered a look of deep skepticism.

"It's all legit. If you have any concerns, you're welcome to call Detective Tillson with the Atlanta PD." Roy said reassuringly.

The manager looked briefly at the warrant, then handed the passkey to Roy. As Mercer exited, the manager said, "Don't forget to lock the door when you're finished."

After entering the apartment, Mercer methodically checked each room, taking photos of anything that may later prove to be significant or of any evidentiary value.

Roy carefully searched the living room and the bathroom. He searched the bedroom closet, checking all of the shelves and the area behind the clothes hanging neatly in a row. The closet was surprisingly well-organized, especially for a young guy living alone.

As he scanned the closet interior, Mercer spotted a small cardboard box stuffed in one corner. Inside the box, he found an envelope addressed to Jarod Harrington. As Roy inspected the envelope, he noticed something odd. The envelope showed a complete mailing address with a stamp in the corner, but the envelope had never been sealed.

Lieutenant Mercer carefully removed the contents. Inside was a letter written by Cody Beard. The text of the letter revealed Cody's quest to find the identity of his father. The letter described the results of the genetic test Cody had obtained.

The balance of the letter was a true revelation. Cody went on to tell Jarod about Cody's discovery of Jarod's covert life in the gay community in Atlanta. The letter ended with an unequivocal demand for payment of one hundred thousand dollars by a certain date or Cody would disclose Jarod's secret to Clevis Harrington.

The box contained other items. Among miscellaneous paper-clips and notepads were several pieces of paper with handwritten notes inscribed on each sheet. One of the sheets had a notation of the name 'Jarod Harrington' and the name and address of the Rooster Inn in Anniston, Alabama.

This seemed odd to Lieutenant Mercer. The obvious question floated in Mercer's mind. *Why would Cody have Jarod's name written next to a notation of the Rooster Inn in Anniston, Alabama?*

Jarod had told Roy he had only recently met Cody when they had lunch together in Atlanta. Mercer recalled Jarod had mentioned it was during the lunch that Cody revealed he and Jarod were brothers.

At this point, Lieutenant Mercer struggled to assemble the information into a logical picture. Mercer had several unanswered questions swirling in his head.

Why was the blackmail letter never mailed? What does the Rooster Inn in Anniston, Alabama, have to do with this? Did Cody ever deliver the blackmail threat to Jarod?

Mercer didn't have the answers to those questions, but he intended to find out.

Lieutenant Mercer had always had a hunch that Jarod had been less than totally cooperative with him. The existence of Cody's unmailed letter with the blackmail threat raised the possibility that Cody may have delivered his threat by means other than the letter. This time, Roy wanted a face-to-face interview with Jarod.

After returning to Huntsville, Roy contacted Jarod and asked him to come downtown for a follow-up interview. Jarod assumed this would all be routine, so he agreed to meet Mercer at two p.m. at central headquarters.

When Jarod arrived, Lieutenant Mercer escorted him to one of the interrogation rooms. The room was very small- barely enough space for a tiny table and three dilapidated chairs.

Jarod had no idea his father had previously been interviewed about Cody's death. Clevis had never told Jarod that he was investigated in any way regarding Cody.

In Clevis's mind, Cody never existed. So, there was no reason to discuss the case with Jarod or anyone else.

Mercer began the interview. "Thanks for coming in, Jarod. We appreciate your willingness to talk with us today."

"I don't mind, but I don't understand why you need to talk to me again. I've already told you all I know."

"When you and I talked by phone recently, the investigation was still in its preliminary stages. We didn't have enough information to know what questions to ask. We've turned over a lot of stones. I've personally questioned various persons here in Huntsville and in Atlanta. We're getting close to completing the investigation. Or at least we hope that's the case."

Jarod replied, "I'm not sure I'll be much help. As I told you before, I didn't know Cody until he called me to set up a meeting for lunch."

Lieutenant Mercer moved from the opposite side of the table to a chair next to Jarod. "That's what we want to talk about- your meeting with Cody in Atlanta. When I asked you if you and Cody discussed anything other than the fact that he said he's your brother, you said, 'not that you recall' or something to that effect."

Mercer leaned forward with his elbows firmly planted against the arms of the chair, his clasped hands pressed against his chest. "I've got something we discovered that may refresh your memory."

Jarod nervously inquired, "Like what?"

Lieutenant Mercer cleared his throat, his voice reflecting a serious tone. "I just recently completed a thorough investigation of Cody's death in Atlanta. One of the things I did was a search of Cody's apartment. Among several other items of interest was a box I found in his closet. The box contained some slips of paper.

One of those pieces of paper had the notation 'Jarod Harrington, Rooster Inn, Anniston, Alabama'. Is there a reason Cody would have made such a note?"

Jarod looked surprised. "I have no idea."

Mercer pressed on. "Did you have a meeting with Cody at the Rooster Inn?"

"I don't recall."

Mercer stared at Jarod. "Come on. I can tell when someone's jerking me around."

Jarod was visibly shaken by the questioning. He nervously touched his ear.

Mercer continued, "I also found something else in that box."

Roy pulled Cody's letter out of the evidence file and handed it to Jarod. As Jarod read the letter, his facial expression became ashen.

After an extended pause, Jarod began to explain. "Okay. I'll tell you what happened."

"There's more to the story about the lunch meeting with Cody in Atlanta, isn't there?"

Jarod sighed audibly. "After he told me he was my brother and that he had a genetic test to prove it, he threatened me."

"Threatened you? How?"

"He said he had some information about me. He said it wouldn't sit well with my dad. He told me he had a news article he'd found online about a police raid in Atlanta a few years ago. I'd heard about the article. One of my friends told me about it. The raid was an obvious harassment campaign by the Atlanta police department. I guess they were trying to eliminate gay bars in a particular section of Atlanta. The article had the names of some of the guys who'd been temporarily detained the night of the raid."

Jarod hesitated. "My name was included in the list. That's what caught Cody's attention. Cody told me he'd seen a bio on Dad. He figured out that Dad was a hard ass and totally intolerant of anything deviating from the straight and narrow. I have to admit, Cody was on to something. A gay lifestyle was one of those things my dad always derided as unnatural. It didn't take long to figure out that Cody was an operator. He threatened me. He had me where he wanted me."

"What was the threat?"

"Apparently, Cody could see the dollar signs in that situation. He told me he wanted one hundred thousand dollars to keep quiet. I initially told him that was outrageous. But eventually, I decided it would be better to pay the money to make the problem go away."

"Where'd you get the money?"

"It took quite a while to pull it together. But I finally managed. Cody had given me one week to get the money, but it was several weeks before I had it all. We'd agreed to meet about halfway between Huntsville and Atlanta. We met at the Rooster Inn in Anniston, Alabama. I gave him the cash. After that, he just walked away. I felt I'd just been robbed."

Mercer sat quietly, continuing to stare directly into Jarod's eyes. "You've got a lot of resentment about being blackmailed like that, don't you?"

Jarod clenched his teeth. His nostrils flared. "You damn right. After a few days, I regretted having paid the money. I knew he couldn't be trusted. I figured he'd be back for more. You can't trust a guy like that. He's an opportunistic parasite."

Mercer shifted his jaw to the side, cradling his chin between his fingers. "Did he make any other threats?"

Jarod paused. He touched his chin and looked pensively down at the floor. "He said, that since he's a biological child of Dad's, he could make a lot of trouble after Dad was dead. He said the estate could get very messy."

Mercer got up from his chair. He walked slowly over to the side of the room and leaned against the wall. "Jarod, you've been less than transparent with me. You originally said you didn't recall having any further conversations with Cody. Turns out the two of you met later in Anniston, Alabama. So, you lied to me about that. What else have you not told me?"

Jarod shifted uncomfortably in his chair. "Nothing. That's it. I've told you everything."

Mercer walked abruptly toward Jarod. "Did you kill Cody?"

Jarod pounded his fist on the table. "No!"

Mercer leaned into Jarod's face and shouted, "Did you kill Cody?"

Jarod's upper lip began to quiver. "Damn it! I'm telling you. I didn't kill anyone. Cody blackmailed me, but I didn't kill him."

Mercer turned away, walking back to lean against the wall. "You just told me Cody successfully blackmailed you. He threatened to make a lot of trouble after your dad was gone. That sure seems to me like a good reason to kill Cody. Cody was screwing up your life. Isn't that true?" Lieutenant Mercer picked up his notepad and moved toward the door. "I don't have any further questions for now. Based on our conversation today, I think you should know you're a suspect in the murder of Cody Beard."

It was obvious to Mercer. Jarod was through talking. At least for now.

Mercer suspected Jarod may have committed the murder or hired someone to do it. Roy just didn't have enough evidence at this point. Formal charges would have to wait.

Lieutenant Mercer ended the interrogation. Jarod walked out of police headquarters a free man. But freedom can be a fleeting thing. Jarod was now a prime suspect in Cody's death. If Mercer has his way, that freedom will soon end. Only time will tell.

CHAPTER 14

Jarod returned to his daily routine at the company. He couldn't afford to be away for any extended period. The level of responsibility imposed on him by Clevis was almost overwhelming. To add to the pressure, he noticed that his father had become even more remote and distant.

Cleve had sunk to a new low. He was totally preoccupied with his thoughts. He had good reason for his sullenness. The business had become extremely challenging.

The aerospace market was either feast or famine. Recently, it had taken a turn for the worse. Cleve was operating on a razor-thin profit margin. He was financially maxed out, particularly with his conventional lenders.

In a desperate effort to keep the company afloat, Cleve resorted to a cadre of very unconventional lenders. After extensive research, he found a financing source- a venture capital group, Allied Funding Partners XB, LLC, based in the Cayman Islands. Clevis was drawn to Allied. He'd discovered the company was known for undertaking high-risk capital financing.

Allied's costs were multiple times higher than traditional

lenders. But Cleve was desperate. He had to obtain an infusion of new money to save his company.

Following several days of contemplation, Cleve contacted Allied. During the loan application process, he learned that one condition for the loan was that Allied would receive a cut of the property's value as part of the total financing. This was prohibited in most jurisdictions, but not in the Cayman Islands.

After completing the loan application, Chris McField, the lender representative, asked Cleve to plan to meet with him at the company's headquarters in George Town on Grand Cayman.

Cleve thought that was very odd. Typically, lenders were willing to complete the loan transaction remotely.

But Cleve was desperate. He'd fully expected a big payout by now on Veronica's life insurance. That payout was on hold. The investigation of the cause of Veronica's death was still ongoing. Cleve reluctantly agreed to fly to the Cayman Islands. As he saw it, he had no other choice.

Due to business conditions in Huntsville, Clevis had little discretionary time to fly anywhere. He booked an early departure direct flight to Grand Cayman for a two-day turnaround. Clevis told Jarod he'd be out of the office for a few days on a business trip but didn't reveal the true purpose or destination.

Upon arrival on Grand Cayman, Clevis was met at the airport by Jose Delgado, a loan officer with Allied. As they drove toward the company offices, Clevis couldn't help but notice the grandeur of the island. Grand Cayman was truly picturesque.

The natural beauty of the tropical growth engulfed the perimeter on both sides of the highway leading from the airport to the central business district of George Town. Every available space not occupied by a physical structure was alive with the sumptuous growth of a vast array of indigenous species of flowers and plants. In all directions, the landscape was accentuated by ironwood trees, oleander bushes, silver thatch palms, agave plants, and banana orchids, forming a botanical mosaic resembling a master's work of art. The entire island was a stunning cornucopia of sandy beaches, crystal-clear coral-blue water, and lush tropical splendor.

It was midmorning when Cleve and Jose arrived at the main office of Allied Funding. The corporate headquarters building was an imposing structure, emanating a palatial aura befitting the image of royalty.

The hexagonal-shaped edifice was enshrouded in a sunset yellow exterior accented by sea-foam green glass curtain wall windows, which gleamed in the reflection of the morning tropical sun. The stunning four-story structure proudly displayed a colonnade main entrance encircling a lavishly landscaped front façade. It was apparent to Cleve. This was a highly profitable lending operation.

As the two entered the building through the rear parking garage, Clevis was uncharacteristically apprehensive. Jose led him into an outer waiting area just off the main hallway on the first floor.

Jose announced Clevis's arrival. "Ms. Hughes, this is Mr. Harrington. He's scheduled to meet with the loan committee today."

Ms. Hughes replied, "Oh yes. Thank you. Please have a seat. Can I get you some water or coffee?"

"No thanks. I'll pass for now."

It seemed to be an eternity until Clevis was summoned into the main conference room. The large wooden double doors leading into the meeting room suddenly swung open. Chris McField, Senior Loan Officer for Allied, motioned for Cleve to come inside.

Clevis stepped into the massive room. As he passed through the doorway, he immediately noticed the conspicuous opulence of the space. The teakwood conference table engulfed the bulk of the rear portion of the room.

Seated at the conference table were eight individuals. Six men. Two women. All were dressed in business casual tropical attire. White legal pads were strategically positioned in front of each committee member.

McField announced, "Mr. Harrington, this is our loan committee. They'll be asking you some questions. Ultimately, the committee will decide if the funding you requested will be approved."

Clevis sat down at the far end of the table opposite the loan committee. The inquiry lasted for a little more than two hours. Every imaginable area of Clevis' business and personal financial life was extensively probed.

The information revealed the obvious truth. Harrington Industries was in a precarious financial situation. The loan committee appeared to be unphased by that revelation.

At the end of the interview, McField admonished Clevis, "Mr. Harrington, we must inform you that Allied Funding is a lender of last resort. That is our niche. The company is willing to make loans to distressed companies such as yours in exchange for a higher-than-market return. Also, as you will see, our loan documents require the payment of a portion of any appreciated value of the loan assets in the event you sell the property or at the time of maturity of the loan."

Clevis responded, "I understand."

After the meeting, Thomas Bodden, who had led the loan committee discussion, told Cleve the committee now had all of the information they were seeking. Mr. Bodden mentioned that Clevis would be notified within six to ten days regarding the decision of the committee.

Bodden then escorted Clevis to the outer waiting area.

As Clevis turned to leave, Bodden said, "One more thing, Mr. Harrington. If we approve your funding request, we like to emphasize the importance of faithful adherence to the loan repayment obligations. It's imperative you not default or delay in any way. You must have all designated payments in our possession by wire transfer no later than the close of business on the specified payment dates. If you deviate from those responsibilities, the consequences could prove dire. We have an excellent track record regarding the collection of the money owed us and the fees and costs associated with our loans."

The following day, Clevis flew back to Huntsville. Cleve was no stranger to playing hardball in his business affairs. But based on Allied Funding's comments regarding the consequences of a loan default, Allied seemed to be taking that concept to a whole new level. They seemed obsessed with maintaining a pristine record for loan proceeds repayment.

The experience with the loan committee was unnerving and very bizarre. Clevis could see that he was dealing with an extremely unorthodox lender group. He knew of the existence of niche venture capital lending, but this group was strange beyond description with a culture bordering on cultism.

On the flight back to Huntsville, Cleve fell deep into deep contemplative thought about the company's current financial troubles. He couldn't stop pondering the crisis at his company.

I've got to get out front of this mess. The most problematic thing is the fact the company's current debt-to-cash flow ratio is way out of whack. The money from Allied is my last chance. Without this loan, the company is doomed to foreclosure and possible bankruptcy.

Up to this point, Cleve had done a remarkable job concealing the dismal financial status of Harrington Industries. Even Jarod had not been told how dire the situation had become.

Consistent with their word, Allied notified Clevis eight days after the loan committee meeting. The email notification stated the loan had been approved for five million dollars, subject to stated conditions. Essentially, Allied was requiring that their office be notified in the event Harrington Industries received a notice of default or was sued for foreclosure on any existing mortgages.

Within days, Clevis had signed all of the necessary documents and was scheduled to receive the first installment of the loan proceeds. Clevis was highly conflicted about the whole thing. But he was relieved to get this funding behind him.

Following approval of the Allied loan, Cleve quickly became immersed in the daily routine of the company. At first, things seemed to smooth out just a bit. The incoming revenue from active production orders was sufficient to service the debt for the conventional loans and the Allied Funding obligation.

But not long thereafter, things began to sour for Harrington Industries. Clevis received notice of cancellation of a sizeable order for the fabrication of aeronautical component parts for a particular model of the Adelphi 5000 corporate jet. This was a devastating blow.

After six months, he received the final disbursement of the loan funds from Allied. The funds were quickly depleted to make payroll and pay the outstanding invoices from key suppliers for Harrington's manufacturing and production activities.

Clevis knew this was indisputably the all-time low point in the history of Harrington Industries. Additional funding sources simply didn't exist. If things didn't turn around quickly, the debt load of the company was unsustainable.

In his desperation, Cleve contacted the life insurance company regarding possible payment of the life insurance proceeds for Veronica's policy. The response from the life company was not what Clevis wanted to hear.

He was decimated to learn that the forensic investigator for the company had decided to recommend refusal to pay policy proceeds. The stated reason was the unresolved status of the death of the insured. Cleve considered turning the matter over to his attorneys but concluded there was little that could be accomplished by undertaking protracted litigation.

Cleve realized he had to pursue new avenues to capture additional business. He desperately needed more income quickly to stop the bleeding.

Over the years, Clevis had accumulated a long list of representatives of aerospace and aeronautical companies. In desperation, Cleve began to spend long hours making personal cold calls to those representatives.

Despite all the effort, he had little to show for it. Business was simply down across the board. It was the nature of the industry.

As time passed, nothing seemed to improve in any measurable way. The pressure on Cleve to keep the company liquid and viable transformed him.

He became an even more driven person than he had typically

been. Volatile outbursts became the norm. Jarod dreaded having to engage with his dad.

Cleve had developed a tendency to blame Jarod for anything and everything that went wrong. Clevis never let Jarod forget that the crane accident cost the company millions of dollars and propelled the company into a downward spiral.

The accident had become a significant distraction for an extended period of time. It remained a substantial unpaid liability of the company.

Jarod had not been able to shake his increasing resentment, bordering on disdain for his father. He knew that was not the way a father-son relationship should be.

He found himself having very dark thoughts, especially after his dad belittled or humiliated him over practically nothing. His morale and self-esteem couldn't have been lower.

Jarod remembered the comments he'd once made to his mother: "I wish I'd been born the son of a factory worker and not the son of the founder of a juggernaut company with the Harrington name emblazoned all over the main entrance."

He recalled one particularly troublesome encounter with his dad. Clevis was on a roll that day. He had just received notification of the cancellation of the Adelphi Aeronautics contract.

Clevis walked into Jarod's office. Jarod could tell Cleve was livid.

"Jarod, what in the hell have you been telling the production division department heads in your management meetings? Someone said you told them you're launching some kind of enhanced quality control initiative."

Jarod was blindsided by Cleve's accusation.

"Engineering told me there's been a lot of issues with substandard output on the production line for the horizontal stabilizer hydraulic cylinders. I'm trying to troubleshoot the problem to get ahead of it. Before we get pushback from the customer."

Clevis exploded. "I don't give a damn about minor problems. Don't tell me about any problems. All I want around here is to see everyone goddamned one of you pushing the product out the door. Tell the managers to get their asses down on the production floor to make sure that happens! Jarod, don't give me any of that pussyfoot bullshit ever again. You better toughen up, or you'll find yourself looking for a job!"

Jarod never forgot that encounter. His dad seemed to be careening out of control. Jarod felt Clevis had become his own worst enemy. His wild outbursts and irrational thinking would likely take the company down.

What a prick. Why couldn't I just have a normal life? Sometimes, I wish my dad was dead.

CHAPTER 15

The financial condition of Harrington Industries was spiraling into oblivion. `In his desperation, Cleve weighed his options. He knew his only choice was to create a new revenue stream. The question was how? The customer orders were drying up industry-wide.

He considered some kind of merger to save the company. But a merger with who? Harrington Industries already dominated the market in the area of design and production of aeronautical parts.

With everything on the line, Clevis turned in a different direction. His obsession to succeed by any means seemed to erase any qualms about crossing the line into illegality.

Cleve knew there was a lucrative black market waiting to be tapped. If only he could devise a plan to sell to offshore customer groups.

He decided to explore opportunities for sales to companies operating in countries with trade bans for products manufactured in the United States.

Cleve realized he had to have Jarod on board for such an operation. When Jarod heard Cleve's scheme, he was stunned at his dad's total lack of integrity and blatant disregard for federal trade laws and regulations.

Jarod was convinced his dad had become unhinged. He'd crossed the line. How else could someone conceive of such a risky and diabolical plot?

Jarod's frustration was obvious. He stormed into Cleve's office. "Sell to Iran? How could you even think this plan would work? We'd have to concoct a whole series of fabricated documentation. We'd have to make it appear as if we were selling to a company in a country outside of the trade ban."

Clevis smiled. "Yeah, that's the point. I've thought this whole thing through. I've worked out all the details. There's a company in Germany, Nottendam Enterprises SX, LLC. They're willing to help us. We'll ship our product to that company. The shipment will be relabeled and then shipped on to Iran."

"Dad, listen to me! That won't work. Germany can't export to Iran."

"That's not our problem. Nottendam said they have a way to get this done."

"That's insane! The chance of long-term success is minuscule. Damn near non-existent. Any third party handling our shipments could become suspicious, and the whole thing would unravel. What you're proposing is an illegal smuggling operation. It won't work. Forget it."

Cleve gave little credence to Jarod's concerns. He was determined to carry out his plan. He was certain Jarod would come around.

Clevis proceeded with his scheme. His contact person with Nottendam Enterprises SX was Hans Wagner. Hans told Cleve they were willing to convert the shipments from U.S.-based status to appear to be originating from Germany. The quoted fees for this surreptitious activity were extremely high.

However, the revenue generated from the ultimate buyer in Iran was more than sufficient to cover the costs. The margin of profit under this plan was astronomical compared to the typical legitimate deal based solely within the United States.

Clevis reported back to Jarod, "The deal's going forward."

In a futile attempt to thwart the plan, Jarod told his father, "I want no part of this. Count me out."

Jarod was unnerved by the manic look in Cleve's eyes when Jarod spoke those words.

"If you're not on board, you can pack up and get out!" Clevis shouted.

Jarod was painfully aware the company would likely be doomed if this illegal scheme was detected.

I've dedicated my life to this company. If I don't do something to stop this insanity, he's going to take the company down and me with it.

Ironically, Cleve had told Jarod on several occasions the company came first.

The way Jarod viewed it, Clevis's proposal would not save the company. It would ultimately destroy it.

The likely scenario would be an investigator would ultimately follow the money and determine that the actual funding source was the Republic of Iran.

It was obvious to Jarod. Clevis had become trapped in a death spiral. A web of incoherent and deranged thinking totally detached from reality.

After two months of strategic planning and numerous phone calls, the production process for the Iranian-bound component parts commenced. Once the plan was fully implemented and production was well underway, Clevis's stress was not alleviated. In fact, it had reached an unprecedented level.

Soon after the scheme was implemented, Cleve realized how difficult it was to maintain effective concealment of the ultimate destination of the Iranian shipments. The shipping department was simply instructed to label all Germany-bound products to be addressed to the attention of Hans Wagner, production manager at Nottendam Enterprises SX.

Cleve's biggest problem was the fabrication of what would appear to be legitimate invoices and payment protocol. The German-based company was to bill and collect the proceeds for payment from the Iranian buyer. In turn, Nottendam Enterprises

SX would remit the proceeds, less their fees and costs, to Harrington Industries based on falsified invoices showing the intermediary company as the ultimate purchaser.

Jarod couldn't believe what was happening. He'd become even more distraught as his dad's scheme swung into high gear. He'd seen enough. He wasn't giving up without a fight.

Jarod walked into Cleve's office. He sat down and stared directly at his father. "You've got to stop this before it's too late. The whole setup is too complicated. It's filled with risks and opportunities for failure. The whole damn thing is against the law. Just think about it, if someone anywhere in the process noticed something didn't look quite right, the whole damn thing would be blown wide open."

Clevis sat quietly, his hands clasped together, his eyes locked on Jarod.

Jarod could see that his dad's expression reflected a haunting vacancy as if he were in a distant, unknown place.

In a very surreal way, Clevis seemed to be looking right through Jarod. The weird aura emanating within the room was more than Jarod could tolerate. After several unnerving minutes of uneasy silence, Jarod walked out of the room without saying another word.

At this point, Clevis and Jarod were no longer speaking directly to each other. Their communication was limited to emails and text messages.

Clevis knew Jarod wanted to keep a safe distance from Cleve's illicit activities. But, as Vice President of Operations, Jarod had no choice. He was responsible for overseeing all the activities of company production, including the Iranian shipments. Finally, Jarod had reached the breaking point. The stress had become unbearable.

CHAPTER 16

I t was late fall in 2011. The oak, poplar, dogwood, and maple trees in the Huntsville area were adorned with the spectacular colors of amber, scarlet, crimson, and maroon, creating a natural mosaic of leafy brilliance rivaling the random and abstract beauty of a painter's pallet. Dawn was breaking as the first rays of sunlight burst over the horizon in the eastern sky.

It was an especially cold Saturday morning. A motorist passing by the stately grounds of the Harrington residence in the opulent district of Highland Place noticed smoke pouring from the northern gable along the upper roofline of the imposing ante-bellum estate.

A call came into the 911 emergency center.

"What's your emergency? Police, fire, or ambulance?"

The motorist responded frantically, "I was driving down the road in the Highland Place subdivision. There's smoke coming from the roof of the house at 8618 Arbor Pointe Lane. I don't see any flames, but there's a lot of smoke."

"A unit is on the way."

As the firetrucks pulled onto the long winding drive leading up the hill to the house, the flames began to flicker along the apex of the ridgeline of the structure. The firefighters on one of the pumper trucks immediately connected the hoses to knock down the flames engulfing the interior of the northern portion of the house.

One of the firefighters smashed the window outside of the master bedroom to allow the high-pressure stream of water to be directed onto the flames. It took more than an hour to fully extinguish the inferno.

The north end of the residence was severely damaged by fire, smoke, and water. Once the flames were sufficiently under control, a firefighter entered the structure.

In the process of searching, the firefighter made a gruesome discovery. He came upon the smoking ruins of a king-size bed in the master bedroom. Lying on the bed was a body. Although the bed was heavily damaged by smoke and water, the body appeared to have escaped the direct effects of the flames.

The corpse showed conspicuous signs of trauma. The face and neck of the person were drenched in blood. It appeared the skull had been crushed by some type of blunt object. Based on the evidence, the unit captain contacted the Huntsville police for further investigation.

At two-thirty p.m., the call from the fire captain came into the Huntsville police department. The matter was referred to the homicide division. Sergeant Morrison took the call, but handed it off to Lieutenant Mercer.

After reviewing the initial incident report, Mercer shook his head in amazement. He realized he recognized the homeowner's name, 'Clevis Harrington'. The report stated the death appeared to have involved foul play.

Mercer knew bad things happened in threes. In the process of investigating the homicide of Veronica Harrington and Cody Beard, he never envisioned he would eventually be investigating the horrific homicide of Clevis Harrington.

Lieutenant Mercer stopped what he was doing. He rushed to the Harrington residence. It was very important to conduct the initial investigation while the body remained on site.

As Mercer drove down the street in front of the property, the image of Harrington's house appeared borderline surreal. Crime scene tape looped throughout the property, resembling a yellow spider's web, engulfing the house and extending toward the street.

The Huntsville CSI unit had just wrapped up its preliminary investigation. As he approached the house, Mercer stopped to talk with Walter Connelly, the CSI team leader on duty that day. "What's your take on this?"

Connelly replied, "We found one fatality. A middle-aged male. He was found in the master bedroom. At first, we thought he'd died from smoke inhalation. But it didn't take long until we could see that wasn't the case. You'll see what I mean when you get in there."

"What do you mean?"

"It appears the victim had been severely beaten with some type of blunt object. The face was extremely disfigured. It has all the signs of a revenge killing. Kind of strange."

Mercer grabbed his notebook and walked toward the rear entry of the house. "Okay. I'll see what we have. This is a bizarre situation. I knew this guy. I've got an active investigation involving members of his family. The thing that's so damn strange is this is the third homicide for the Harrington family. This whole thing's like a Greek tragedy. Everyone dies in the end."

Mercer walked into the house. The stench of smoke and charred wood was overwhelming. Most of his investigations over the years didn't involve fire fatalities.

As Roy entered the master bedroom, he approached the bed to get a closer look at the body. Harrington had clearly been bludgeoned to death. His face was so badly deformed from the multiple blows, Roy couldn't recognize him. The forehead and cheekbones were partially collapsed.

The cartilage of Harrington's nose was obliterated. Fragments of cranial bone, scalp, and hair were scattered onto the bloody pillow and the surrounding bedding. Blood spatter and brain tissue were splayed onto the wall behind the bed as a morbid epithet to the vicious actions of the killer. Whoever had done this was intentionally and extraordinarily brutal as if the killer wanted to convey a message.

Lieutenant Mercer had seen his share of killings in his lengthy career. Only a handful had involved the level of cruelty and animus exhibited in this case.

He realized the heinousness of this homicide would likely prove to be a significant factor in solving the crime. The critical question was- Who harbored such deadly hatred for Clevis Harrington?

Roy continued his search of the crime scene. As he moved around the room, he noticed the telltale signs of the use of an accelerant to ignite the fire. It appeared the fire most likely started in the bedroom.

The floor near the outer walls suffered the heaviest damage. Roy's first reaction was that the perpetrator likely poured some type of flammable liquid along the perimeter of the room before igniting it.

Cleve rechecked the initial crime scene report. The report noted the presence of a vinyl glove found several inches from the burned area along the wall opposite the bed. The glove was intact and undamaged.

As Lieutenant Mercer continued his search, he noticed the flames of the fire appeared to have migrated upward through the ceiling and into the attic of the residence. The interior of the bedroom had been spared from the full destructive effect of the fire.

After his initial inspection of the scene, Mercer returned to central headquarters to examine the evidence collected by CSI. In particular, he wanted to inspect the vinyl glove found at the scene.

Consistent with investigative protocol, Roy donned protective gloves before handling the evidence. Upon opening the bag containing the glove, he immediately noticed the strong smell of gasoline.

The following day, Mercer returned to the Harrington residence to expand his inspection of the property. His primary focus was the rear storage area of the garage. He suspected if the killer used gasoline as the accelerant for the fire, he most likely returned the gas can to the garage before fleeing the scene.

Using sterile techniques to avoid contamination, Mercer searched through all the miscellaneous items stored in numerous boxes and on the shelves in the garage. He moved anything that obscured his view.

As he cleared items out of his way, Roy found a baseball bat tucked behind a wooden storage crate against the back wall. The bat appeared to be free of visible blood or tissue. There were no residual signs the bat had been used as the murder weapon.

Lieutenant Mercer continued his search through the boxes and cabinets. He spotted a gasoline can on a lower shelf. It appeared haphazardly placed. The base of the can teetered close to the edge of the shelf. The filler spout was missing. The can was empty.

Roy paused to contemplate the situation.

That's odd. That can is conspicuously out of place.

Lieutenant Mercer took photos of the shelf as it appeared at the time of his arrival on the scene. He collected the can and the bat for further analysis back at the crime lab.

CHAPTER 17

Two days later, Mercer stopped by the crime lab to discuss the case with Bob Evans, crime lab forensic unit manager. "Hey, Bob. Just wanted to stop by to check on the lab test results. You got anything on the Harrington homicide?"

"Your timing is excellent. Just got the report back today on a couple of things."

"What I'm most interested in is, did you find anything on the baseball bat and the gasoline can from the victim's house?"

Evans thumbed through the printout of the report. "Let's see. Looks like our initial tests showed nothing was picked up on the bat. It appeared to us it may have been wiped clean. So, we did a luminol test. Found minute traces of blood. The bat's made of aluminum. The surface is kind of porous at the microscopic level. We found blood embedded in the small pores of the metal. We did a DNA test for the blood on the bat. We got a match for Mr. Harrington. We have no doubt the blood traces on the bat are Harrington's."

"What about the gas can? Anything on it?"

"Yeah. We hit paydirt on the can. Our fingerprint technician lifted one partial print from the handle."

Roy responded enthusiastically, "Excellent! You've made my day. I'm anxious to get feedback on that print. Hopefully, our killer's in the database."

"I have to warn you. It may be a while before we can get the results back on the print. The database retrieval has been ridiculously slow the last couple of weeks. We'll let you know as soon as we hear back."

"That's all we can ask. Good work, Bob."

Roy returned to central headquarters. He knew it was time to piece this all together. Consistent with Roy's time-tested approach, he constructed a 'likely scenario' of what went down at the scene.

Mercer discovered over the years this method allowed him to create a mental picture of the crime. It proved to be essential to establish a chronology of events before and during the homicide.

Lieutenant Mercer had just turned the corner in the narrow hallway of central headquarters when Sgt. Brad Morrison stepped out of his office. Morrison quickly caught up with Mercer and followed him toward his small office at the end of the hall. "Roy. I'm glad I saw you. I've been wondering how the Harrington case is going. Or should I say, cases?"

Mercer rolled his eyes. Morrison was still considered to be a rookie cop. Kind of a pest in his effort to learn all he could from the veteran detectives assigned to the homicide unit.

"I just got back from the scene."

"What'd you learn?" Morrison asked impatiently.

Mercer walked into his office and motioned for Morrison to have a seat in one of the two small chairs tightly crammed into the small space between Mercer's desk and the wall.

"I spent several hours searching the property. Checking the layout. Inspecting the contents of each room. Trying to visualize what happened on the night of the homicide."

"Well, what'd you learn?"

Lieutenant Mercer held up his hand, resembling a patrol officer directing traffic in a busy intersection. "Hang on. I'll get to that. As you should know by now, any detective worth their salt would try to put himself or herself in the shoes of the perpetrator to get the feel of the dynamics of the crime in real-time."

"So, what'd you figure out?"

"Well, I've given this a lot of thought." Roy leaned back in his chair, his right hand cradling the back of his head. "I'll tell you how I think this all came down. Keep in mind, this is just my best first impression. I may have to tweak my theory as more evidence is uncovered."

Morrison leaned forward toward Lieutenant Mercer's desk. "You got this figured out just walking around the property?"

"No. I didn't say that. I said I've got a working theory. What I think may have happened was this. The evidence I've seen so far shows the killer planned the hit well in advance. He either had first-hand knowledge of the property or was able to obtain some strategic information from some unknown source about the layout of the house."

Mercer suddenly sat upright in his chair. "Whoever committed the murder had detailed information about the personal habits of Clevis. He apparently had figured out Harrington's general daily schedule. The killer also had a basic knowledge of the security system for the personal residence. Based on what I saw, it appears the perpetrator discovered a point of entry through the side door of the garage. That door had been temporarily disconnected from the active entry alarm system. I noticed the kitchen area is being remodeled. My guess is the alarm system was either inadvertently disabled in the construction or intentionally disconnected by a contractor for easy access to the home. For whatever reason, it wasn't working." Lieutenant Mercer turned toward a side table to briefly review his notes. He asserted confidently, "On the night of the attack, the killer wore vinyl gloves to avoid leaving telltale fingerprints. Also, the killer ---_"

Morrison interrupted, "How'd you know that?"

"I found a discarded glove in the bedroom. I'll get to that in a minute." Roy paused briefly to collect his thoughts. "As I was saying, the killer forced open the side door to gain access to the house. No alarm was triggered. The killer must have searched the garage and found an aluminum bat in the rear storage area."

Sgt. Morrison furrowed his brow. "A bat?"

"Yes. It appears the bat was the murder weapon. The victim's death was due to blunt force trauma. My theory is the killer found the bat and made his way to Harrington's bedroom. He came upon Harrington as he slept in his bed. He raised the bat and began violently striking the victim in the head. After the first blow, Harrington was rendered unconscious, or worse. In any case, he was unable to defend himself. There were no visible defensive wounds or injuries on Harrington's hands and arms."

Morrison asked, "Harrington didn't fight back?"

Mercer ignored the question. He continued his description. "Blood spatter and brain tissue had sprayed onto the wall adjacent to the bed. The blood spatter on the wall behind and beside the bed indicated there were repeated impacts of the bat into Harrington's skull. We don't yet have the coroner's report. It's likely Harrington was killed after the first violent strike of the bat. The killer must have repeatedly delivered blows to the victim's head. This indicates a sick and perverse desire to mutilate the body. The condition of the deceased demonstrated classic evidence of a revenge killing."

Sgt. Morrison inquired, "The killer showed up at the house to commit a murder and didn't bring a weapon?"

Mercer nodded. "Apparently so. It looks like the perpetrator may have been acting spontaneously out of sheer emotion. A crime of passion. Or, I suppose it could have been committed by someone wanting to make it look like a crime of passion." Lieutenant Mercer paused, taking an ample breath. "We also found a blood-soaked towel on the floor next to the bed. The killer used a towel to try to wipe the bat clean. I guess he thought wiping the bat with a towel would eliminate any blood or tissue from the bat's surface. At some point after the attack, the perpetrator returned to the garage to hide the bat behind the wooden storage crate."

"That's where you found the bat?"

"Yes. There was unmistakable evidence of a deliberately set

fire in the house. It's a common misconception that a fire can destroy evidence of a killing. It appeared to me the killer found the gasoline can in the rear area of the garage. Based on the fire pattern, it looked like he poured gasoline onto the carpet along the walls in the room. I'm sure he thought the room would be engulfed in flames once the fire was set."

"The fire didn't destroy the room?" Sgt. Morrison queried.

"Not at all. The walls were badly charred, but my guess is the fire quickly moved into the attic. One thing I did notice, he'd spilled some fuel on his right hand."

"How'd you know that?"

"I looked at the vinyl glove found at the scene. Apparently, the gasoline had begun to partially dissolve the glove. He pulled the glove off of his hand and tossed it onto the carpet along the wall. That's where we found it. It's for the right hand. He must have assumed the glove would be destroyed in the fire." After he set the fire, he returned the gas can to the shelf in the garage. After the fire was ignited, I have no doubt he quickly fled the scene through the side entry door in the garage."

Roy noticed Morrison's expression of surprise and admiration.

"Damn. That's pretty amazing, if you ask me. It'll be interesting to see if your version turns out to be the way it really happened."

Roy hoped this scenario would be substantiated by the evidence collected at the site. Also, the general condition of the body of the victim supported his version of what happened that night. The key thing Mercer lacked was the results of the fingerprint analysis from the crime lab.

Another week passed. The crime lab finally reported to Roy. The fingerprint on the gas can was no match- too indistinct for a true analysis. Mercer was disappointed but undeterred.

The next week, Roy returned to the Harrington residence with a CSI fingerprint technician. He instructed the technician, "Check for prints on the interior doorknob of the side entry garage door. That's the point of entry that makes sense when you consider the layout of the house."

After careful inspection of the door, the technician found several prints on the knob. This was not unusual. It was to be expected due to the normal use of the door.

All of the print specimens were sent to the forensic lab for analysis. Five days later, Mercer received the report.

The fingerprint database generated more than one possible match for one of the prints. The lab report noted they weren't able to isolate the print to one person due to smudging of the sample.

The report showed there were five possible matches for the partial print. Roy was genuinely disappointed that the doorknob print was not conclusive.

Out of frustration, he threw the report onto his desk and walked down the hall to discuss the case once again with his colleague, Sergeant Morrison.

Lieutenant Mercer stepped inside the entryway of Morrison's office and leaned against the doorframe. "Brad, I've got a real dilemma. I'm up to my elbows in the Harrington homicide. I want to bounce something off you. To see what you think. As you know, we've done the preliminary investigation. I previously told you the apparent murder weapon was an aluminum baseball bat. We checked the bat for prints. Didn't find any." Mercer moved closer to Brad's desk. "We also checked a gasoline can I found in the garage. Picked up a partial print. It was not complete, so it couldn't be processed through the database. I returned to the crime scene to check one more location for possible prints. I mentioned to you earlier that the killer entered and left through a side door in the garage. We know he'd discarded a vinyl glove while setting the fire in the bedroom. Based on that information, I thought there might be some additional prints on the doorknob when he escaped through the side door."

Sgt. Morrison slowly looked up from his work. His expression reflected mild aggravation.

"Oh, I'm sorry. I just barged in on you. Did I interrupt something?" Mercer asked.

Brad shook his head. "No, I'm good. Did you find any prints?"

"Yeah, we did. But it wasn't complete. The lab said the print was smudged. The perpetrator had gasoline on his hand when he touched the knob."

"That's a damn shame."

Mercer walked over and leaned against the wall. "The print analysis said there was one person with prints that may match the print on the knob. The problem is, due to the low resolution of the print, the lab wasn't certain that the match was accurate."

"I may still be a rookie, but I know you'll need solid proof of the killer's identity. If the lab can't confirm the perpetrator's identity based on the partial print, what will you do?"

"I'll definitely need something more. The prosecutor will need ironclad evidence of the ...." Lieutenant Mercer stopped in mid-sentence, pausing briefly, immersed in thought. "You know, I've got an idea."

"Like what?"

"CSI didn't say a thing about security video. I don't know why. That's kind of odd. The house had cameras mounted inside and outside. There was no security camera in the master bedroom. I did see one in the hallway leading to the bedroom, and another one in the garage. I need to check to see if anyone reviewed any available footage. There could be some usable images. You never know."

Sgt. Morrison rose from his chair as Mercer turned to leave. "Good luck, Roy."

At this point, Lieutenant Mercer had sufficient information to obtain a search warrant for Harrington's office and computer. Roy had already completed an exhaustive search of the personal residence. What he really needed was access to any communications Cleve kept at his office.

But first, Mercer concluded it would be useful to interrogate Jarod one more time. The immediate family members of a homicide victim are always primary suspects. At least until evidence cleared them from suspicion.

Based on information Mercer gleaned from past conversations with Jarod, Jarod had a clear motive to commit the crime. He had a caustic relationship with his father. Jarod was the most logical person to have committed the killing, possibly by his own hand.

Roy had to move quickly. Mercer wanted to get a reading on Jarod's demeanor soon after the death of his father. If Jarod's behavior was inconsistent with a grieving and shocked son of the victim, the likelihood that Jarod was the killer is significantly enhanced.

Roy called Jarod to schedule the interrogation. Jarod agreed to come to police headquarters that next day at ten a.m.

The following morning Jarod arrived at police headquarters at nine forty-five. After the previous police interview regarding Cody's homicide, Jarod assumed he'd never have to return to the station for further questioning. He'd been through this before. He just wanted to get this whole thing behind him.

Jarod was nervous as he walked into the reception area of headquarters. He was confused about the purpose of the interrogation. His father had been brutally murdered. He hoped Mercer didn't suspect he knew anything about this. Jarod instinctively knew he needed to deflect the investigation away from him.

Upon entering the interrogation room, Lieutenant Mercer motioned for Jarod to have a seat. Mercer pulled a small chair from across the room and sat down a foot away from Jarod. He wasted no time with small talk.

"Jarod, we're sorry about the loss of your father. As you probably already know, the crime scene showed that the homicide was exceptionally violent. Your father was brutally beaten to death. To say it was macabre is an understatement."

Jarod shook his head. "It was a terrible shock. Of course, I haven't been out to Dad's house since the day of the murder. I don't know if they'd let me in. Anyway, I don't want to see it. It wouldn't serve any meaningful purpose."

Mercer said reassuringly, "Well, we aren't asking you to view the crime scene. I just felt you should know the facts of this killing. I do have a few questions for you. The obvious one is where were you in the early morning hours last Saturday?"

"What do you mean by early morning hours?"

"From about midnight to eight in the morning."

"I was at home, sleeping."

"Was anyone there with you?"

"No, I was alone. I'd gone to bed at about eleven-thirty. I got up at about seven-forty-five that next morning."

"So, you don't have anyone who can verify your whereabouts at the time of the death of your father?"

"I didn't have anyone at my place overnight if that's what you're asking."

Mercer turned to retrieve his notepad lying on the table positioned against the wall. "Okay. Let me ask you this. It's an obvious question. Do you have any idea who would want to murder your father?"

Jarod responded emphatically, "Lord, no. I can't begin to fathom who would want to do that. I know my dad could be a tough guy. I'm sure he stepped on some toes along the way. Probably a lot of toes. But murder? It doesn't make sense to me."

Mercer paused and leaned over to study the back of Jarod's hand. "I noticed you have some scratches and abrasions on your right hand. How'd you get those?"

"I don't recall. I may have scratched my hand down at the plant. A couple of guys were moving some equipment around on one of the production lines. I helped them get some crates loaded onto a dolly. That may be how it happened."

Lieutenant Mercer methodically scribbled a note. "Uh-huh. We'll want to get some photos of your hands before you leave today if you have no objection."

"I don't see the point of that. Am I a suspect?"

Mercer sat up straight in his chair. "It's too soon to know for sure. I'd say you're a person of interest at this point. One last question. I know you and your dad didn't always have the best relationship. As I understand it, the two of you clashed fairly regularly. Is that correct?"

"I guess you could say that. We had our disagreements, mostly about how things should be handled. He and I didn't always agree on the long-term direction for the company."

"Did either one of you ever threaten the other with physical violence?"

Jarod shook his head. "No. But he did threaten to fire me more than once. Nothing ever came of it."

Lieutenant Mercer quickly scanned his notes. "Jarod, the way we see it is you had a lot of disagreements with your dad. You didn't like the way he ran the company. You resented the fact he treated you like crap. You felt you needed to do whatever it took to get him out of the way in order to save the company, didn't you?"

Jarod stiffened. "I told you over and over, I didn't kill my father!"

Mercer abruptly rose from his chair. "I think that's all I have for now. We'd like to get fingerprint samples from you today. If you don't want to give us prints, we can obtain a court order if we have to."

Jarod waited briefly while the lab prepared to take his prints. Afterward, he walked slowly toward the front entrance of police headquarters. He was conflicted about what to make of Mercer's questions.

He came away from the interview knowing Lieutenant Mercer suspected he'd killed his father. Why else would Mercer have asked those questions? For the first time, Jarod thought maybe he should get his own lawyer before he talked any further with the homicide division.

Roy's theory that Jarod may be the killer was bolstered by the fact Jarod's demeanor was not typical. He was very controlled and methodical when discussing the death of his father. Roy expected Jarod would have shown more emotion when he heard the graphic description of how his father died. Instead, Jarod was matter-of-fact in his comments. Mercer believed the animus between Clevis and Jarod had festered for a long time, eventually erupting into rage resulting in the killing of Mr. Harrington.

After the interview, Lieutenant Mercer called it a day. He was exhausted. The fast pace and endless hours of the investigation were taking their toll. He was anxious to get home to his wife and a good home-cooked meal.

The following day, Roy filed the necessary papers to get a search warrant for the offices of Harrington Industries. Any information Clevis had in his possession related to Jarod might provide a basis for a search of Jarod's home and computer.

As expected, he was able to get the warrant. The court authorized the warrant based on the reasonable belief that the records at Cleve's office may contain relevant and probative information regarding the crime.

Mercer also wanted to look for any evidence that might help solve the unresolved case of the death of Veronica Harrington. It'd now been several years since the drowning of Veronica. That case had lingered without resolution for far too long.

Roy knew he could have simply walked into Clevis's office with the search warrant. But he decided to call Harrington's personal assistant, Ms. Goodman, to arrange a convenient time for his arrival. Mercer was confident that, after Harrington's death, there was little chance anyone had tampered with potential evidence.

The next morning, Mercer called Ms. Goodman. "This is Lieutenant Roy Mercer with the homicide division of the Huntsville police. I'm investigating the recent death of Clevis Harrington. I've obtained a search warrant for the corporate offices. The purpose of my call is to arrange a convenient time to come by to look through some files and records."

Ms. Goodman dutifully replied, "I was expecting your call. I'm still in shock over the death of Mr. Harrington. I've been his personal executive assistant for many years. I still can't believe he's dead."

"I'm sure the news of his death was totally unexpected. What day and time will work for you?"

"Well, I'm available about any time. There are no appointments on the schedule now that Mr. Harrington is no longer here. How about nine a.m. tomorrow?"

"That will work. I'll see you at nine."

Roy was excited about the chance to search Clevis Harrington's files and records. He'd tried to get a warrant in the investigation of the death of Veronica. The court denied the issuance of that warrant. Roy was still ticked about that. He was convinced the court had simply refused to go against the power structure of the money elite of Huntsville.

The next day at the appointed time, Roy arrived at Mr. Harrington's office. Ms. Goodman escorted him from the outer waiting area into the lavishly appointed office suite.

Roy couldn't help but notice the large brass plaque, ' Clevis Harrington-President, ' mounted on the massive hand-carved wooden double doors of Cleve's personal office.

In her typical business-like manner, Goodman told Mercer, "I don't quite know how you want to do this. I've never been served with a search warrant before. Just tell me what you are looking for. Maybe I can help you find it."

Mercer patiently explained, "The way this works is I'll be looking through everything in this office, including the data on any computers or phones. I don't have any specific item in mind. That's why it's called a search warrant. I'll be doing a general search for anything relevant to the case. I'll take the computers and phones with me for forensic analysis."

Goodman turned to exit the inner office. "Well, okay. I'll be right here if you need anything."

Lieutenant Mercer began the search. He created a make-shift logistical drawing of the office layout. He snapped several wide-shot photos to preserve the general orientation of the space. To avoid contamination of evidence, he donned a pair of vinyl gloves.

Roy began methodically sorting through all the documents in the hard copy file cabinets. He soon realized that Clevis was old-school in his record-keeping and a bit of a pack rat. There were reams of paper records dating back several years stored in his personal file cabinet. As Roy began reviewing the documents, he noted that Clevis had carefully labeled every file folder and arranged them alphabetically.

Mercer pulled each file. He scanned the contents looking for anything relevant to the investigation. He paused as he came across a file labeled "Life Insurance-Veronica."

The file included an application for life insurance, with Veronica Harrington as the proposed insured and Clevis Harrington as the sole beneficiary. The application was for ten million dollars.

At the bottom of the file folder, Roy found the issued policy showing an effective date of January 13, 2005. He checked the terms of the policy. The insuring provisions included a double indemnity clause. The policy would pay double the face amount for accidental death.

Lieutenant Mercer already knew that Clevis held a life insurance policy on Veronica. That information was revealed in the investigation of her death in 2005.

What he didn't know was the policy would pay double in the event of an accident. That alone created a powerful motive for Clevis to kill his wife for the insurance.

Roy was confused by this obvious paradox. He struggled to find the answer.

The puzzling aspect of all this was, why would such a successful man as Clevis Harrington want to kill his wife for the insurance? From the outside world's perspective, Clevis was a very successful business owner. The word on the street was he had a personal fortune of around 1.5 billion dollars.

But Roy had been around long enough to know things aren't always as they appear.

Mercer continued searching the files. He hoped to come across something that would break the case wide open. Roy knew luck played a big role in any successful investigation, but plain old hard work was how most crimes were solved.

The hours passed quickly. Mercer was exhausted. He had reviewed six drawers of file folders. Most of the documents were routine. Some were downright boring. Just what you'd expect in any business. After many grueling hours, Roy finally took a break to get some fresh air.

When he returned to the inner office, he asked Ms. Goodman, "Do you know if Mr. Harrington had any other place where he stored records? Any off-site storage facilities?"

Goodman replied, "No. We had the really old records

shredded after five years. Of course, I ordered shredding only on the files Mr. Harrington gave me. It's possible he had some old files in his possession that are still around."

"Could there be any other storage units or file cabinets where hard copy records would be held?"

Goodman paused briefly, appearing to be in thought. "I don't think so. However, I know Mr. Harrington kept a large floor safe in a backroom outside his office. I don't know what's in it. He was the only one who had the combination to the safe. I remember one time I was looking for him for a phone call. He was in that back storage area with the safe open. I couldn't see much, but I could see the safe had quite a few files and boxes in it."

"So, you don't know the combination to that safe?"

"No. Mr. Harrington always kept that information to himself."

"You realize our search warrant is for a general search. We have the right under the law to open the safe."

Ms. Goodman nervously touched the side of her face with an expression of unease. "Well, okay. If you must, I can't stop you."

After several more hours of searching, Lieutenant Mercer eventually left for the day. He returned the following morning with a locksmith.

After a quick check of the safe, the locksmith commented, "That's a fairly old safe. It's one of those that's not all that easy to open. Hard to feel the tumblers. We could drill the lock if that's okay."

Roy didn't hesitate. "Do whatever's necessary to open the safe."

Within a half-hour, the lock had been drilled out. The safe was open.

Lieutenant Mercer peered in. The yawning jaws of the open safe revealed numerous files and envelopes. Before removing any contents, Roy photographed the shelves and compartments of the inner sanctum of Harrington's personal hiding place.

As Roy sorted through the contents, he hoped this would yield some meaningful results. From what he could see, Mr. Harrington had used the safe as a highly secure repository for sensitive information. The kind of thing all forensic investigators hoped to find.

Nothing in the safe was labeled in any discernable fashion. Most of the contents had been haphazardly placed simply to secure the items away from public view. In one of the wooden drawers in the back wall of the safe, Roy found a small manila envelope.

He removed the envelope from the drawer. A label was attached to the front of the envelope. The handwriting on the label had been blacked out with a permanent marker.

When Mercer opened the envelope, an SD video card fell to the floor. He retrieved the card and returned it to the envelope. He placed the envelope into a labeled evidence bag for further analysis.

In the back corner of the safe, Mercer found a file folder containing what appeared to be a series of email communications and some loose-leaf business letters. In total, there was more than a ream of loose sheets of paper.

There's a lot of stuff here. It's going to take time to review all this.

Roy sat the folder to the side with other items he intended to take to the office for comprehensive analysis.

The search continued. Lieutenant Mercer methodically checked the contents of the drawers in Harrington's desk. He discovered that the drawer on the upper left side of the desk was locked.

Mercer summoned Rita Goodman. "Ms. Goodman, do you know if there's a key to Mr. Harrington's desk?"

Goodman shook her head. "I don't have one. Mr. Harrington kept his keys in his pocket."

"There's one drawer in his desk that's locked. I could check with CSI to see if they found any keys at Harrington's residence, but it would be a lot easier to get the locksmith back out here to open it. I'll be back tomorrow as soon as I can arrange for that."

The next day, at mid-morning, Mercer returned to continue the search. The locksmith quickly opened the locked desk drawer.

At first glance, the drawer's contents seemed unremarkable. However, Mercer did notice a letter to Harrington showing a return address for 'Allied Funding Partners XB'. The curious aspect was the address for Allied- 'Grand Cayman, Cayman Islands'. The letter had been sent by certified mail, return receipt requested.

Mercer opened the envelope and read the letter. He was stunned by the tone and content revealed within. This was no ordinary business letter.

The text emphasized, in unequivocal terms, that Allied Funding had made numerous demands to Clevis for payment of the balance of a past-due loan obligation. It emphasized that Clevis had failed to timely pay the debt owed to Allied.

The wording of the letter was foreboding in content and apocalyptic in tenor. The demands of the letter reflected an unmistakable mafia style. The letter was unlike anything he'd ever read. Roy placed the letter in the stack of documents to be reviewed back at his office.

Lieutenant Mercer told Ms. Goodman, "I'm through for now. I've made a list of the files I'm taking with me. I'll leave the list with you so you'll know what I took. I'll let you know if I need to return for a follow-up search."

On his way back to the office, Roy couldn't stop thinking about the obliterated handwriting on the envelope found in the safe. *Why would someone think it was necessary to black out the handwriting on that envelope? What were they trying to hide? And from whom?*

Mercer had a couple of hours left before the CSI lab closed for the day. He stopped by the lab to discuss the possibility of recovering the text under the permanent marker redaction.

Arriving at the lab, Roy spoke with CSI lab team leader Walter Connelly.

"Walt, I found an interesting thing in this investigation. I discovered an envelope in a safe at Clevis Harrington's private office. The envelope contained an SD video card. We're going to review the contents of the card very soon." He handed the envelope to Connelly. "It would be very helpful if you could find out what's written on the envelope. I need to know what's been blacked out on the label. Can you help with that?"

Connelly looked at the envelope, holding it up to an overhead light. "I think we can. There's a fairly new technique called impression analysis. We can give it a try."

"Yes, please do. Anything you can find out will help us immensely. By the way, how does impression analysis work?"

Connelly elaborated, "What we do is take the bottom half of the envelope, which was under the upper layer where the handwriting was done. We'll energize the bottom layer with an electrostatic charge. We then pour plastic beads covered with printer toner over the impression area. As the beads roll down the piece of paper, the toner adheres to the indented portions of the page. This should create a readable version of whatever was written on the upper layer of the envelope. We'll take photos for your file if we get a legible impression."

Mercer smiled. "Great. That sounds like that might work. Let me know how it turns out."

After three days, Walt contacted Roy to report the results. "Good news. The lab was successful in deciphering the text on the envelope. The handwriting image was not totally distinct. The image on the lower portion of the envelope was barely discernable, but we did determine the substance of the text. It read- 'Mobile Bay, June 2005.'"

Based on the information he'd obtained in his earlier investigation of the death of Veronica Harrington, Lieutenant Mercer realized the date on the envelope was around the time of the family getaway trip to Mobile Bay. That homicide investigation had gone stone cold.

No new developments surfaced after the court determined that the facts of the investigation did not establish probable cause for the issuance of a search warrant. Roy hoped the video card found in the envelope would provide additional information regarding the cause of Veronica's death.

CHAPTER 18

It was mid-afternoon the next day. Roy sat alone at his desk, reviewing the evidence in the file. There were a lot of bits of information floating around. He desperately needed to piece all this together.

As he contemplated the evidence, he had a gut feeling it would be worthwhile to conduct another interrogation of Jarod. The problem was Jarod had turned 'hardball'. Mercer decided, this time, that using a "tag-team" approach to the questioning would be more effective.

When asked to come back to the station, Jarod was reluctant to subject himself to more questioning. He knew he was a person of interest in the death of his father. But once again, he agreed to appear voluntarily.

After the last interview, Jarod had considered hiring his own lawyer. He decided against that, realizing that it would likely increase suspicion of him. He was hoping his cooperation would disarm and distract the detectives, putting him in the best light.

As the interview commenced, Mercer introduced his colleague, Sergeant Brad Morrison. "Jarod, this is Sgt. Morrison. He and I will be asking you some follow-up questions today."

Jarod responded, "I thought when we last talked, you were through with any questions for me."

Mercer clarified, "This investigation is ongoing. The facts are evolving. We just want to try to tie up a few loose ends. But before we start, I want to be sure you know your rights." Lieutenant Mercer handed a card to Jarod which listed the Miranda rights.

Jarod commented, "I know what that says. That doesn't intimidate me. I know I'm innocent."

Mercer continued, "The last time we talked, you told us you were at home sleeping at the time of the murder of your father. You recall we found some scratches and abrasions on one of your hands."

"Yeah, but I told you how that happened."

"I guess you realize the fact you don't have a valid alibi puts you in the alpha position as a possible suspect in the homicide of your father." Mercer paused, then leaned forward with a somber expression. "Sergeant Morrison and I have been discussing this situation. The way we see it, you had the opportunity, means, and motive to kill your dad."

Jarod emphatically declared, "I told you. I did not kill my father!"

Lieutenant Mercer forcefully countered, "The facts point in the other direction. We've discussed this before. From what we've been able to determine, you had a very combative relationship with Mr. Harrington. That alone is a sufficient motive for a child to kill his parent. We've seen it many times in the past. Besides that, after the death of your mother and your half-brother, the only person standing in the way of the inheritance of the entire Harrington empire was your father. That's motive number two."

Sergeant Morrison interjected, "Jarod, we obtained some video footage of the interior of the Harrington residence on the night of the murder. The images show a male figure. About your height and build. Since you don't have an alibi, there's no way you can convince us that the image in the video was not you. Correct?"

Jarod nervously bit his upper lip. "I'm telling you, I was at home in bed."

Mercer stood up, moving toward Jarod. "We were able to lift some fingerprints from the crime scene. We found your finger-prints on the interior doorknob in the garage."

Sgt. Morrison added, "Jarod, it would be much easier for you if you were straight with us. If you admit your involvement now, the prosecution may take that into account."

Lieutenant Mercer continued, "Look, Jarod, we're getting tired of screwing around with you. We've been more than patient in this whole process. All we've gotten in return is your stonewalling. This crap's got to stop."

"I've told you the truth. I'm not stonewalling."

Mercer moved ominously close to Jarod. "I've asked you before, but now we have solid evidence on you. Did you kill Clevis Harrington?"

"Absolutely not." Jarod asserted.

Mercer propounded, "You killed your dad, didn't you?"

Jarod slammed his fist against the table. "No!" After a brief pause, Jarod said, "I have nothing more to say."

Mercer and Morrison knew there was no purpose in continuing. Jarod was not going to confess.

After the interrogation of Jarod, Morrison confided to Roy, "As you're aware, we don't know for sure what's on the video. I told Jarod the image of the person on the footage was similar to his height and build just to get his reaction. I'm sure you knew what I was trying to do. I thought he might break down and confess. That tactic has worked well in the past. Jarod's a lot tougher than I imagined."

Lieutenant Mercer added, "He's going to have to feel the heat before he sees the light."

Mercer and Morrison felt they had a good track on solving this. Unless something else surfaced, they were convinced they'd be able to construct a case against Jarod sufficient for prosecution.

Another week flew by. No new evidence emerged. Lieutenant Mercer was genuinely frustrated by the slow pace of progress.

As Roy exited his office at the end of a long day, he stuck his head in Sergeant Morrison's office. "Hey Brad, we've been working damn hard for a long time. If you're about to wrap it up for the day, how about grabbing a beer over at The Brew House?"

Sgt. Morrison quickly responded, "Man, that sounds great. I need a break."

Roy and Brad walked the short distance to the local watering hole.

It was an extraordinarily beautiful evening. The temperature was in the seventies with a gentle breeze from the southwest. The crimson rays of light of the setting sun glinted off the mirrored glass of the surrounding high-rise buildings, creating a golden hew of iridescent splendor.

The two rounded the corner at the intersection of Market Street and Union Avenue. They entered through the heavy wooden door into the relative darkness of the bar.

Roy commented, "Let's grab the booth over in the corner."

The two sat down as the waiter approached.

"What can I get you guys this evening?"

Lieutenant Mercer quickly replied, "I'll take a dark lager on tap."

Brad confirmed, "That sounds good. Same for me."

The two couldn't resist talking about the Harrington case. Lieutenant Mercer had many years of service. Despite that fact, he'd never experienced true burnout. He lived and breathed his work.

Still a rookie detective, Sgt. Morrison was anxious to learn all he could from an old veteran like Roy.

Mercer took a generous swig of his frosty mug of beer. "You know, I get so immersed in the details of a case, sometimes I forget to back off and look at the big picture."

Brad asked, "What do you mean?"

Roy leaned forward with his elbows firmly ensconced on the rough-hewn surface of the wooden tabletop. "I don't know how to explain it. I guess sometimes I feel like I'm operating from some type of playbook for police personnel. Kind of like a robot. On cruise control. It's easy to get stuck in a rut. You probably know what I mean. You've been around long enough to learn the basic ins and outs of this crazy business."

"Yeah, but not nearly as long as you."

Roy continued, "It's too easy to overlook the obvious in search of minute detail. My problem is I tend to focus on each element of evidence as if it's going to reveal the whole story. I should know better by now. I have to remind myself to back off, to connect the dots to see the big picture."

"Well, from what I've seen so far, I'd say you do a pretty damn good job. The solve rate for your cases is the highest in the division."

"That's nice of you to say. One thing I've tried to avoid is becoming hardened in this business. That can definitely cause you to develop tunnel vision, to jump to conclusions based on the first piece of evidence you find."

Morrison nodded affirmatively. "I think I see what you mean. I suppose a good example would be the Harringtons. I've learned quite a bit about the case just by talking to you. It's a damn fascinating story. The patriarch of the family was brutally murdered. His wife mysteriously drowns while on a family getaway. Clevis Harrington had a love child shot to death in Atlanta. The only person still around is Jarod."

"Yeah. I've given that a lot of thought. I can't remember the last time I was assigned to a case where three members of the same family met their demise by homicide or suspected homicide. I'm not sure where we'll end up with that. I do think a break may come at any time."

"I hope so. I know there's been a hell of a lot of groundwork done up to this point."

"Well, Brad, that's why they pay us the big bucks."

The waiter glanced over and noticed the near-empty mugs. "Can I get you guys another beer?"

Morrison instantly replied, "Sure, we're not in any hurry to get home."

Mercer shifted in the booth, his legs extending out with his back against the interior wall. "As I was saying, police work is a tough job. I don't know about you, but I'm damn glad I'm not a patrol officer. It's been quite a few years since I worked a beat."

Morrison nodded. "I worked my butt off to make detective so that I didn't have to ride around in a patrol car all day. The risk is too high. I don't want to get shot by some worthless piece of shit who should've never been born. It goes without saying that police officers all over the country now have a bullseye on their backs."

Mercer observed, "See, Brad, now that's what I'm talking about. That's pretty damn harsh. I didn't realize you had such a hardass view. It takes real effort to avoid getting too cynical. Being a police officer can make you jaded, especially working a beat. After a few years on the force, everyone seems like a bad guy up to no good. I've done my best to avoid that syndrome."

Morrison hesitated. "Yeah, I guess you're right. But you'll have to admit, there are a lot of hardcore bad guys out there. We see the results of their actions every time we're called in to investigate a homicide."

The conversation paused. Lieutenant Mercer gazed toward the ceiling. He uttered philosophically, "I've been around a long time. Long enough to see a lot of change. Societal change. Back in the early nineties, it was all about getting tough on crime. Both at the state and federal level. But now, change is underway. It's been evolving for quite a few years."

"I'm not sure what you mean."

Roy reflexively glanced at his watch. "I see a conflict developing between "old school lock 'em up" laws and the new age push for flexibility in policing and sentencing. I call it coddling the criminals. The whole damn thing puts the police in an impossible situation trying to balance the interests. It's damned if you do and damned if you don't. How can you be tough and touchy-feely at the same time?"

Morrison declared, "Whether we like it or not, we're the public face of law enforcement. The tip of the spear. Especially the patrol officers. The thing that frustrates me is the pressure of trying to be effective at our job. The old guys, now retired from the force, had it a lot easier. We have to deal with arresting the criminals, but yet show empathy toward the victims of crime."

Roy quickly downed the last of his second beer.

"That's what I'm saying. The touchy-feely thing. It's a load of crap. A big load of crap! Speaking of empathy, it's been a challenge to adjust to changing attitudes about what they're calling 'alternative lifestyles'. I've been thinking about that ever since I interviewed Jarod. He told me about a blackmail scheme his half-brother, Cody, pulled on him. Cody had discovered that Jarod was his half-brother. From what Jarod said, Cody must have been a real piece of work."

"A real bad dude?"

Mercer spontaneously rocked his empty beer mug from side to side as he spoke. "According to Jarod, someone had told Cody about an online newspaper article from some underground scandal sheet in Atlanta. The story talked about a crackdown by the Atlanta police on some gay bars in one end of town. Jarod ended up getting detained by the police on what apparently was some bogus charge of public intoxication." Roy leaned back in the booth. "When Cody found out about the gay bar situation, he used that to his advantage. Jarod told me that Cody had learned through one of his friends that Clevis Harrington was ultra-conservative. Mr. Harrington had no tolerance for any deviation from the straight and narrow. Cody figured Jarod would be in a lot of trouble with Mr. Harrington if Clevis ever found out about his son's personal life."

"What do you mean?"

"Jarod told me if his father ever discovered he was gay, his dad would disown him. No questions asked. That's how friggin' rigid Harrington was. When you look at this whole situation, it's easy to see that Cody was a master manipulator. He'd size up the situation and figure out how to screw someone out of some money. Everything I've seen tells me he was ruthless and greedy."

Morrison nodded. "That's the impression I got."

"Jarod had a lot at stake. True to form, Cody attempted to con Jarod out of one hundred thousand dollars. It was hush money. If

Jarod didn't pay, Cody threatened to tell Clevis everything he knew."

"Jarod paid the money?"

"Yeah, he did, unfortunately. He told me he regretted that decision. He knew Cody was an opportunistic snake. It was only a matter of time until Cody would be back for more money. Jarod said Cody mentioned that, after Clevis was gone, Cody could make a lot of trouble for Jarod by claiming an interest in the family estate. He didn't know if that was an empty threat or a prediction of things to come."

"What a piece of work!"

"Jarod said his dad totally refused to accept the fact that Cody was his biological child. As I understand it, Clevis never bothered to change his estate plan to exclude Cody. To do that, Harrington would've had to admit that Cody was his son."

"So, that's why Jarod is a suspect in the homicide of Cody."

Roy nodded. "That's right. Jarod had more than one good reason to eliminate Cody. By the way, this whole thing about gay lifestyles is out of control nowadays in popular media. As you know, I'm no new-age kind of guy, but in my opinion, the Atlanta police were way out of line. They had no justification for harassing the patrons of those gay bars."

"It happens."

"My take is a person has a right to decide how they want to live their lives, so long as they don't harm anyone. I've made a point to not let that aspect of Jarod's life taint my thinking. As far as I'm concerned, it's the right way to handle this. What it comes down to is, Jarod's sexual preference is not the issue. It's really none of my business at a personal level. But you can't escape the conclusion that Jarod's sexuality was a gift to Cody. It provided the perfect opportunity for Cody to play Harrington's rigid attitude against Jarod."

"This whole thing is a convoluted mess."

Roy glanced over at Morrison. "Yes, it is, my friend. Yes, it is."

CHAPTER 19

The investigation of Harrington's murder was advancing, but at an unacceptably slow pace. From Roy's perspective, a suspect should be in custody by now. The frustration was palpable. Due to the notoriety of the Harrington family and the iconic industrial complex Mr. Harrington built over the years, the Huntsville Times carried a series of stories about the homicide.

For weeks following the homicide, local television stations aired numerous reports about the unsolved death. The news media was particularly focused on the fact there were three unsolved homicides in the same family.

The unyielding news coverage triggered unprecedented public awareness and interest in the multiple deaths. The Huntsville police tip line was inundated. More than one hundred calls had been received specifically regarding the murder of Clevis Harrington.

Two and a half weeks elapsed with no new developments. Finally, a uniquely useful tip was received. The tipster described what he saw on the night of the homicide.

In the pre-dawn hours on the Saturday morning Harrington was killed, the tipster was driving down the road bordering the front of the Harrington estate. He noticed the shadowy image of a person quickly exiting an SUV parked on the street near the front entrance of the property.

As the tipster's car approached, the person ran up the long driveway toward the Harrington residence. The caller thought it was extremely odd someone would park on the street in the darkness of night and run all the way up the long driveway. The tipster described the person as tall and wearing a hoody.

The tip information was referred to Lieutenant Mercer as the lead investigator. Mercer contacted the informant through the anonymous communication network set up for the tip line. The tipster was very cooperative. He agreed to answer any questions the police might have.

When Roy spoke with the caller, the eyewitness mentioned he'd seen news coverage of the homicide. He also mentioned that, at first, he didn't think much about the story. But eventually, he realized he may have useful information. He decided to let the police know what he'd witnessed.

The informant told Lieutenant Mercer he became concerned because he knew no one in that neighborhood typically parked on the street. He noticed that all of the homes were set back several hundred feet from the street entrance. To the caller, it didn't make sense for someone to park so far away.

Mercer was not one to jump to conclusions. But, given the timeline, he thought this shadowy figure wearing the hoody was most likely the killer. The description of the person and the timing of the sighting were consistent with the information Mercer and the CSI unit had gathered from their investigation.

Roy felt confident the killer assumed the residence would have an extensive set of security cameras deployed around the property. Mercer's working theory was the perpetrator chose to park on the street to avoid identification of his vehicle.

Lieutenant Mercer's analysis reinforced his ongoing suspicion of Jarod Harrington. As Mercer saw it, everything was coalescing to support the theory that Jarod was the most likely person to have committed the homicide. Jarod knew the layout of the Harrington residence. He had good reason to avoid detection of his vehicle on the security video.

Roy gathered all the files and notes he'd created during the investigation. He commandeered a large conference table in the media room at headquarters.

With all of the documents spread out sequentially along the table, Roy began to create a timeline. Each critical event leading up to the actual homicide and the date of each occurrence were noted.

In the process of reviewing all the evidence he'd accumulated, Roy came across the SD video card he'd found in Harrington's safe. Roy had become so involved in the effort to solve the murder of Clevis; he'd neglected to check the card to see if it contained legible images.

Roy reviewed his notes to refresh his memory. The notes showed the forensic lab had determined that the text on the envelope containing the SD card referenced 'Mobile Bay, June 2005'. Roy recalled that was the date on which Veronica drowned during the family retreat on Mobile Bay.

Mercer had previously determined that the cameras on Harrington's boat were motion-activated. In his inspection of the Harrington yacht, Mercer had concluded that there was only one recording unit.

After considerable effort, Roy located a computer with a compatible port for the video card. In reviewing the footage, Mercer could see there was content on the card, but the images were less than optimal.

The card was labeled as high capacity. Consequently, the memory included a large number of extraneous images extending over several days.

Despite the pressing need to review the accumulated evidence for the homicide of Clevis Harrington, Roy sat for hours watching the Mobile Bay video. Toward the end of the imaging sequence, Mercer observed a scene captured by the aft camera showing what appeared to be a wide shot of the rear portion of Harrington's cabin cruiser.

The scene showed Clevis and Veronica sitting comfortably in the chairs mounted on the aft deck. No sound was available. The lighting was faint as the sun set into the western sky. The camera image showed the couple drinking cocktails and appearing to be enjoying the evening.

As the video progressed, the image showed Clevis walking out of view toward the front of the boat. Minutes later, Veronica also moved out of camera range.

In a subsequent scene, Veronica was being led by Clevis back toward the rear of the boat.

From the grainy video, Mercer was able to conclude that Veronica was under the influence of alcohol. Her movements were slow, deliberate, and unsteady.

The balance of the video was very graphic and revealing. It appeared to be compelling and irrefutable evidence of a homicide.

The grisly scene showed Clevis aggressively grabbing Veronica by her shoulders. He shoved her forcefully toward the edge of the boat. A frantic struggle ensued. Veronica valiantly fought back in an attempt to avoid falling overboard. Clevis's bulky body was no match for Veronica. He was considerably bigger than her petite frame.

In mere seconds, Veronica was flailing in the water, her hands frantically searching for any stable object to avoid sinking into the murky deep. The video left no doubt she'd been intentionally pushed overboard.

Veronica desperately struggled to pull herself back onto the boat. At each attempt to save her own life, Clevis blocked her access.

At one point, Clevis aggressively stepped on Veronica's hands to prevent her from clinging to the boat's railing. Veronica instinctively thrashed her arms through the air as if trying to swim back to the safety of the vessel.

Clevis countered every desperate attempt to survive. After one final frantic effort to avoid sinking into the watery abyss, Veronica suddenly disappeared from view.

A short time thereafter, Clevis could be seen calmly walking back toward the bow of the boat. Within seconds, he was beyond the camera's range.

The end of the video reflected the glassy stillness of the water, belying the violent incident that had just occurred.

After viewing the video, Lieutenant Mercer paused to collect his thoughts. He was stunned. He shook his head in amazement and disgust. He'd seen more than his share of gruesome crime scenes in his career. Rarely did he have video documentation of the actual crime in progress.

Roy mused, *I can't figure out why Harrington didn't destroy the video card. I guess he's the victim of his own arrogance. It's a damn shame he's no longer around to face justice for this brutal slaughter.*

The video left no doubt as to the perpetrator in the homicide of Veronica Harrington. The death was no accident. The compelling issue remaining was the motive for the murder. Mercer had a hunch the answer would lie in the sequence of events occurring in the months leading up to the killing.

Roy had finally determined what really happened to Veronica on that fateful night. He needed to let Sergeant Brent Palmer know what he had discovered.

Lieutenant Mercer placed a call to Palmer. "Brent, this is Lieutenant Mercer in Huntsville. How's it going?"

"About the same as usual. Just chasing the bad guys."

"I'm sure you remember the drowning incident of Veronica Harrington on Mobile Bay."

"You bet. I've been wondering how that's going. I planned to give you a call to see if you'd made any progress."

"Well, we found what we needed. We did a search of Clevis Harrington's private office. You remember when you did your initial investigation, you noticed that the recording unit for the security cameras on Harrington's boat didn't have a video card?"

"Yeah. I remember."

"As it turns out, I found the missing SD card. It was hidden in Harrington's safe in his office. At first, I didn't know what it was. But after I viewed it, I could see it was from the boat."

"What was on the card? Anything useful?"

"Absolutely. There was a video of what happened that night. Fortunately, the security camera on the aft end of the boat caught everything. It was kind of grainy, but good enough to see what happened. The video showed that Harrington forced Veronica off the end of the boat. She tried to climb back on board, but Harrington blocked her. In the end, she was no match for him. She couldn't fight him off. She drowned that night as Clevis stood there and watched it happen. It was a barbaric act of unspeakable cruelty."

"My God! Do you know why he did it?"

"We don't know for sure. I've got a theory. It appears Harrington needed money. Veronica represented a big payday, provided she was dead."

"Life insurance?"

"Appears to be. We've seen it all before, too many times. Money trumps love when you get your ass in a financial wringer."

"No surprise there. Okay. Thanks for the update. I'm sure we'll talk again soon."

Mercer began to piece together all of the elements of evidence to create the big picture. To connect the dots. He couldn't help but speculate. Did Jarod know, or at least suspect, his father murdered his mother?

The onboard video camera showed a violent encounter. Veronica struggled for her life. She had to be screaming for help. Undoubtedly, there was a lot of noise.

These haunting conundrums spun in Roy's head like a Ferris wheel out of control.

Did Jarod know Clevis had purchased a life insurance policy on Veronica before she died? Was Jarod telling the truth when he told Roy he'd slept through the drowning? How could Jarod not have heard something that night? Did he hear the commotion and refuse to intervene? If so, why?

Based on the timeline of the evidence Mercer had accumulated, at the time of Veronica's death, it appeared only Clevis knew the severity of the company's burgeoning financial problems.

Lieutenant Mercer's mind was overwhelmed with questions.

Had Jarod contemplated the likelihood that his mother would inherit the Harrington estate at the time of his father's demise? Did Jarod acquiesce in the death of his mother and later kill his father to inherit what Jarod thought was potentially a very valuable estate?

Roy desperately wanted to establish any possible connection between Veronica's death and the subsequent death of Clevis. The first question was, what was the motive for the murder of Veronica? An obvious motive was life insurance. Another was the money from Veronica's multi-million-dollar settlement from her car wreck in Memphis.

Roy found it puzzling that Clevis Harrington was perceived to be a highly successful businessman with a vast personal fortune. Mercer had a gut feeling he was on the cusp of discovering the answer to some of these haunting questions.

During his intense review of all of the evidence, Roy discovered that the contents of Harrington's private safe were very telling. Lieutenant Mercer focused on one particular folder containing numerous individual sheets of paper. Upon inspection, Roy determined that the documents in the folder consisted of printed copies of several emails and letters.

One of the letters contained a notice sent by a lender informing Harrington that he was in default on the payments for his primary operating loan for Harrington Industries. The letter went on to state that if the loan was not brought current, the lender would initiate foreclosure proceedings on the property covered by the mortgage.

Mercer was stunned to discover that Clevis Harrington and Harrington Industries were in the throes of serious financial issues. The public perception persisted that the company was financially sound and prosperous. The documents in Cleve's private safe showed that the image of financial prosperity for Harrington Industries was not consistent with reality.

The multitude of questions continued to populate Roy's mind.

Had Harrington's financial empire collapsed to the point he was desperate for cash? If Harrington Industries is in dire financial straits, why would Jarod want to kill his father?

Roy knew Jarod and Clevis had a contentious relationship, but was that a sufficient motive for murder?

Among the email threads found in the file folders in Cleve's safe was a series of email communications between Clevis and Nottendam Enterprises SX, LLC, a company headquartered in Munich, Germany. The emails outlined a plan Clevis had concocted to sanitize what appeared to be illicit sales of airplane parts by Harrington Industries to an unidentified buyer.

Initially, Roy didn't fully understand the implications of those communications. The comments in the emails made it clear. Financially, Harrington Industries was on the ropes. In desperation, Harrington had resorted to an ultra-risky and unlawful scheme to raise much-needed revenue.

Included in one of the files was another series of emails from a venture capital group, Allied Funding Partners XB, LLC. The emails covered a period of two years.

The subject of the emails was the obligation of Harrington Industries to pay a substantial debt owed to Allied Funding. The tone of Allied's earlier emails was businesslike but sternly matter-of-fact. As time progressed, the language of Allied became very demanding.

The responses Harrington provided to Allied were accommodative in tone. Harrington emphasized the unfortunate circumstances of his business. He repeatedly mentioned that the aerospace industry had taken an unforeseen turn for the worse. Roy could see Clevis had made every attempt to reassure Allied that the money would soon be repaid.

He tried to explain that his business was cyclical in nature. Harrington desperately reassured the lender that, given enough time, his company would rebound to a profitable level. The replies from Allied were direct and increasingly unforgiving.

After Mercer discovered the documents in Harrington's office, he knew he needed access to more information. Roy asked Jarod to meet with him for some follow-up questions. To Roy's surprise, Jarod reluctantly agreed. Mercer had decided, at this point, it would be best to avoid any further accusations that Jarod had killed Clevis.

As the interview began, Roy explained, "Jarod, I think you're aware of the fact we've searched your dad's office. We found several items which raise some pretty significant questions. I'm not sure how much you know about some of the items we discovered. Your father had a safe in the back room of his office. We'd obtained a search warrant to open the safe. Apparently, your father used the safe to store his more sensitive documents." Roy turned to thumb through a stack of papers on the table. "Among the documents was a series of emails between your father and a company called Allied Funding Partners XB. Did you know anything about that company?"

Jarod responded ruefully, "Yes. He'd mentioned he was planning to apply for additional funding from Allied. Based on what he told me, Allied Funding was some type of venture capital operation. Dad had tried to get bridge funding to cover expenses for suppliers and payroll, but his traditional sources of money were maxed out. He couldn't provide additional unencumbered collateral to support any new money. He later heard about Allied, so he applied for a loan."

"What happened with that?"

"He had to go through a rigorous application process. After completing all the paperwork, Allied required Dad to meet with them at their corporate headquarters in Grand Cayman. I didn't know anything about that trip until Dad got back and told me he'd sought financing through Allied."

"Why Grand Cayman?"

"Apparently, that's their headquarters. For some reason, they wanted to meet him in person. I know that was very unusual for a lender."

Lieutenant Mercer methodically entered the information in his notebook. "Did he get the funding?"

"Yes, but by that time, the company's finances were getting

worse. He had to use all the new money to cover outstanding supplier invoices and meet payroll."

"So, you're saying he was still in financial trouble?"

"Yes."

"The company was still operating but in trouble? What was your dad doing to avoid foreclosure or bankruptcy?"

Jarod paused, took a deep breath, and exhaled audibly. "By that time, he was getting very desperate. He began to look for other ways to increase revenue for the company."

"One of the things we found in your dad's safe was a series of emails to a company in Munich, Germany. Do you know anything about that?"

"Well, sort of. I don't know what that has to do with your investigation of the homicide."

Mercer stood up and began pacing back and forth within the cramped interrogation room. "That's what we are trying to find out. From the emails, it looks to us that your dad had arranged for some type of product sales through the German company. The emails didn't set out all the details. Who was the ultimate buyer for the products?"

Jarod swiveled nervously back and forth in his chair. "I'd prefer not to say." He hesitated briefly. "But I guess it doesn't matter now. You apparently already have information about the German connection. Dad kind of going off the rails by that point. Actually, more than kind of. He would do whatever it took to save the company. He came up with a plan to sell airplane parts through a German company."

Lieutenant Mercer reached for a sheaf of papers stacked precariously close to the edge of the table. "The emails mentioned a company named, let's see … it's on the email. Nottendam Enterprises SX in Munich, Germany. What can you tell us about that company?"

Jarod uttered an audible sigh. "That's the company that agreed to handle the transaction."

"What transaction?"

"Dad had come up with a plan to sell aeronautical parts."

"To whom?"

Jarod sat silently, nervously biting his bottom lip.

Lieutenant Mercer abruptly interjected, "You haven't answered my question. Who was the buyer for the airplane parts?"

Jarod hesitated with his hands tightly clasped together. "It was the Republic of Iran."

Roy leaned closer to Jarod. "No shit? Your dad was selling parts to Iran? That takes some world-class balls! Your dad must have been beyond desperate to save his company."

Jarod shifted in his chair, leaning to the side, his clenched fist pressed tightly against his face. "When I found out about the scheme, I tried to talk him out of it. He'd already made up his mind. He didn't give a damn what I thought. All he wanted was to get some more money in the door. It was crazy. You can't imagine how manic he'd become. His whole life was tied up in Harrington Industries. He was determined not to lose because of financial problems."

Mercer turned and sat down in one of the chairs near the table. He sat silently for a full minute, staring directly at Jarod. He contemplated what Jarod had just described.

Did Jarod kill Clevis in some misguided effort to save the company?

"That's all the questions we have for now. Do you have any questions?"

"Yeah. Am I still a suspect in the investigation?" Jarod asked tentatively.

"You are for now."

Roy was well aware that Jarod was more than just a bit idealistic. It was obvious Jarod knew his dad had become delusional. To Roy, it was logical that Jarod may have believed it was up to him to save the company. Jarod likely saw it as his personal mission to save Harrington Industries and the Harrington dynasty from his father's impulsive and irrational behavior.

Lieutenant Mercer's search warrant investigation of Clevis's office uncovered valuable information on Harrington's computers. Roy had delivered the computers to the forensic lab for review.

The lab reported they found emails on the hard drive from Allied Funding Partners XB covering an extended period of time. Many of those emails were the same as the hard copies found in Harrington's safe. In addition to the Allied Funding emails, the lab reported additional messages were found between Nottendam Enterprises SX and Harrington. The emails revealed an extensive series of communications outlining the logistics for the delivery of aeronautical parts from Harrington Industries to Nottendam.

One of the emails contained a detailed description of the process by which the shipped aircraft parts would be relabeled to "recharacterize" the products to disguise the fact the United States was the country of origin.

The lab also mentioned the search of Harrington's phone was not particularly remarkable. There were numerous text messages between Crystal and Clevis. The lab stated those text messages involved an apparent personal relationship that didn't appear to be relevant to the case.

The investigation of the death of Clevis Harrington had become virtually all-consuming for Roy. His trademark style had always been borderline obsessive- Take a deep dive into the latest homicide investigation and not let go until the suspect was in custody.

To add to the frustration, Lieutenant Mercer was coordinating with the Atlanta police in his probe of the yet-unsolved death of Cody Beard while attempting to devote the bulk of his time to the Harrington murder in Huntsville. The investigation of Clevis Harrington's death had reached an exasperating stage. There were more questions than answers. To Mercer, that circumstance was totally unacceptable.

CHAPTER 20

I t was a cold, dreary December morning in 2011. The icy
winter wind sent dead leaves and remnants of trash scurrying
along the ground to their ultimate resting place against the chain
link fence on the easterly side of police headquarters.

Roy had just returned to his office. The phone rang. "This is
Lieutenant Mercer."

On the other end was Detective Tillson.

"Hey Roy, this is Jay Tillson down in Atlanta. How's it going?"

"I've been up to my elbows in the homicide investigation of
Clevis Harrington. I guess you know who he was ...Cody's dad."

"Oh, yeah, that's right. So, Cody's old man was killed? That's
kind of shocking. Do you have any leads?"

"We're gaining on it. Mr. Harrington was beaten to death with
a baseball bat. He was sleeping at his home at the time. I'm telling
you Jay, that crime scene was gruesome. Whoever killed him
showed no mercy. His son, Jarod, is a prime suspect. We have
some fingerprint evidence and some video from the residence.
We're hoping for a break in the case soon."

Tillson replied curtly, "Kind of amazing, isn't it? Cody was shot dead here in Atlanta. Now his father in Huntsville was beaten to death. That family must be cursed."

"Yeah, I'd say someone has definitely put a hex on the Harrington bloodline."

Tillson explained, "The reason I called was to let you know we just got the lab reports on Cody Beard."

"They finally got those done? The lab was right. It did take them a hell of a long time to do the tests. What'd you find?"

"Apparently you hit pay dirt. You were on track to get those tests done. Charles Martin with Atlanta CSI lab asked that you give him a call for the details."

"Will do. Thanks for all your help."

Roy planned to call Martin that afternoon. He was more than anxious to hear what Martin had to report on the tests for Cody.

Despite the enticing prospect of getting valuable information from the Atlanta CSI lab on the Beard homicide, Lieutenant Mercer remained consumed by the perplexing unanswered questions on the brutal beating death of Clevis. Mercer had some additional thoughts on the Harrington case. He wanted to convey that information right away to Walter Connelly with the Huntsville CSI division.

"Walt, this is Lieutenant Mercer over in Homicide. In the Clevis Harrington case, I noticed the residence had several security cameras. Did anyone check the footage on those?"

"You bet. We found current footage. Looked like images of an intruder. The date and time stamp showed it was around the time of the homicide. The images weren't all that great. Very grainy. The cameras did have night vision capability."

"Well, I'd think that would help." Lieutenant Mercer responded.

"Even with that, we couldn't really get a good look at the face of the perpetrator. The killer wore a hoody. He obviously was concerned about security cameras."

"Could you see his face at all?"

"Not really. We did notice tattoos on his neck. It was too grainy to make out any detail."

"That might help. At least we know we're looking for someone with neck tattoos. That cuts down the number of suspects. Hey, thanks, man."

Roy hung up the phone and immediately called the forensics division at Huntsville CSI. They agreed to send the video to a specialty lab for digital analysis.

CSI mentioned the video lab could eliminate any visual "noise" to concentrate the key elements of the images on the footage. It was explained to Roy that the specialty lab uses an artifact-free low-light video restoration algorithm to increase the sharpness and contrast of the images.

The enhancement process was not quick. It was five days before Roy received the newly-processed video. When Mercer viewed the images, he was able to discern much more detail, particularly of the neck tattoos.

Unfortunately, the subject's hoody partially obscured the tattoos. However, the front portion of each tattoo was sufficiently visible to establish identification.

Using sequential still shots of the video, Lieutenant Mercer could see the dominant feature of the tattoo on the right side of the neck was an eagle with arrows in its talons. Roy knew this symbolized strength, power, and dominance. The tattoo on the left was skull and crossbones, meaning danger and death.

Armed with that information, Mercer ordered copies of any mugshots available for the five suspects tentatively identified by the partial print on the doorknob.

After two and a half days, central records sent all available mugshots of the suspects potentially matching the partial fingerprint. Roy carefully studied each of the photos. As Lieutenant Mercer scrolled through the photos, he suddenly stopped. One of the photos showed a suspect with distinctive neck tattoos. Roy compared the photo with the still shots of the suspect captured from the enhanced security video at the crime scene. Lieutenant Mercer found it difficult to make out the full detail of the tattoos, but he thought it looked like a match. The name associated with the mugshot was Toni Riviera. His rap sheet showed he was a two-time convicted felon.

A warrant was issued for Riviera's arrest. Roy knew the drill. At this point, it was a waiting game. He hoped Riviera could be picked up quickly. Mercer was anxious to interrogate Riviera, provided he was willing to talk.

Two weeks later, Riviera was apprehended. It appeared Lady Luck was with Roy on this one.

Riviera was arrested by the Alabama state police after a routine traffic stop on Highway I-20, just east of the Mississippi state line. The state police transported Riviera back to Huntsville.

Lieutenant Mercer quickly arranged for an interrogation in Interview Room C at Huntsville police headquarters. Riviera, wearing leg shackles and handcuffs, was escorted into the room by jail personnel.

The two security officers clung tightly to Riviera's upper arms as they positioned him in front of one of the chairs and motioned for him to sit down.

Shortly thereafter, Roy entered the room. The stench of days-old body odor emanating from Riviera's unwashed frame hung in the air like a heavy fog over a stagnant swamp.

Lieutenant Mercer, breathing shallowly to avoid the full impact of the foul smell, found it difficult to speak. Riviera looked like he'd been on the run for quite some time. His tattered clothing was haphazardly draped across his torso, like the wind-whipped canvas of a shipwrecked sailing vessel.

Mercer quickly realized that Riviera may be their man. An early middle-aged male with greasy disheveled jet-black hair accentuated with small patches of gray along his temples, Riviera looked the part of the stereotypical tough-guy thug capable of committing such a vicious and brutal attack.

Prior to questioning, Roy sat quietly reviewing his notes and the arresting officer's report. The arrest records showed that Riviera was six foot, two inches tall. About the right height to match the person seen in the security camera video.

Mercer looked over at Riviera. The tattoos on Riviera's neck were the most prominent feature on his body. Toni couldn't have concealed such audacious inkings if he'd tried.

Roy thought, *It's world-class stupid for a criminal to have face or neck tattoos. Big-time felons think they're smarter than the rest of us. Sporting tattoos that aren't easily concealed blows that myth right out of the water.*

Riviera sat uncomfortably in a stiff-back chair crammed against the wall. A wooden table bearing nicks and gouges from too many years of action sat in the far corner.

"Toni, you've been read your Miranda rights. You can talk with us now or you can wait until you have a lawyer. It's your choice."

Riviera asserted, "I don't need no damn lawyer. I'm innocent!"

Mercer proceeded, "Okay then. I'm sure they told you why you were arrested. You've been charged with first-degree murder for the homicide of Clevis Harrington."

"I don't have nothin' to say, except you got the wrong man."

"We don't think so. We've got some solid evidence you killed Harrington."

"Like what?"

Lieutenant Mercer reached for a chair. "I'll ask the questions. Where were you in the early morning hours of October 13, 2011?"

Riviera smirked. "I don't know. I'll have to check my social calendar."

Mercer sat down several feet from the interview table, his elbows propped against the chair arms, and fingers intertwined. "Listen, Toni. Don't get smart with us. We have a lot of solid evidence that placed you at the scene on the morning of the murder."

"Kiss my ass!" Riviera snorted.

Lieutenant Mercer methodically continued, "Let's get down to the facts. We were able to lift a fingerprint from the doorknob in Harrington's garage. The print matched a print we had on file for you and ----"

Riviera interrupted, "So what?"

Mercer ignored Riviera's question. "Also, Mr. Harrington had several security cameras strategically located around the property."

Toni mindlessly scratched his upper left arm. "Get to the point."

"One of the cameras showed a person about your height running up the driveway. Another camera showed that same figure entering through the side garage door."

Riviera declared assertively, "I was at home in bed. That ain't me."

"The footage showed that the person entering the garage was wearing a hoody. We could see that the person in the video had a tattoo on the right side of his neck. The tattoo was of an eagle with arrows in its talons. Sort of like the one on the right side of your neck."

Riviera slumped down lazily in the chair, his hands clasped together. "I guess it's a popular design. I know a lot of people with eagle tattoos on their necks."

"I'll bet you do. The positive fingerprint identification and your distinctive tattoo on the security video gave us all we needed to know. You're the person who killed Clevis Harrington." Lieutenant Mercer rose to his feet and walked toward the wall next to the interview table. "Also, we found what we believe to be the murder weapon. An aluminum bat in the garage. It was tested for blood residue. The bat had minute traces of blood. DNA tests showed a match for Clevis Harrington." Mercer approached Riviera, standing directly in front of him. "Look, Toni, we have everything we need to convict you."

Riviera sat in silence, biting the side of his lower lip and shaking his head from side to side. It was obvious he knew. It was inevitable. He'd be tried on the murder charges for the death of Clevis Harrington.

"Toni, you're no stranger to this process. You have two prior felony convictions. You need to cooperate with us if you hope to have any chance of avoiding the death penalty."

As Roy uttered those words, Riviera's demeanor totally changed. The wise-guy attitude and cocky grin were gone.

"Why don't you tell us what you know? Did someone hire you to do this?"

Toni exclaimed, "I want a deal if I'm gonna talk."

Mercer emphatically pointed his index finger at Riviera. "You know how this works. We can't promise you anything. Only the district attorney's office can make that decision. If you cooperate and tell us everything you know or you provide corroborating information which leads to the arrest of someone who helped you, the prosecutor could consider that."

"Why should I trust you guys?"

"Think about it, Toni. You have no choice. The DA calls the shots."

Riviera sat quietly, looking down at his lap, then back at Lieutenant Mercer. "It wasn't my idea to kill Harrington."

"Okay, whose idea was it?"

"I was hired to do the job. Someone called me. Said they needed to eliminate a guy in Huntsville."

"Who called you?"

"I don't know. He didn't give me his name."

"What'd he say?"

Riviera straightened in his chair; his expression turned somber. "He told me there was this fellow he wanted me to eliminate."

"Did he say why he wanted to do that?"

"Not exactly. He said I was to make it gruesome. You know, so anyone who saw this would know, this was a revenge killing. I thought that was kind of odd. A little creepy, if you ask me. This guy said he wanted to send a message."

Lieutenant Mercer paused. "Why did you set the fire?"

"That was my idea. I thought it would destroy everything. I didn't want nothin' left behind tying me to the scene."

"Well, it didn't work. The report showed the flames quickly moved into the attic. CSI said there wasn't enough oxygen in the bedroom for the fire to get going in there."

Riviera smirked as he spoke. "That's a damn shame if you ask me."

Mercer shook his head. "Did you get paid for the job?"

"Yeah, in cash. I ain't no damned idiot! I get my money upfront."

Roy moved toward the door. "Okay. I think that's all the questions for now."

Lieutenant Mercer left the room. Riviera was taken back to the police van for transport to the detention center.

After the encounter with Riviera, Mercer knew he needed something to confirm or refute the veracity of Toni Riviera's confession. Roy's experience told him people don't generally confess to something they didn't do. But there have been cases where small-time thugs give false confessions to achieve a warped sense of infamy.

Upon returning to the office, Roy sat at his desk, analyzing what he knew. He re-read the Allied Funding letter. The final paragraph contained an irrefutable threat of death if Clevis failed to pay in full by a date set out in the letter. The deadline had long since passed.

Mercer was confused. Had he just found the missing piece of the puzzle for the motive to kill Cleve? Roy considered the possibility that Allied Funding arranged for the killing of Harrington in retribution for his failure to repay the loan owed to Allied.

Roy queried, *What good is it to kill Clevis if you want your money?*

Mercer realized that Allied Funding was no run-of-the-mill lender. They play hardball 24/7. The documents in the file made that very clear.

Roy's mind continued to process the anomalies of the case.

"Legitimate lenders don't issue death threats to collect from their borrowers."

From Roy's perspective, the evidence collected at the crime scene eliminated any doubt that Toni Riviera killed Clevis Harrington. The obvious question remained: Who hired Toni? Allied Funding? Or Jarod Harrington?

Lieutenant Mercer intended to find out.

CHAPTER 21

Lieutenant Mercer had the killer of Clevis Harrington. Toni Riviera was in custody, charged with first-degree murder. However, the gangland-style killing of Cody Beard continued to haunt Roy. The elimination of Cody had all the trappings of a professional hit job disguised as a drug deal gone bad. Jarod remained a key suspect in that homicide.

After interviewing Jarod, Mercer was convinced he had more than one motive to eliminate Cody. The way Roy saw it, despite the fact Clevis was dead, Jarod considered Cody to be an ongoing threat as long as he was still around.

Cody had been an opportunistic criminal all his life. He successfully blackmailed Jarod. Jarod admitted to Mercer that, prior to Cody's death, he knew Cody was a threat. Cody had made it clear. He was a potential claimant to a portion of the Harrington estate.

Roy knew Jarod was an idealistic young man. From all indications, Jarod intended to rebuild Harrington Industries. Jarod definitely didn't want Cody in the picture to screw that up.

Mercer considered calling Jarod back to headquarters to put

pressure on him. To see if he'd slip up and say something implicating himself in the killing of Cody.

Roy decided to skip that. He was certain Jarod would simply deny any involvement. If Jarod hired the hit on Cody, Mercer needed more tangible evidence before he questioned Jarod any further.

LIEUTENANT MERCER HAD BECOME SO CONSUMED LATELY BY recent developments in the Clevis Harrington homicide, he'd neglected to call Charles Martin with Atlanta CSI. Roy's typical method of operation was laser-focus attention on one case at a time. Based on his style, it wasn't natural for Mercer to whipsaw back and forth between two unsolved homicides.

To advance the Atlanta case, Mercer needed the lab's findings on Cody Beard. Roy walked down the hall to his office to call Atlanta. Based on what Jay Tillson had told Roy in their phone call, Roy hoped the lab had some solid information.

"Charley, this is Lieutenant Mercer in Huntsville. Detective Tillson asked that I give you a call. Sorry I didn't get back to you sooner."

"No problem. It's not as if we didn't have anything else to do." Martin replied.

Mercer continued, "I understand you have lab results for the Cody Beard homicide."

"Yeah, that's right. Hang on a minute. I'll pull the file."

After several minutes, Martin was back. "Let's see. You requested we check for any gunshot residue on Cody Beard. We checked the subject's face and neck. The results were negative. No residue. We did find trace evidence of residue on his right hand and wrist area."

"That's helpful."

"You also asked us to test a strand of hair found in Beard's vehicle. On the hair sample, you're in luck. The hair follicle was intact. We were able to collect enough DNA for a test. Unfortunately, we didn't get a match when we ran the results through the

Georgia central DNA database. But, when we ran the sample through the national database, we got a hit. According to the national base, there was a match for a male by the name of Sonny Desoto. Records show he goes by the alias of "Ace."

Mercer replied enthusiastically, "Man, that's great news. Thanks for your help."

Following that conversation, Mercer ran a background check on Desoto. DeSoto had a long criminal record, including several felony convictions. The records also revealed Desoto's ethnicity and physical characteristics. Lieutenant Mercer knew that information would be critically important in locating the suspect.

That afternoon, Roy pulled the file on Cody Beard. It had been quite a while since he'd personally viewed the crime scene in Atlanta.

As Roy looked through his notes, he was able to reconstruct what might have occurred on that lonely stretch of road just outside the metro area of town. The way Roy saw it, Cody most likely had been lured to that remote location on County Road 412 under the pretense of a cocaine buy.

Mercer had previously read Cody's autopsy report. The toxicology portion of the report showed a sizeable level of cocaine in Cody's body. It was obvious Cody had a substantial drug habit. Cocaine was his drug of choice.

Lieutenant Mercer deduced that Cody needed a personal reserve of cocaine to maintain some level of equilibrium in his daily life. Based on the test results and the evidence found in and around the car, Mercer created a plausible sequence of events.

At that point, Lieutenant Mercer needed a sounding board. He picked up the phone and called Morrison

"Brad, you got a minute?"

"Sure. What's up?"

"I'm kind of stymied. As you know, I'm working with Jay Tillson down in Atlanta on the homicide of Cody Beard. We got some test results back. If you're available, I'd like to run some things by you."

Morrison replied, "I've got a meeting later this afternoon, but I'm free right now."

Roy responded, "Great. I'll grab the file. Be right down."

Lieutenant Mercer liked to run fact situations by Sgt. Morrison. He'd done that in the past. Brad had a good analytical mind. Based on their collective experience, Morrison could help Roy mold the evidence into a reasonable scenario of what actually happened to Cody Beard.

Roy walked briskly into Brad's office. He sat down in front of Morrison's cluttered desk and laid his bulky file on the edge. "Well, Brad. I've got another dilemma. Or maybe this one's an enigma. The homicide of Cody Beard. It's not like Clevis Harrington. We don't have a video of the suspect. I guess you remember I told you Cody is the son of Clevis Harrington. That's the reason I'm involved in the investigation of the Atlanta killing of Cody. He had family ties, of sorts, here in Huntsville. His half-brother, Jarod, is a suspect in Cody's death."

"Yep. I remember you telling me about that. What do you have so far?"

"Well, actually, we have some really good evidence at this point. I've tried to piece everything together. Let me run this by you to see what you think." Roy pulled a handful of papers from his file. "After the murder of Cody, I went to Atlanta to inspect the crime scene. While I was there, I viewed Cody's body prior to burial. I have some test results. I think they'll be very helpful. Or, at least, I hope so. One real plus is we now have an identification of the homicide suspect." Mercer paused to review his notes. "Here's how I see it, based on the information I have and my best guess as to what happened."

As he spoke, Lieutenant Mercer periodically glanced at his notes. "This all happened out on a rural road on the outskirts of Atlanta. Cody was lured to the scene by the killer under what appeared to be a pretense of an opportunity to buy cocaine. Cody arrived at the designated site for the drug transaction. Cody stopped his car along the edge of the dirt road next to the bar ditch. At some point, another vehicle pulled up directly behind

Cody's car. Sonny "Ace" Desoto, a stocky young Hispanic male about five feet, two inches tall, emerged from his vehicle."

Sgt. Morrison intervened with a question. "How'd you know DeSoto's name?"

"I'll get to that in a minute." Roy paused momentarily, glancing down at his notes, then back up at Morrison. "Cody remained in his car with the engine running just in case he needed to make a quick getaway. We know from Cody's criminal record that he was no stranger to drug purchases. Cody was naturally cautious. Drug deals can go off the rails in a millisecond. A passerby who came upon the scene after the homicide reported that Cody's engine was still running. So, I concluded that Cody never shut his car off at any point in the transaction. As soon as Ace stepped up to the driver's side door of Cody's car, Ace pulled what I believe was a .38 caliber revolver."

"How did you know that?"

"We found two matching shell casings. They were both .38 caliber." Mercer flipped to the back section of his file to check for additional information. "Apparently, Cody realized he'd been set up. Cody couldn't help but see the pistol aimed right at him. It's my theory that Cody figured if he tried to speed away, Ace would have shot him in the back of the head. At that moment, I think Cody lunged out of his car, jamming the front driver's side door against Ace's midsection. It looks to me like Ace was temporarily knocked off balance. I found evidence that Cody grabbed Ace by the hair and jerked him backward toward the ground."

"Wait a minute. How in the hell would you know that? You weren't there at the time."

"I'll get to that. As I was about to say, as Ace stumbled, Cody grabbed Ace's wrist attempting to force him to drop the gun. In the struggle, the pistol fired one round into the air. Cody must have lost his grip on Ace's wrist. At that moment, Ace was able to jam the pistol into Cody's chest long enough to fire the second round. Ace then pulled Cody's limp body back into the driver's seat of the car. He positioned the body to make it look like Cody had been shot while seated in the car."

"Why do you think he did that?"

"I'm not exactly sure why he bothered to do that. I guess he thought it would look more like a bad drug deal. CSI found no fingerprints for Ace. My guess is Ace showed up at the scene wearing some type of vinyl or latex gloves."

Brad looked askance at Roy. "How did you figure all that out? I mean the details of the shots fired."

Mercer replied confidently, "Well, we found one shell casing in the ditch. I figure that was the casing ejected from the gun when it fired overhead as Cody struggled to force the gun from Ace's hand. I think Cody had grabbed Ace by the hair. The single strand I found in the car was Ace's. The DNA test showed that. The hair apparently was transferred from Cody's hand to the car as Ace pulled Cody's body back into the vehicle."

"What makes you think Cody was outside the car when Ace shot him? Maybe Ace just walked up and shot Cody as he sat there."

Mercer smiled. "When I viewed the crime scene photos from the Atlanta CSI report, you could see that Cody's right arm was tucked behind his back in an unnatural position. Basically, his right arm was stuffed behind him. That wouldn't have happened if Ace had simply walked up and shot Cody. Also, CSI Atlanta found gunshot residue on Cody's right hand and wrist. If Cody had been sitting in the vehicle at the time he was shot, he wouldn't have any gunshot traces on his right hand. Another thing the CSI report noted was the presence of a sizeable amount of blood on the carpet on the driver's side. Only a small amount of blood was found on the roadway. That tells me Ace shot Cody and quickly pulled his body back into the vehicle where he bled out."

"You've got this all figured out, don't you?"

"Well, we'll see. The photos showed Cody's car door was shut at the time of the initial investigation. My theory is Ace closed the door after he placed Cody's body in the driver's seat. Ace forgot one detail. The driver's side window was intact. If Ace shot Cody while he sat in the car with the door closed, the window would likely have been up and would have been shattered by the bullet."

"The window might have been down at the time of the shooting."

"Could be, but it's highly unlikely Ace would have taken the time to raise the window after he shot Cody. Besides, the angle of the bullet entry into Cody's chest didn't match the angle of someone standing outside of the car firing downward."

Sgt. Morrison nodded in agreement.

Roy sat quietly, deep in thought, staring toward the ceiling.

"There was one really odd thing. We found several plastic packets containing cocaine on the ground near the driver's side of the car. It looked like Ace had tried to stage the scene as a drug deal gone bad. It appeared to be an attempt to disguise the true nature of what went down that day. After the shooting, I'm sure Ace quickly fled." Lieutenant Mercer leaned back in his chair as he continued, "This all fits together, as far as I can tell. The existence of the second shell casing suggests a struggle must have ensued outside of the car. The inspection of Cody's car didn't reveal any additional bullet penetration holes for the second shot. The gunshot residue on Cody's right hand and wrist and the location of the shell casing in the ditch near the car are pretty convincing that Cody's hand was near Ace's gun when it discharged into the air."

Morrison shook his head. "You're amazing, Roy. You've really thought this through. That's damn good police work."

Roy smiled confidently. "There was additional confirming evidence. No blood spatter was found on the car's seats, dash, or headliner. If Cody had been shot while sitting in the front seat, blood spatter would be visible on several surfaces within the interior. The most significant evidence was the single strand of hair under the driver's seat. As I mentioned, some hair had apparently been torn from Ace's scalp when Cody grabbed Ace. That single strand of hair was transferred to the car when Ace repositioned Cody's body back into the driver's seat. The DNA match for the hair indisputably tied Sonny Desoto to the scene of the crime."

Sgt. Morrison asked, "Isn't it possible the hair just fell off Ace's head as he pulled Cody's body into the car seat?"

Mercer hesitated. "Well, I suppose so. But it doesn't really matter. The obvious struggle for the gun on the roadway told me Cody most likely grabbed Ace by the hair in an effort to get the gun. In any event, that hair strand put Ace at the crime scene."

Based on all the evidence, Lieutenant Mercer was convinced the homicide played out basically as he envisioned. After fully analyzing all the available evidence of Cody's murder, Detective Mercer directed his attention to possible motives for the killing. The operative question was, who wanted the victim dead? Roy needed to take a deep dive into the circumstances leading up to the murder. He knew who committed the murder, but why? There was solid evidence that Sonny DeSoto shot Cody. Lieutenant Mercer believed Jarod Harrington was somehow involved. Jarod had made it clear that Cody was a critical threat to him. Cody possessed the ability to upend Jarod's life. The stakes could not have been higher.

Following receipt of the lab results, Lieutenant Mercer coordinated with Detective Tillson to find and arrest Sonny "Ace" Desoto. The charge was first-degree murder.

Twelve days after the issuance of the arrest warrant, Mercer received a call. It was Detective Tillson.

"Roy, we got Desoto. He was picked up at his home on the east side of Atlanta. I know you're working an angle on this homicide with your prime suspect in Huntsville. We plan to interrogate Desoto either tomorrow or the next day. I thought you'd want to be here to ask some questions."

Mercer exclaimed, "You damn right! I've been waiting for this opportunity. What time do you plan to start?"

"If you can get here tomorrow afternoon, we can start at one. Will that work?"

"I'll make it work. I'll try to be there around noon."

The next day Lieutenant Mercer arrived ahead of schedule at the central division of the Atlanta PD. He'd gotten an early start out of Huntsville to avoid the traffic on I-75 into Atlanta. He was totally pumped. Finally, he would have the chance to interrogate the accused killer of Cody Beard.

At straight up noon, Roy walked into the lobby of the central division. "I'm Lieutenant Roy Mercer, here to see Detective Tillson."

The desk clerk responded, "I'll page him. It'll be just a minute. Please have a seat."

Ten minutes passed. Jay Tillson entered the lobby to greet Mercer. "Good morning, Roy. You made good time getting here. Our session is still on for one this afternoon."

Lieutenant Mercer stood up to shake hands with Tillson. "I woke up early, so I decided to hit the road. If you have a few minutes, I'd like to discuss the case before the interrogation."

Tillson and Mercer walked back to Tillson's office. Detective Tillson pulled a chair toward a small conference table and gestured for Roy to have a seat. "Roy, it's good to see you again. We've talked by phone a number of times since you first came to Atlanta right after the shooting. Can I get you a cup of coffee?"

Mercer sat down and placed his file on the corner of the table. "That sounds good, thanks."

As Lieutenant Mercer cradled the warm cup of coffee, he began, "You know Jay, I've given this case a lot of thought. I interviewed Cody's mother about his death. She had a lot of information about Cody's life growing up with her as a single mom. She said she had a hell of a time trying to rein him in. She made it clear that Cody had a wild side. She said when Cody got to be a teenager, he was out of control. Hanging out with gangs in Atlanta. Doing petty crimes."

Tillson nodded. "Fits the profile, wouldn't you say?"

Mercer shrugged. "I guess so. As you know, I viewed the crime scene on County Road 412. Based on what I found, it looked like the whole thing was a gangland-style hit. The CSI photos showed there were some packets of cocaine scattered on the ground near Cody's car. That looked like the scene had been staged after the shooting. To make it appear as a drug deal gone bad."

Tillson poured a cup of coffee and sat down next to Roy. "You'd mentioned you had a theory about what went down at the time of the killing."

"Yeah. There were two shell casings at the scene. When I found the second casing, I realized this was not a simple walk-up-and-shoot situation. There had to have been a struggle outside the car. There was no evidence any shots were fired into the vehicle. The casing was ejected in a direction that would require that the pistol be pointing in a direction parallel to the car. I figure Cody managed to get out of his car long enough to try to get the gun away from Desoto. Obviously, it didn't work. Cody ended up taking a lethal shot to the chest."

"So, if Cody was out of his car, what's your theory on why the body was found in the car?"

Mercer continued, "You're right. It's just a theory. After Cody tried to wrest the weapon out of Ace's hand, Desoto was able to overpower Cody long enough to fire the fatal shot. Ace then quickly pulled Cody back into the car to position the body to make it appear that there was a single shot fired into Cody as he sat in his vehicle."

"Sounds plausible."

"I recently took another look at the autopsy report. The angle of entry of the bullet into Cody's chest didn't match up with someone firing a gun down into the car."

Detective Tillson furrowed his brow as he slowly nodded. "Yeah. That's an interesting observation. You mentioned in our phone conversation the other day that you found a strand of hair."

"Right. I checked the car at the impoundment yard. I used my flashlight to get a good look inside the vehicle. I went through the car from one end to the other. That's when I spotted the single strand of hair. Under the front portion of the driver's seat."

"That was the source for the DNA match?"

"Yep. We got a match. That's how we identified Sonny "Ace" Desoto as the homicide suspect."

Tillson commented wryly, "Cut and dried at this point."

Lieutenant Mercer shook his head. "I'm not so sure about that. I still have my hunch that Jarod Harrington may have some involvement. That's one of the reasons I wanted to attend the interrogation today. I want to see if Desoto says anything that might implicate Jarod."

Tillson smiled broadly. "Roy, I really appreciate all the work you've done on this case. You've put a lot of time into this. We've been so swamped with case assignments here in Atlanta recently. I'm not sure we'd be this far along in the investigation without your help."

After lunch, Sonny Desoto was transported from the detention unit of the central division to Interview Room Two. The room was dingy from too much use and too little maintenance. Chipped and peeling paint covered the scuffed-up walls. Gapping spaces appeared intermittently on the floor where tiles once lay.

Desoto was seated in a straight-back chair pushed tightly into the corner of the room. His right arm was handcuffed to a chain tethering device mounted to the wall.

Detectives Mercer and Tillson sat in chairs facing DeSoto.

"Sonny, I'm Detective Jay Tillson. This is Lieutenant Mercer. Our records show you've been read your rights. You don't have to talk to us today if you choose not to."

DeSoto glanced up at Tillson with a look of unmitigated disdain.

Tillson continued, "We have some questions for you regarding the homicide of Cody Beard. What can you tell us about Cody's death?"

Desoto clenched his jaw. His breathing became labored and pronounced. He spoke with a thick Hispanic accent. "I don't know what you're talking about."

The two detectives exchanged glances.

"You're in jail without bond on first-degree murder charges. It'd go a lot better for you if you cooperate."

Desoto shook his head and shrugged without comment.

"The CSI lab placed you at the scene of the murder. We found a hair strand in Cody's car. The DNA test identified you. It's your hair they found. How'd that happen?"

Desoto looked down with feigned disinterest. "I have no idea. I wasn't there."

Tillson pressed further, "What'd you do with the murder weapon?"

DeSoto reached up with his free hand to casually scratch the side of his head. "I don't own a gun."

Lieutenant Mercer interjected, "I have a few questions. Where were you on the day of the homicide? That would have been July twenty-third."

Desoto shook his head. "I don't remember. That was more than a month ago."

Mercer leaned toward DeSoto. "I see you have a tattoo on your arm. It's some kind of a symbol with the letters, ATV. What is that?"

Desoto cocked his head back proudly. "That's my brother-hood, la fraternidad."

"What does that mean?"

DeSoto's nostrils flared. He bit his lower lip. "It's the Antau-vio. That's my crew."

"You're a member of the Antauvio gang? They're well known in the Atlanta area for drug running out of Mexico."

Detective Tillson turned toward Lieutenant Mercer. "They're the most violent gang in this area."

DeSoto declared, "If you say so. I wouldn't know."

Mercer added, "I have one more question. Did you kill Cody Beard?"

Desoto emphatically waved his hand in the air. "Hell no. I ain't killed nobody!"

After that exchange, it was obvious to Mercer and Tillson that DeSoto had no intention of cooperating. It was the honor code in the intricate structure of the gang world. Keep your mouth shut around the police.

DeSoto was escorted back to the jail unit.

After DeSoto left the room, Mercer said, "Jay, that went nowhere. I suggest we check the Georgia Bureau of Investigation records to see what they have on Desoto and the Antauvio gang. Hopefully, we can get something to move this along."

It had been a long day with a very early start. Mercer quickly packed up his file. "I'm headed back to Huntsville. Give me a shout if you have any new developments. I can drive back to Atlanta if GBI gets anything further on this."

The following day, Tillson contacted the Georgia Bureau of Investigation. He was seeking information regarding Desoto's possible connection to other known members of Antauvio.

The records department of the GBI came back with several names of possible Antauvio gang members in the Atlanta area. One of the names caught Tillson's attention. It was Javier Cabello, an Atlanta-based underworld thug with a long criminal history and multiple felony drug-related convictions.

On a sheer hunch, Tillson decided to try to contact Cabello to get an interview. He ran a check on Cabello and found outstanding arrest warrants. Detective Tillson issued a BOLO bulletin to all units for Javier to be picked up.

The Atlanta police had no luck finding Cabello. He had simply disappeared.

After several weeks, Cabello was arrested outside of Augusta. He was brought in for booking on the existing warrants.

Tillson contacted Mercer to let him know. "Roy, we got a lead on the Beard homicide. We ran the records on known Antauvio members. We found a character named Javier Cabello. Picked him up on outstanding warrants. I think he may know something about DeSoto. He's a member of the Antauvio gang. He's in our jail now."

Mercer exclaimed, "Good job! Sounds like it would be worth my time to drive down to Atlanta. I can be there early next week. I've got several things to wrap up here. I can be in your office by Tuesday morning."

"That'll work. See you Tuesday."

Mercer arrived in Atlanta well before lunchtime. Cabello, wearing handcuffs tied to a waist restraint, was brought into the interrogation room.

Roy was surprised by Javier's appearance. He was expecting the typical heavily tattooed and gold-chained attire of the run-of-the-mill drug gang member. Cabello was immaculate in appearance. No visible tattoos. He could have easily blended in at any executive business conference.

Tillson began the interview. "Javier, do you know why we picked you up?"

Cabello sat expressionless.

Detective Tillson explained, "We brought you in because we know you're in the Antauvio drug cartel. Do you know Sonny "Ace" DeSoto?"

Cabello slowly rubbed his wrists around the snuggly-fitting handcuffs. "We've met a couple of times."

Tillson sat erect in his chair, his left leg perched on his right knee, twirling an ink pen. "What's your relationship with DeSoto?"

"Just friends. Compadres."

"Do you know anything about the murder of Cody Beard?"

"No. Never heard of him."

Lieutenant Mercer added, "We believe DeSoto killed Cody Beard. It was a gangland-style hit."

Javier shifted uncomfortably in his chair. "I don't know a thing about that."

"Come on, Javier, you and Ace are in the same gang. You're lying to us."

Javier leaned forward. "I'm telling you, I don't know what you're talking about."

Mercer stated forcefully, "Well, maybe I can refresh your memory. We think you were involved in this killing. You know a lot more than you've let on. If you don't tell us what you know about the shooting, we can charge you with being an accessory to felony murder. You better get your shit together and tell us what you know!"

Javier mumbled under his breath, "Oh, Mary, mother of God, please protect me."

Mercer declared, "Get on with it, Javier. We need answers."

Cabello rotated his cuffed hands upward in a gesture to stop.

"Okay! Okay!" Cabello sat quietly for a minute, clenching his jaw. "I know what going on. I'm being set up. If I talk, Ace will find me and take me out. That's no shit, man. That will happen once Ace learns I met with you guys. If I say nothing, you guys are going to throw my ass in jail. I don't like either of those options. I ain't talkin'. I'll take my chances in jail. It's safer than on the street after talking to the cops."

Detective Tillson asserted, "Well, Javier, looks like you'll be staying with us for a while. By the way, we picked up DeSoto last week. He's in the same jail as you. Let us know if you change your mind."

Cabello was booked on accessory charges. After two days in custody, Javier was ready to talk.

Lieutenant Mercer had agreed to stay in Atlanta for a few days to coordinate with Atlanta CSI regarding the outstanding details of the investigation.

Cabello was brought back to headquarters and placed in an interview room.

Detective Tillson began the interrogation. "Okay, Javier, we gave you a chance to tell us what you know. Now's the time to come clean. Did Ace kill Cody?"

Javier sat in his chair, nervously tapping his foot on the floor. "I'm damn sure not telling you nothing unless you can protect me from Ace. You said he's in this jail, but I ain't seen him."

Tillson drummed his fingers on the table as he stared at Cabello. "I'll tell you what. We'll ask the DA to drop the charges on you if you give us the information. You could go free. As I told you, Ace is in custody here in our jail right now. I can assure you Ace won't be out on bail on this one."

Javier took a deep breath. "Okay, okay, but I don't want to go back to jail. Not with Ace in there."

Tillson confirmed, "You won't have to if you talk to us."

Cabello scratched the side of his face, looking down at the floor. "I hope I don't regret this. God, I hope I don't regret this." Javier paused, shaking his head. "Ace is a Don in Antauvio."

Lieutenant Mercer pressed Javier. "What do you mean, a Don?"

"A boss, a kingpin. The man. Ya know what I'm sayin'?"

Roy glanced over at Detective Tillson. "So, he's a leader?"

"Yeah. He controls the operation. Ace personally eliminated Cody." Javier hesitated, then exclaimed, "This shit better not get back to Ace! He threatened me. More than once. He said if I told anyone about the plan to eliminate Cody, he'd kill me. Cut me up into little pieces and feed me to the dogs. I'm telling you, Ace is a badass! He's a mean son-of-a-bitch. The most brutal human I've ever known. He's killed at least two people, execution-style, not including Cody. I'm screwed if he found out I ratted on him."

Detective Tillson replied reassuringly, "You don't have to worry about that. As I said, Ace is in our jail, and he's not getting out anytime soon." Tillson pulled his chair closer to Cabello, leaning within inches of Javier's face. "Why'd Ace kill Cody?"

Javier looked down at the floor. "Cody had become a competitor to Antauvio. He ran heroin out of Mexico into Atlanta. Cody had gotten really good. Made a name for himself. Big shipments of product. Ace began to complain. Cody's action was getting into Antauvio's profits. Ace needed to eliminate the competition."

Lieutenant Mercer followed up, "So, Ace killed Cody because Cody was moving in on Ace's business in the heroin drug trade?"

"Yeah, that's about it. Cody died from his own damn success."

Mercer challenged Javier, "We don't believe you. You're still lying."

"I'm telling you, damn it, I'm not lying!" Cabello retorted emphatically.

Tillson glanced at Lieutenant Mercer. Tillson hesitated briefly, then queried, "Would you take a lie detector test?"

Javier, without hesitation, responded, "Yeah. Why not?"

Later that day, the polygraph examiner conducted a lie detector test for Javier. The examiner noted that Javier was conspicuously nervous. During the inquisition, he fidgeted in the chair, bouncing his right leg rapidly up and down in a nervous tick.

When asked if Ace acted alone in killing Cody, the results showed Javier's answer was not deceptive. However, the results were inconclusive when Cabello was asked if anyone had hired Ace to do the hit. The examiner certified that Javier was generally truthful, but some of the answers did not support or refute his veracity.

Following the interrogation of Javier, Roy considered, for the first time, the possibility that Jarod may not have been involved in the murder of Cody Beard.

Cody had made his share of enemies during his short life. He'd screwed around a lot of people.

Mercer figured if Ace hadn't eliminated Cody, Jarod might have done the job himself. Lieutenant Mercer had a hunch that maybe Jarod was just lucky. Ace had beat him to the punch.

CHAPTER 22

I t had been several weeks since the death of Clevis. Jarod returned to the office at Harrington Industries to face the backlog of emails and unanswered interoffice memos. He was very aware that nothing would ever be the same without his father at the helm.

Jarod had never enjoyed a truly congenial relationship with his dad. Not even close. Despite all the animosity, Jarod realized that Clevis would be missed at some level. His dad had been the glue that held all the pieces together at the company. Despite all the problems over the years, Clevis had achieved quasi-legendary status in the aerospace industry. Everyone knew him. Many had heard the story of his self-made career. Among the employees of the company, some admired Cleve, and some were truly intimi-dated by him.

Following the death of Clevis, Jarod had unprecedented access to all of the company's records. Over time, that access revealed that Harrington Industries had been in deep financial trouble for an extended period. After several long days, with the able assistance of Ms. Goodman, Jarod finally managed to work his way through all the mail and memos. The task was gargantuan, but Jarod met the challenge.

During the search of Harrington's records, Lieutenant Mercer had made duplicate copies of any files he had taken for further review at police headquarters. To Jarod's utter surprise, the copies of his father's records disclosed numerous communications and written demands for payment of overdue balances from the company's conventional lenders. It was immediately apparent that Clevis had been struggling for years to save the company from a financial meltdown.

To establish the perception of stability, Jarod knew he had to create an atmosphere of continuity among the employees and executives at Harrington Industries. He met with each department head, one on one, to answer any questions and to provide some level of reassurance.

Many of the senior executives had been with the company since Jarod was a young boy. He was keenly aware that it would be very difficult to gain the respect he needed to be perceived as a trusted leader.

In the daily routine of reviewing incoming mail at the office, Jarod came across a conspicuously odd-looking letter. The envelope was made of brown parchment paper. The recipient's address showed Harrington Industries, Attention: Jarod Harrington. The return address simply recited a post office box on Grand Cayman Island.

Jarod hesitantly opened the envelope. He was well aware that Cleve's venture capital lender, Allied Funding, was based in Grand Cayman. He had no idea why someone from that locale would be sending a letter directly to him.

As Jarod read the letter, his expression transitioned from curiosity to the unmistakable look of fear and shock. The letter provided a detailed synopsis regarding the loan transaction Clevis had made with Allied and the subsequent default in repayment. The contents of the envelope included a summary sheet showing all of the disbursements of loan funds and the due date for repayment. Each of the due dates was over-stamped in red letters with the words, "Past Due!"

The writer of the letter was Chris McField, the principal loan officer for Clevis Harrington and Harrington Industries. Jarod didn't know McField. Clevis had dealt exclusively with him. McField reminded Jarod that Clevis Harrington had defaulted on the loan Allied had made to Harrington Industries.

McField went on to mention that Mr. Harrington had died under unusual and unfortunate circumstances. The closing paragraph of the letter was beyond apocalyptic. As he read the words, Jarod felt the unmistakable chill of sheer terror.

McField had issued an unequivocal ultimatum: "Pay in full, by wire transfer, all outstanding sums of the loan no later than the end of the month or prepare to suffer the same fate as your father."

Jarod was stunned. He was horrified beyond description. His eyes glazed as he stared into the distance, searching for answers to the obvious question- *Why is this happening?*

His hand trembled as he slowly placed the letter on his desk. He could not stop thinking about the barbaric death of his father. The ultimate question loomed in his head: *Had Allied ordered the killing? Did Dad unwittingly forfeit his life in his misguided efforts to salvage the company?*

Until he read the infamous letter, Jarod had not known the full details of the loan with Allied. He knew Harrington Industries was experiencing major financial difficulties but was unaware of the extent of his father's failure to pay.

Clevis had done a masterful job of hiding the dire financial circumstances of Harrington Industries and, in particular, his involvement with this predatory mafioso lender.

After reading the ominous letter from Allied, Jarod needed time to assess his options. It was virtually impossible to think clearly under the circumstances.

At that moment, Jarod was startled when Ms. Goodman stepped into his office. "Jarod, I'm leaving now. It's been a long day. I think we've made a lot of progress working through the backlog. Your father didn't share much information with me on the big issues. He mostly told me to manage the front office and answer the phone. That's made it more difficult to get a handle on everything now that Mr. Harrington is gone."

Jarod looked up at Ms. Goodman with a thousand-mile stare. His face displayed a zombie-like expression. The look of total shock.

Ms. Goodman immediately noticed his odd demeanor. She was unnerved by the haunting appearance lodged in Jarod's eyes. Goodman spoke haltingly with concern, "Are you okay? You look like you just saw a ghost."

Jarod's lips quivered as he spoke. "I'm okay. I guess I'm a little overwhelmed by all the issues Dad left unaddressed. I'll see you in the morning. Thanks for all your help, Ms. Goodman."

As Goodman turned to leave, Jarod's eyes closed. With head bowed in a prayerful pose, he cradled his forehead in the palms of his hands. He sat silently in the empty office for what seemed like an eternity. His thoughts ran wild.

Jarod attempted to focus. His ability to think critically and logically had vanished. After reading the letter from Allied, any analytical or objective thinking was totally impossible. The unmitigated stress of the situation was overwhelming.

As Jarod sat alone, he was quickly overcome by a sense of desperation bordering on panic. He saw no obvious way out. The imminent danger he faced from Allied's death threat was unrelenting. He struggled to shake off the oppressive sense of fear that had captured his mind and spirit. He desperately tried to think lucidly and methodically. Jarod never felt more alone and untethered.

Life experiences had taught Jarod that there comes a moment in time in most people's lives when overwhelming dire circumstances lead to hopelessness and despair. As Jarod sat alone at his desk, agonizing images consumed him.

Jarod's erratic introspection of the situation led him to the conclusion that there was no way out. His thoughts raged out of control.

"I don't have a solution for this. I'm a prime suspect in the death of Cody.

Lieutenant Mercer is convinced I killed him to prevent another blackmail attempt. Mercer still thinks I murdered my father to save the company. The letter from Chris McField might convince Mercer I didn't kill Dad, but Lieutenant Mercer can't protect me from McField's threats. Allied's outlaw operation in Grand Cayman is way beyond the reach of the Huntsville police."

The ominous death threat from Allied and the continuing suspicion that Jarod arranged for the killing of his father and his brother Cody weighed oppressively on his psyche.

His ability to think cogently or to logically process the information revealed to him was jaded by the gripping fear of the looming possibility of arrest for the multiple homicides. Or, worse, his own brutal death at the hands of a hired killer sent by Allied to even the score.

In a last-ditch effort to convince Lieutenant Mercer that he had not killed his father, Jarod mailed a copy of the Allied letter to Mercer. At the very least, Mercer would finally realize that Jarod was not the one who hired Toni Riviera to kill Clevis Harrington.

Three days after the Allied letter was mailed to Lieutenant Mercer, unbeknownst to Jarod, Roy had arranged for a second interrogation of Toni Riviera. Riviera was brought back down to police headquarters for additional questioning.

When Toni came into the interrogation room, Lieutenant Mercer was seated near a small table against the wall opposite the entry door. The metallic clanging of Riviera's leg irons dragging across the concrete floor interrupted the stillness in the air. The detention officer escorting Riviera motioned for Toni to sit down.

Mercer began the interview. "Toni, we've spoken with the district attorney's office. After some soul-searching and a lot of questions for the detective division, the DA agreed to offer you a deal. If you tell us the name of the person who hired you to kill Clevis Harrington, the DA won't seek the death penalty."

Riviera scowled as he gazed over at Mercer. "Yeah, right. Like I'm supposed to believe the DA? Is this a setup?"

"No, Toni, we've got the offer from the DA's office in writing. It's the real thing."

Riviera pressed back in his chair, slowly scratching the side of his mouth. "You know, I don't really trust you bastards. My gut tells me to keep my damn mouth shut. Why should I tell you anything? After I talk, I'll probably get whacked anyway."

Lieutenant Mercer responded, "No. That can't happen. The DA agreed to not ask for death."

Toni sat motionless, gazing upward toward the ceiling, deep in thought. "I want a copy of that agreement. I want to see the damn thing before I say another word."

Lieutenant Mercer immediately left the interrogation room. He returned a short time later with a copy of the prosecutor's email stating that pursuit of the death penalty had been waived.

Mercer thrust the email toward Riviera. "You've got what you wanted. An email from the DA. That's all you're going to get."

"I want something signed by the DA."

"Forget it, Toni. That email is it. Take it or leave it." Roy dropped the document on the table and walked back to his chair. "Now, tell us what you know."

Riviera tilted forward, staring at the email. He carefully studied the document as he stroked his chin with his index finger and thumb. A minute passed. The only sound in the room was the faint ticking of a clock mounted on the wall above the interview table.

Riviera looked up at Lieutenant Mercer with an unsettling stare and then looked back down at the paper lying on the table. He continued to sit silently, apparently immersed in thought. "Okay, but this better be on the level."

Riviera pursed his lips as he shook his head.

"I never met the guy who hired me to exterminate Harrington. We talked by phone. He seemed like a cautious dude to me."

Mercer pressed on. "What did he say to you?"

"He told me he worked as a manager for Clevis Harrington for years at that airplane plant. He said he had a really good job and a damn good life. This guy went on and on about how, out of the blue, Harrington fired his ass for no good reason. This guy said Harrington never really liked him. Harrington had chided him. Called him a pansy-ass and a fruitcake. He said Harrington had made him look like a fool in front of the other managers. The guy was pissed beyond description. He said Harrington screwed up his life big time when he fired him. He said he was going to get even. I could tell he knew how to hold a grudge."

Lieutenant Mercer sat quietly, entering notes as Riviera spoke. "What happened then?"

Toni nervously twisted his lip to one side. "Well, he said Harrington destroyed his life. He said his relationship with his life partner fell apart. He told me he was never able to put his life back together."

"What else?"

"I got tired of hearing his damn bitchin'. I told him I didn't need to hear all that shit! All I needed from him was who's the target and how do I get paid?"

Mercer looked up from his notepad. "What'd he say to that?"

"The guy got really angry. He told me I did need to hear all that crap. He said he wanted me to know what had happened. He wanted me to feel his rage."

"You keep referring to this person as 'the guy'. Does he have a name? We need his name if you expect to get the deal from the DA."

Toni hesitated. "Yeah. I guess it don't really matter now. He didn't want to say. I told him that's okay by me as long as I got paid. The guy finally did tell me his name. He said his name was Carl Brooks. He wanted me to know he'd been some kind of hot-shot supervisor at Harrington Industries. When Harrington fired his ass, Brooks sued Harrington and got a settlement. Brooks said that was not enough. He wanted revenge. He just kept bitchin' about Harrington screwing up his life and his career."

"Is that it?"

"Yeah. That's all I know."

After that interview, Lieutenant Mercer was finally able to connect the dots. He now knew who was responsible for the deaths of Veronica, Clevis, and Cody.

Roy had never heard of Carl Brooks before the latest interrogation of Riviera. To Roy's amazement, he just recently learned that Jarod received a threatening letter from Allied Funding implying that Allied had arranged for the homicide of Clevis Harrington.

After interrogating Toni Riviera, Lieutenant Mercer knew that Carl Brooks had actually ordered the killing. Lieutenant Mercer's mind lingered with an obvious question: How did Allied Funding find out that Clevis was dead?

Looking at all the information, Mercer concluded that Allied knew something was amiss when Clevis stopped responding to Allied's demands for payment of the loan. The emails Mercer had reviewed showed that Harrington always replied to communications from Allied. Harrington was highly motivated to appease Allied to stave off further action by Allied to collect the unpaid loan balance.

Mercer concluded that the uncharacteristic silence of Clevis motivated Allied to find out what had happened to Harrington. Lieutenant Mercer deduced that Allied undoubtedly found news stories covering the murder of Harrington.

As Roy thought about the sequence of events, he reached an inevitable conclusion. *Allied Funding sent the threatening letter to Jarod to create the impression they had killed Clevis. The obvious motive was intimidation to force him to pay the money.*

Roy was certain Allied didn't actually know who killed Clevis or why.

The days following Jarod's receipt of the Allied letter became a blur. Jarod's life was in turmoil. His daily routine suddenly seemed surreal. After a number of robotic days and sleepless nights, Jarod could no longer cope with the pressure of the situation. He'd had taken all that he could stand.

In a moment of unmitigated dread and hopelessness, Jarod was hurled into an abyss of despair. There was only one real solution.

CHAPTER 23

As Jarod drove the usual route toward home, he contemplated what awaited. The crushing weight of all that fell upon him was more than anyone could bear.

He was oblivious to the magic of the warm summer evening in Huntsville. He failed to notice the golden hue of the setting sun or the twinkling glow of fireflies hovering in the distant woods. He was unaware of the gentle breeze licking the treetops, their leafy arms swaying rhythmically to and fro.

He was past the point of any reticence regarding his decision. It was now simply a matter of time and methodology.

That evening, Jarod sat alone in his apartment. The room was oppressively dark.

Lost in macabre and brooding thoughts, the gravity of the situation drained his mind and spirit like a python squeezing the essence of life from its unwitting victim.

As the clock approached eleven p.m., Jarod summoned the strength to press on. He locked the door to his apartment and headed toward his SUV parked nearby.

Exiting the parking lot, he turned north onto Beale Street. His hands and face became enshrouded with the clamminess of unmitigated terror. His mind suddenly entered a dream-like state. His perception became muted, mimicking a transcendental out-of-body experience.

Ten excruciating minutes passed. Jarod reached the city limits of Huntsville. He turned west onto the winding two-lane road known as old Magnolia Drive.

He couldn't shake the overwhelming sense of finality. As he sped along, the pulsing flow of the painted stripes on Magnolia Drive rhythmically emanated out of the inky darkness, momentarily illuminated by the furtive luminescence of the headlights of his speeding SUV.

As Jarod continued along the desolate stretch, thoughts of his life experiences began to race through his head like a video replay on fast-forward-

The early days of yearning for the tenderness of a loving father he never knew. The chiding he endured from his schoolmates calling him names. The harassment heaped on him because he didn't want to play softball at recess. His father asking when was he going to find a girlfriend. The tenderness of his mother's love and understanding. The disgust and anger he harbored when others called him the golden boy. The unyielding stress of striving to live up to the expectations of a cold and demanding father. The precious and fleeting love of his partner, Matt. The unspeakable pressure and frustration of knowing Harrington Industries was teetering on financial ruin. The inescapable fact he remained a suspect in the deaths of Cody and Clevis. And ultimately, the insurmountable pressure of dealing with the impossible task of resolving the enormous loan debt to Allied Funding.

As those images commandeered his mind, his SUV continued speeding down Magnolia Drive as the Rock Island railroad overpass loomed in the distance.

The vehicle abruptly accelerated to speeds approaching ninety miles per hour. Jarod's pulse quickened as he hastily unbuckled his seat belt. The overpass, no more than one thousand yards away, swelled to gargantuan size as the SUV sped toward its final destination.

Jarod closed his eyes as he violently jerked the steering wheel to the right. The vehicle swerved sharply toward the massive concrete structure of the overpass.

As the SUV left the road right-of-way at blinding speed, it swept through the drainage culvert, launched into the air, and careened forward, smashing into the ground just milliseconds before impact with the mammoth concrete buttress.

The explosive sound of crushing metal and shattering glass penetrated the peaceful stillness of the night.

Instantly, the scene was deathly quiet. The only sound was the distant chirping of miniature tree frogs perched in a grove of black gum trees nestled along the small creek near the railroad tracks.

The ubiquitous and unmistakable silence of death permeated the air like the pervasive hush of newly fallen snow. The unyielding darkness of the night was briefly interrupted by the faint red glow of the still-illuminated tail lights of the crumpled mass of glass and steel that once was a functioning vehicle.

The silence was enduring and all-pervading. Nothing stirred. There was no movement. There was no life. Jarod had succumbed to a multitude of forces beyond his control. Jarod was gone forever.

"Born on third base and thought he'd hit a home run." More than one person said that about Jarod. Unfortunately, perception was not always reality. Reality for Jarod was anything but a home run. The son of a cold-hearted tyrant. The brother of a sociopathic manipulative ne'er-do-well. Raised in an environment of toxic masculinity. Misunderstood by everyone except his mother and his life partner. Identified as a prime suspect in two homicides. Received a death threat for financial problems he didn't cause and could not resolve. Unable to find the true purpose and meaning of his existence. Life for Jarod proved to be hell at times. Third base was no home run. Not at all.

EPILOGUE

In the end, Lieutenant Mercer realized his suspicion of Jarod as the likely person committing the homicide of Cody was woefully misplaced. Unbeknownst to Jarod, Lieutenant Mercer had recently concluded that Javier Cabello was, in fact, telling the truth. Ace Desoto had indeed killed Cody to eliminate competition in the drug smuggling business.

Objectively, Roy was simply doing his job. The evidence and circumstances at the time did, in fact, point to Jarod. Jarod had the opportunity and motive to eliminate Cody. Cody's lifestyle of living on the edge with little regard for the law proved to be the fatal element of his chaotic existence.

The death of Clevis Harrington was a total surprise to many who knew him. In the end, Clevis had become his own worst enemy. Jarod tried to be the dutiful son. But, ultimately, the manic decline of Clevis' psyche under the pressure of the ominous and ongoing failure of Harrington Industries proved to be too much.

Harrington's relentless life-long drive to succeed was his prescription for ultimate failure. Cleve's ruthless pursuit of success spelled the demise of his loving spouse and the unwarranted belief that Jarod had ordered the brutal death of his own father.

The real tragedy in Jarod's life was the timing of critical events. If Jarod had been able to summon the strength to persevere until the full picture was revealed, the outcome would have played out in a very different way.

IN THE FINAL ANALYSIS, WHAT PASSED AS ACCEPTABLE POLICE procedure sometimes fell short at the human level. Roy Mercer's remorse weighed heavily on him. He deeply regretted not having enough time remaining to tell Jarod what he now knew about the identity of those involved in the killing of Clevis and Cody. That might have saved Jarod's life. Roy knew he could not undo what had happened to Jarod. He could only move on.

Thank you for reading *Deadly Dynasty*. Written reviews are critically important for an author's continued success. If you enjoyed this book, please go to Amazon.com/books and write a review.

ACKNOWLEDGMENTS

I extend my sincere appreciation to Alicia Dean for her valuable assistance in the editorial process for the production of this book.

ABOUT THE AUTHOR

D. L. Astle is an attorney based in Tulsa, Oklahoma. During his lengthy career, he has written extensively, with numerous publications to his credit covering various law-related topics.

He has now turned to the creative side of writing as his literary focus, drawing back the veil to pass from the rigid infrastructure of law into the ethosphere of free-flowing creativity and world-building without limit.

Deadly Dynasty is his debut novel and the first in a series in the murder mystery genre featuring Lieutenant Roy E. Mercer.